# THE
# **GOOD**
# LIFE

# MARIAN THURM

# THE
# **GOOD**
# LIFE

THE PERMANENT PRESS
*Sag Harbor, NY 11963*

For information, address:
  The Permanent Press
  4170 Noyac Road
  Sag Harbor, NY 11963
  www.thepermanentpress.com

Library of Congress Cataloging-in-Publication Data

Thurm, Marian—
    The good life / Marian Thurm.
    ISBN 978-1-57962-428-6
      pages ; cm
      1. Marital conflict—Fiction.  2. Upper class—Fiction.
    3. Domestic fiction.  4. Suspense fiction.  I. Title.

PS3570.H83G66 2016
813'.54—dc23                                    2015041947

Printed in the United States of America

*For Robin Rue, the agent of my dreams*

## ACKNOWLEDGMENTS

Heartfelt thanks to Robin Rue, Genevieve Gagne-Hawes, and Beth Miller, all at Writers House; to Lisa Shea, Joe Olshan, Joe Olshan, Amy Bloom, Dan Chaon, Josh Henkin, Joanna Hershon, Teddy Wayne, Stacy Schiff; to Yona Zeldis McDonough, Henry Landsman, Kate Axelrod, George Axelrod, and Marty and Judith Shepard. And to Barbara Anderson, copyeditor *par excellence*.

While his wife, Stacy, is busy with their young son and daughter at the egg-shaped swimming pool adjacent to his mother's condo, Roger Goldenhar will drive in his rented Toyota to an indoor, air-conditioned shooting range in Pompano Beach where they also happen to sell guns and ammo—a fact he will learn on the Internet the night before he and Stacy and the kids fly out from JFK to Fort Lauderdale.

At the shooting range—to which he will return to pick up the handgun after a mandatory three-day waiting period and official approval from the Florida Department of Law Enforcement—he will be encouraged to take a class offered on-site that will teach him all about loading, unloading, and firing his weapon. He will politely decline, explaining that long ago, back when he was thirteen or fourteen and went to summer camp in Maine, he used to fire a .22-caliber rifle at paper targets with the image of a vivid orange Popsicle at the center. And was actually awarded a marksman's badge in riflery. Oh, and also a complimentary junior membership in the NRA.

Thanks anyway, he will say to the guys behind the counter at the range; even though he's never shot this particular pistol before today, he's quite certain he doesn't need any formal training in the handling of firearms. Though of course he'll take a good long look at the instruction book that comes with it.

But wait, someone will ask him, don't you need ammo to go with that newly purchased 9 mm semiautomatic Glock?

Oh, thanks, one small box of 9 mm bullets, please.

# ~ 1 ~

Of all the things they had in common—and there were many, including the fact that they'd both grown up on Long Island, Roger in the sixties and early seventies, Stacy a decade later—the crazy thing was that they were both born on April 20th, in, believe or not (and at first neither one of them could), the same hospital. This was Lenox Hill, on Manhattan's Upper East Side, just a few blocks from where, in the early years of the twenty-first century, Roger and Stacy Goldenhar would eventually buy a three-bedroom apartment and begin to raise their children together.

*Kismet, karma, fate, destiny*, call it what you will, these two had it, baby. In spades.

April 20th also happened to be Adolf Hitler's birthday, a fact which was news to Stacy.

"What? No way!" she'd kept insisting to Roger the afternoon they first met. "How could I have missed something like that? No way!" It was 1998, the first week in June, and each of them had made it to Cambridge for their respective reunions; Stacy had been an undergrad at Harvard in the mid-eighties, just a couple of years before Roger had attended the Business School. They were seated now at a table for two in a muffin shop in Harvard Square, where the cashiers and employees behind the counter were dressed in Revolutionary War costumes, and the wallpaper was patterned with images of Washington, Jefferson, and Adams at the Continental Congress. Stacy and Roger had introduced themselves less than half an hour earlier, when each of them had ordered a glazed lemon drop muffin and an iced tea to go. While waiting in line at the cashier, absently fooling with her key ring, a two-inch plastic Pinocchio dangling from it, Stacy's keys and wallet had slipped from her hands and onto the unvarnished wood floor of Ye Olde Muffin Shoppe. Where her imitation suede wallet then fell open, several credit cards and Stacy's New York State driver's license spilling out as the wallet hit the ground. And Roger, in his gentlemanly way, had bent down to retrieve her things for her. After a quick thank-you from Stacy and a spirited conversation about 1) their mutual birthday (which of course Roger had gleaned from her license) 2) the fact that they both currently lived in Manhattan 3) Lenox Hill Hospital 4) Hitler, and 5) the sprinkling of grated lemon peel they both liked in the muffins' glaze, Roger suggested they sit down at a table together. Stacy, who had recently broken up with the work-obsessed, hard-to-please legal aid lawyer she'd been dating for about a year longer than she should have, silently admired the startling turquoise-green of Roger's eyes and also his small ears with their delicate, attached lobes. He was taller than she was by four or five inches, she calculated—well over six feet—and she found that alluring, too. Stacy was almost five nine, and always on the lookout for men who hit the six-foot mark and then some. None of these features she was admiring in Roger had any weight to it, moral or otherwise, she understood, but, even so, she found herself willing to settle into a rickety, uncomfortable seat opposite him and explore the possible pleasures of his company.

As he talked, with great enthusiasm, about his job as a commercial real estate developer, Stacy stared at his clean-shaven, angular face, and realized she had no idea how old he was: Thirty-eight? Fortyish? How could you tell? She herself was thirty-three and, frankly, not getting any younger, as Lauren, her occasionally exasperating sister, liked to remind her. Lauren hadn't celebrated her thirtieth birthday yet but already had a husband and two children—a pair of dark-haired, identical twin girls who were enrolled in the Kiddie Kollege Preschool in the suburbs of Connecticut, where they studied the alphabet and rode tricycles and finger painted, from nine in the morning until two in the afternoon, Monday through Friday, while Lauren worked as an assistant teacher in the classroom next door.

The life her sister inhabited, deep in the suburbs of New Haven County, was one that Stacy—who'd never owned or operated a Chevy TrailBlazer or Ford Explorer, or changed a single diaper or coaxed a burp from a newborn baby—was entirely unfamiliar with. And did not aspire to. Unlike her college roommates, most of whom, it seemed, had ended up in med school, law school, or investment banking, Stacy had found a job after her senior year with a nonprofit, earning $19,000 a year working with Manhattan's homeless population. And taking satisfaction in helping what her mother, Grace, had referred to as "those poor souls"—many of them Vietnam vets with schizophrenia and severe substance abuse problems whose wretched lives Stacy tried so hard to improve by securing housing and medical care for them even when they didn't seem to much want what she was offering.

"I can't believe no one ever told you that you and *der Führer* shared a birthday," Roger was saying now, while adding a packet of Sweet'N Low to his iced tea. He followed that with two more packets, and stirred vigorously with an extra-long spoon suitable for use with an ice cream soda.

Stacy laughed.

"What? You think I'm a wuss because I like my tea sweet?" Roger said. "Or do you think I'm an idiot because there's a possible link between artificial sweeteners and cancer in laboratory rats?"

"We've known each other for, let's see, twenty-seven minutes or so," Stacy pointed out after checking the stainless steel Timex on her wrist. She noticed the white-gold Rolex around Roger's, but it held little meaning for her. (Weeks later, when they were lying in bed together and she asked, out of simple curiosity, how much a watch like that actually cost, she was shocked to learn that this Rolex Daytona, as he proudly identified it, came with a $15,000 price tag. *That's a joke, I assume?* she said. *I mean, who in their right mind would ever pay that kind of money for a watch? And, more importantly, why?* Roger explained—eagerly, without hesitation—that, for him, it was a measure of his success out there in the world, and that he loved to feel the weight of it around his wrist. *You understand that, right?* he said, and she very politely pretended that she did.)

"The truth is, I wasn't thinking anything about you and your apparent fondness for Sweet'N Low," she continued now. "That laugh of mine was just one of those nervous laughs, I guess, that came out of nowhere." But this was a lie; she was actually thinking about those eyes of his—she'd never seen such a memorable, light bluish-green before. "Can I ask you something personal?" she said.

"Feel free," Roger said. He took a sip of his iced tea, and made a face. "You wanna know what undrinkable tastes like?"

"Big surprise, right?" Stacy offered him some of hers, pushing the glass gently toward him, though only a moment later it seemed to her an oddly intimate gesture between two strangers, albeit ones who shared a birthday and birthplace. "So where'd you get those, um, really beautiful eyes from?" she asked, and watched as his lips touched her iced tea. "Or is that too personal a question?"

"I thought you were going to ask me how old I am," Roger said, looking relieved. "And then I'd feel compelled to tell you the truth."

"Well, *I'm* thirty-three, as you already know from my driver's license," said Stacy, lowering her voice just a bit. Years from now, she suspected, she'd long for the days when she could still announce that she was thirty-three; right now, though, she couldn't quite believe that her thirtieth birthday had actually come and gone several years ago. Hanging around Harvard Square this weekend, slipping in and out of bookstores and cafés with teenagers and twenty-somethings everywhere you looked was a little depressing, as was contemplating the decade that had already passed since she and her friends had been students here. Which reminded her that several of them—including her longtime best friend, Jefrie-Ann Miller, with whom she'd lived off campus in a run-down Victorian house on Mass Ave their senior year—were waiting for her at the Coop, where they were going to shop for toddler-sized Harvard sweatshirts for their respective kids.

Roger confessed that he was forty-two. "But of course forty's the new thirty," he told her, and smiled hopefully.

Walking in their direction now was a beefy guy in a gray T-shirt imprinted with the words "STILL PISSED AT YOKO!"

Stacy gave him the thumbs-up, and the guy winked at her as he found a seat for himself and his tray of coffee and minimuffins toward the back of the small, crowded room.

"I get it," she reassured Roger. "Prime of your life and all that." She was suddenly thirsty, and wanted more of her iced tea. Roger was gulping it down without apology; perhaps he'd forgotten that it was hers. "And actually, I thought you were younger," she said. Now that she knew how old he was, she wondered if he'd been married before, or even if he were married *now*, though the ring finger of his left hand was unadorned. There was nothing, after all, preventing a married person from pretending he or she was single. "Hey you, you're not married, are you?" Stacy heard herself say.

"Divorced."

His voice didn't sound even the slightest bit rueful, a good sign, she knew. Because the last thing she needed in her life was some guy pining for the ex who'd so cruelly demolished his big dumb heart.

Just before Stacy left to catch up with her friends at the Harvard Coop, Roger suggested they exchange "contact info"; returning home to her apartment in New York the following night, she found a playful e-mail inviting her to dinner next April 20th to celebrate their birthdays. Or, Roger proposed, instead of waiting those eleven long months between now and then, they could have dinner at the end of the week.

Sure, why not?

✍

*They have been married for nearly nine years, and have two children, a daughter who is named Olivia, and a son named Will, two very good kids, Roger and Stacy will always say, though they both agree that Will, who is in preschool now, can be stubbornly rambunctious at times. Devilish, you could say. One time, a year ago, when he was only two and a half, he'd been sitting with them in a crowded Hamburger Heaven in midtown, and a gray-haired woman at the next table waved and asked him his name. Will flashed her his friendliest smile, inserted a single french fry into the side of his mouth like a cigarette, and said, with exquisite nonchalance, "My name is shit, lady."*

*Parenthood. Who knew what they were getting themselves into?*

*Boarding the JetBlue plane now for their six fifteen* A.M. *flight to Fort Lauderdale, Stacy is loaded down with a sturdy canvas carry-on bag filled with children's books, crayons and a thick sheaf of drawing paper, and a portable mini DVD player with a twelve-inch screen so that Olivia and Will can watch their favorite episodes of Yo Gabba Gabba and Dora the Explorer. She has Olivia by the hand; behind her, Roger's hand is circling Will's small wrist. All four of them are exhausted after a cruelly attenuated night's sleep and two separate alarms set to awaken them at three* A.M. *so they could get to the airport in time. Early departure, early arrival, Roger's idea of a good time. But Stacy has other ideas; frankly, southern Florida is one of her least favorite places in the universe. (God's waiting room—whoever came up with that was spot-on.) If it* weren't for her mother-in-law's condo that is theirs to use anytime they please—sparing them the expense of a hotel room—she would never have agreed to fly down here. But money is an issue these days; they've been living mostly on credit and there's no denying it.

Stacy is trying desperately not to think about it, not to talk about it, not to worry about it. And that's only because Roger worries enough for both of them. He's often on the Internet until four thirty or five in the morning, conducting business on the other side of the world. (Most recently, something to do with alternative energy sources, one more subject that he declines to discuss with her in any great detail.) Roger sleeps for a few hours a day, from five A.M. until nine or so, and then takes the subway to his office in Long Island City, where, Stacy fears, he worries even more. (She pretends to be half-asleep when he finally crashes in their bed at five in the morning, pretends that she doesn't feel his heart thudding when she rests her palm so lightly on his chest.)

He just can't mellow out, no matter how hard she tries to persuade him.

Money-wise, things are bad, despite all his efforts to improve them, he's told her again and again.

But life can be good nonetheless, she thinks. Compared to the homeless she worked with for so long, their lives, hers and Roger's and the children's, are still privileged.

Just not as privileged as they were before.

And it's not as if they're completely destitute, right? They can still pay their rent, can't they?

Just deal with it, she'd like to tell Roger. And has told him, from time to time, though very delicately, probably too delicately to make much of an impression on him. She keeps her voice as gentle, as moderate, as can be, because Roger's distressed enough as it is, and she doesn't want to make things any more difficult for him.

◆

She has no idea how much Xanax he swallowed this morning before they left for the airport, or what he'd be like without it. Or how much is currently required just to get him through the day.

She doesn't have a clue.

⚮

"Welcome, y'all," the flight attendant says as Stacy and her sleepy family step onto the aircraft. The woman, whose name badge identifies her as Doe, doesn't look as perky as she should; her eyes are a little glassy, and the cranberry polish on her nails is chipped here and there, Stacy notices.

See, looky there, everyone has his or her problems, she'd like to point out to Roger.

Even twenty-five-year-olds named Doe with soft-looking, highlighted hair.

When the plane lifts off, Stacy, Olivia, and Will are seated all in a row, with Roger just across the aisle. Later, a half hour or so after takeoff, when the flight attendants come around with complimentary bottles of water, and tiny foil bags of chips or cookies (take your pick, but you can't have both), Olivia and Will are already dozing, Will with his head against the Plexiglas window, Olivia with hers listing against Stacy's shoulder.

Across the aisle, Roger smiles wistfully at all three of them. "Love you guys," he says, though only Stacy is awake to hear him.

# ~ 2 ~

Allyson Stewart, Roger's ex-wife, was a know-it-all of sorts. Their brief marriage had ended when Allyson, who worked as an administrator in a prep school in Riverdale, fell in love with someone named Warren Whitcomb, a geometry teacher who was from a wealthy, distinguished family and never cashed his paychecks, turning over every last one of them to the school's headmaster on the final day of the term each June. Breaking up with Roger one night in their den on West End Avenue as they were watching Jay Leno chatting amiably with Tom Hanks, Allyson made a point of this, of what a saintly figure Warren was, working for free like that year after year; how could Roger deny that saintliness, that generosity of spirit?

Well, he couldn't.

He was blown away by the news of Allyson's betrayal that night in their apartment, having thought, mistakenly, that they had a rock-solid marriage, one of those marriages that, he explained to her, was "built to last." (*You sound like you're talking about a car,* Allyson mocked him. *Or a washing machine.*) As Roger spoke to her, reeling from the shock of her announcement about this Whitcomb guy—someone he'd never met, and could only picture next to a blackboard littered with diagrams of isosceles triangles, the tips of his fingers coated in chalk dust the color of spoiled milk—Allyson scanned his face briefly. And then shrugged in a way that was so half-hearted, so utterly lacking in regret and compassion, it was as if Roger had merely said, "*Wait, I don't understand, you mean we're NOT having filet mignon for dinner tonight?*"

Allyson and her new love, Warren, never did marry, though they lived together in a house in Scarsdale that had been in the Whitcomb family for generations. Roger heard all about the pleasures of their suburban life after running into the two of them on Broadway, in the lobby of the Nederlander Theatre, where he'd taken his mother to see *Rent* for her birthday. He and Allyson, the know-it-all, got into an argument about Jonathan Larson, the creator of *Rent*, who'd died, so tragically, of a torn aorta, though Allyson insisted it was a brain aneurysm. They argued for several minutes in the lobby about Larson's death, Roger's mother and Warren Whitcomb looking on impatiently, until Roger shrugged and said (even though he knew damn well that Allyson was dead wrong), "Fine, you win; if you say it's an aneurysm, who am I to doubt you?"

He fell in and out of a series of relationships, not one of them what he would have called "serious" and most of them lasting weeks rather than months. A couple of years later his fortieth birthday came and went, with a modest celebration in his parents' dining room on Long Island. Surrounded by his mother and father, his sister, brother-in-law, and six-year-old nephew, Roger himself accompanied by a somewhat strident publicist he'd been dating for several weeks and had already grown tired of, it hit him that, because of bad luck, bad karma, or whatever it was, he might never find himself in love ever again.

This sort of thinking turned out to be unduly pessimistic on his part, because, as it happened, a little more than two years after that disappointingly subdued birthday party, Stacy accidentally dropped her wallet and Pinocchio key ring onto the floor of the muffin shop, while Washington, Jefferson, and Adams looked on gravely from the blue-and-gray wallpaper behind her.

∾

The rental car they pick up at the airport smells like "something bad," Olivia complains, and Will immediately agrees with her, though neither of them can explain exactly what they mean by "bad." Maybe just hot and plasticky.

"Anybody hungry for breakfast?" Stacy asks, but no one answers. She asks Roger to power down all the windows to get rid of the imaginary smell, puts on her sunglasses, and gazes into the rearview mirror at her three-year-old and five-year-old in the backseat, both of them light-haired and blue-eyed, and looking nothing like her at all. Both of them beautiful, she thinks. She might be just one more deluded mother blinded by love for her son and daughter, but, in her case, she actually has official confirmation of her children's beauty: both Will and Olivia were signed by a top-drawer modeling agency in Manhattan a year ago and have worked plenty of jobs—Gap Kids, Ralph Lauren, Calvin Klein, lots of catalogue work for department stores she'd never heard of in the Midwest, and once, for Olivia, the cover of the New York Times Magazine. (Stacy would never have gone after this sort of thing on her own; it was only that someone who worked for the children's division of the modeling agency happened to approach her with his card one day when she'd taken Olivia and Will to a playground at the edge of Central Park.) On occasion she's had to pull both kids out of school in the middle of the day for these jobs of theirs, and has been feeling guilty about that lately, especially about Olivia, who is in a fast-track reading program and shouldn't be missing a single thing in the classroom. And so Stacy has made a promise to herself to put an end to all of this as soon as they return to New York after vacationing this week in Florida while the kids are on spring break from school.

Call her superficial, but she gets a thrill from hearing the stylists and photographers at the modeling shoots admiring her kids; after all, what parent wouldn't?

The truth is, there's another reason she's pulling the plug on the kids' far-from-lucrative careers; there's an urgent need for her to go back to work herself. She's been happy enough as a full-time mother these past five years, though she couldn't have predicted it. The time has come, however, for her to get back out there and start earning a living again.

This isn't simply her opinion, it's a fact.

Roger doesn't want to talk about it.

A couple of nights ago, when she told him she was planning to contact her former boss, and also some head-hunters, he didn't bother to stop typing on his laptop, but merely said, "Fine."

"Did you hear what I said?" she asked him, fixed in the doorway of their bedroom, addressing the back of his head. "I'm going to start checking Craigslist, too, when we get back Sunday."

Roger turned around to look at her. "What?"

"Not Sunday, I mean a week from Sunday," she said, and saw him wince. "I promise I'll find something, okay?"

"Whatever you want, no problem." Turning away from her again, he took his hands off the keyboard of the laptop, picked up his BlackBerry and began texting.

"Who are you texting at one in the morning?" Stacy said. She wasn't expecting a response, but thought she'd give it a shot anyway.

"No one," he murmured.

Now in the rental car, studying her kids in the rearview as Roger drives them out of the airport and onto US 1, she tries to imagine them grown up, tries to imagine a time when she'll be nostalgic for Will and Olivia's childhood selves, a time when they're already teenagers—teenagers not too challenging for her to handle, but struggling a bit to come into their own. She imagines buying a first bra for Olivia, who will have already lost some of the *soft, rosy-cheeked beauty of her childhood but will still be lovely, though in a different way, a thirteen-year-old who wants to shave her legs for the very first time and needs to be shown how . . . And she can see Will with his arm slung around a girl, his voice deepening, his feet filling size-ten Nikes, his T-shirt reeking of adolescent sweat after a game of pickup basketball on a court somewhere in the city. Because of course she's determined never to leave Manhattan, to raise her children there where the pulse of the whole world can be felt every time you step out from the lobby of your building. After Will was born, Roger had made noises about moving out to the suburbs, but has, more recently, stopped talking about it.*

*He understands that he'll have to carry her out kicking and screaming to get her to move to a place where the streets are named Jessica Drive and Bittersweet Lane.*

*NOT going to happen.*

*"Not," she murmurs out loud, and hands over two Juicy Juice boxes, kiwi strawberry for Olivia and apple raspberry for Will, who struggles to unwrap the cellophane from his straw for only a moment or two before Olivia takes over.*

*"What do you say to your sister?" Stacy reminds Will.*

*"Gracias, muchacha," he says, a New York City kid so savvy that at the age of three, he already knows how to roll his "Rs" flamboyantly.*

*Fiddling with her own straw now, Olivia says, "Il n'y a pas de quoi."*

*"Are these kids wonderful or what?" Stacy says. "I mean, how impressed are you with these kids of ours?"*

*"Pretty damn impressed," Roger agrees.*

*In a couple of hours the temperature will hit eighty, and the already humid air will feel like eighty-five, and Stacy will remember some of her chief reasons for hating Florida. For the moment, though, she's happy just to hear her children speaking a little French and Spanish, happy to see the relaxed way Roger angles his elbow out the window as he drives, his impressively thick hair blowing back across the top of his head in the summery breeze.*

Stacy had been instructed by the social service agency she worked for never to dress in a manner that would make her homeless clients feel even worse about their profoundly troubled lives than they already did. So while it was perfectly acceptable for her to come to work in jeans and T-shirts or sweatshirts, it was considered highly inappropriate to arrive at the office dressed in pointy-toed designer pumps and fur-lined leather jackets. Also frowned upon were gold bracelets, diamond earrings, and Cartier eternity rings. Unlike some of her colleagues, who tried to get away with a little bling here and there, Stacy showed up in store-brand sneakers and in Levis ripped at the knees. The faded, gray leather satchel she carried to work had belonged to her grandmother long ago, as had the wrinkly, colorful silk scarves she often wore draped around her neck. (Her mother would have judged Stacy's wardrobe "shlumpy," but, in fact, both of her parents had died—her father of a heart attack while Stacy was in college, her mother, a decade or so later, in a single-engine two-seater piloted by the brand-new boyfriend who, on a fiercely windy afternoon, crashed his plane into the ocean en route to Atlantic City. Stacy frequently reminded herself to lay off the Chicken McNuggets and fries, exercise vigorously and often, and keep the hell away from small planes. She still missed her parents enormously, especially her mother, whose shocking death she hadn't yet made peace with, but what could you do? You still had to go to work every day, and take care of your laundry and the dishes from last night, and savor whatever pleasures were within your reach.)

Because she was advised against dressing with any flare at all during the workweek, she relished her weekend wardrobe, and sometimes went a little too far, outfitting her tall, slender self in short, tight skirts and high-heeled boots, hanging long, sparkly earrings from six of the eight holes in her ears, and overloading each of her arms with more than two dozen thin silver bracelets that jangled seductively whenever she gestured with her hands. Her grandmother, Juliette, who had outlived her daughter and son-in-law, was eighty-three and, thankfully, had all her marbles—not to mention excellent vision and hearing—and she scolded Stacy for dressing as she did.

"A nice pair of pants, a nice pair of flat shoes, what would be so terrible? What are you doing going around like that in those high heels and that skirt up to your *pupik?*" she said one Saturday afternoon when Stacy stopped by to see her.

Juliette lived in Brooklyn, in a neighborhood that was neither hipster-cool nor particularly safe, and Stacy worried about her. It was clear, though, that her grandmother was perfectly content where she was and wouldn't dream of moving to someplace better, like Park Slope, where Stacy lived alone in a small second-floor apartment in a well-kept townhouse.

She and Juliette were sitting in her grandmother's tiny living room now, on a warm afternoon in late September, surrounded by photographs of Stacy's mother and uncle; some of them taken in black-and-white back in the forties, and some in color and far more recent; in almost all of them, Stacy's mother, Grace, wore that sweet, winning smile of hers. She had been gone for nearly two years, but it still hurt Stacy to look at the photographs. Someday, she believed, when her grief over her parents had fully subsided, she would grow accustomed to the idea of her mother and father having vanished from this earth, never to reappear. But like a five-year-old, she thought, she sometimes found herself fantasizing that her parents would be returned to her, like a lost book or favorite stuffed animal from childhood that had inexplicably disappeared, left behind somewhere by, perhaps, her own carelessness. This was how it would go: there would be a voice mail from some vast lost and found somewhere in the ether, and a soothing voice, probably female, would say, *I'm trying to reach Stacy Harrison? Are you missing a mother and father? If so, you're invited to claim them at your earliest convenience. Or, if you like, we can put them on our shuttle and deliver them to you free of charge. Please give us a call at our toll-free number. Operators are standing by . . .*

She watched as her grandmother lit up a cigarette. Stacy rolled her eyes at her.

"Get me an ashtray, will you, please?" Juliette said. "And while you're at it, you can drop that disapproving look, okay? If you think that look of yours is going to get me to quit smoking, you're sadly mistaken, sweetheart. I'm over twenty-one, and I'm allowed. It's been almost seventy years I've been smoking these Parliaments, and I'm still going strong." She turned her head to the side and exhaled a nasty-smelling stream of smoke toward the window.

"Still going strong," Stacy agreed. Her grandmother did her own grocery shopping, her own laundry, and even her own windows; she was small and round and determined, and, like a cat whose tail you'd accidentally stepped on, could turn on you in an instant, showing those razor-sharp claws of hers. Juliette kept a mental list of relatives and friends who she believed had betrayed her in some way and whose company she no longer could tolerate. The list stretched longer and longer, but Stacy made sure her own name was never on it, not even for a day. She was an expert at concealing her anger at, and disappointment with, the people in her orbit. It was a talent she believed she was born with, and she used it lavishly, whenever she found herself bumping up against the prickliness of those who just couldn't chill out and be Zen. That included the guy on the subway today in a thin, shiny black jacket with a skull outlined in winking rhinestones: after he poked his elbow in Stacy's side as they entered the packed subway car, not only did he fail to apologize, he inexplicably growled at her, saying, "Hey, whatever happened to fuckin' etiquette?" Her face burning, Stacy's response was to look down at the tips of her black patent leather high heels, which, she noticed, could have used a quick polishing.

"Do you have any shoe polish?" she asked Juliette, whose Parliament was leaking ash onto the linoleum floor because Stacy had forgotten all about the ashtray until that moment.

"What color polish and why?" Juliette said as she took the ashtray from her; lining it, under a circle of clear glass, Stacy saw, was a photograph of a close friend of her grandmother's whom Juliette was no longer speaking to.

"Answer to question number one: black; question number two: because I'm having dinner with Roger and his family tonight."

"Who's Roger? And no, I don't have any shoe polish for you, black or otherwise."

"You know perfectly well who Roger is," Stacy said, waving away the cigarette smoke as violently and obnoxiously as if she were a reformed smoker.

"I'm teasing you, sweetheart. If you say he's your boyfriend, who am I to dispute that?"

"As grandmothers go, you've very weird," Stacy told her. "And I mean that in the best possible way."

"I mean *this* in the best possible way: you're not planning on meeting Roger's family wearing an outfit like *that*, are you? Because you're too old and too tall to be walking around in a skirt that short, never mind those trampy high heels."

Stacy was insulted, but wouldn't say so. Instead she said, "I'm thirty-three, Gram, okay? By most people's standards, that's young enough to dress any way I like."

"I'm not most people," Juliette said.

Indeed she wasn't. After she'd lost her daughter on that ill-fated and foolhardy flight to Atlantic City, the eulogy she delivered at the graveside service was short and anguished:

*This is the worst thing that could ever happen to a mother. There's nothing left for me now. Nothing. It's just all fucked up.*

As if Stacy hadn't felt bad enough, her grandmother's eulogy was the last thing she'd needed to hear. She remembered, at this moment, her father often and affectionately (well, maybe not so affectionately) referring to Juliette as *a tough old broad.* But her words and demeanor at the cemetery proved him wrong; anybody could see that her grandmother was the furthest thing from a tough broad. What you could see was a broken woman in a black dress with a white handkerchief stuffed into the sleeve, a handkerchief that was soaked through with her bitter tears. She hadn't even allowed a rabbi at the gravesite, only Stacy and her sister, Lauren, and their uncle, and some of her mother's friends, every one of whom flinched at Juliette's raw, ugly words as Stacy's mother was lowered into the space that the bored-looking gravediggers had carved for her.

"Fine," Stacy said now. "I'll change into something a little more subdued when I get home, okay?" The high heels would stay; only the short skirt would go back into the mess of a closet she'd been meaning to clean out for ages now.

Extinguishing her half-smoked cigarette against the photograph of her former best friend that ornamented the ashtray, Juliette said, "Don't do it on my account. It's for you, baby-doll. You just don't want what's-his-name's family to think of you as trashy, you see what I'm saying?"

*Fine.* "I have to go now, Gram," Stacy said. "I'm getting my hair trimmed before the big dinner tonight." She got up from the folding chair she'd been seated on, and leaned over to kiss Juliette good-bye.

Her grandmother squinted at her. "*What* big dinner?"

"I'm not even going to dignify that with a response," Stacy said, and both of them laughed.

"Before you leave, can you get me a pack of cigarettes from the freezer?"

"Get it yourself," Stacy said; honestly, why should she aid and abet that half-pack-a-day habit? But she found her way into the kitchen nevertheless, because her grandmother was, after all, eighty-three, no spring chicken. If Juliette insisted on storing her cartons of cigarettes in the freezer to keep them fresh, alongside a pint of high-cholesterol mocha chip ice cream and a half-pound package of ground sirloin, well, whose business was it anyway?

∽

*His father, a dentist who'd also owned parking garages in midtown Manhattan, had been able to offer Roger and his mother and his sister the sort of comfortable life in Westchester that included a large house on three-quarters of an acre with a swimming pool and tennis court in the back, trips to the Caribbean every winter, and a live-in housekeeper who wore a uniform and served dinner every night. It was hard not to take these things for granted, hard not to go along with the mistaken assumption that, as an adult, this life of comfort and privilege would con- tinue endlessly, no matter what. But his father retired too soon, foolishly sold the garages, invested unwisely and unluckily in the stock market, and lost most of the money that eventually would have gone to Roger and his sister and would have made their already comfortable lives even more so.*

*His father's bad luck didn't matter so much when Roger was doing well. But it sure as shit matters now.*

∽

*Arranging his shirts in what was once his father's closet, and tucking his boxers and socks away in the top drawer of what used to be his father's dresser, Roger pops another Xanax, swallowing it down with a handful of* warmish water from the faucet in the en suite bathroom. And then collapses on the king-size bed, too lazy to kick off his Top-Siders first. There's barely an inch of uncovered space on the bedroom walls, which are painted a minty green and crowded with framed pictures of his mother and father, Beverly and Walter, most of them snapped down here in Florida. He can see how tanned they both were in their unflattering bathing suits and shorts and T-shirts, and also how much weight they both needed to lose—a good twenty pounds or so for each of them, Roger estimates (though at his death, back in the nineties, his father had been nearly skeletal). Overweight or not, his mother had been an attractive woman. As she still is today, never mind the Alzheimer's that has robbed her of everything but her pretty face, and yet has, surprisingly, bestowed upon her a sweetness she never possessed before. Though she shrieks like you wouldn't believe when the caregivers at the assisted-living residence dress her in the morning and undress her at night. ("You're trying to killll meee!" she screams, and fights them every step of the way. Roger just can't stay in her room when she's like that, and, instead, has to escape into the common hallway and pace along the beige-and-gray commercial carpeting until his mother has calmed down.)

Stacy isn't driven crazy like he is by all that carrying on; she goes right into his mother's room at the residence— within walking distance of their apartment in the city and currently paid for, now that Roger can no longer afford to share the costs, entirely by his compassionate, well-heeled brother-in-law, Marshall—and helps to soothe her as the caregivers deal with the rest.

Roger's wife is a good and remarkably generous person. But she doesn't seem to understand the business world he's in, or maybe it's that she—an otherwise smart girl—simply won't allow herself to make the effort to understand; wouldn't allow herself to understand, just a few months *ago, "soft costs" versus "hard costs," and the misery that runs sickeningly through the words "cross-collateralize" and "construction cost overruns." And won't allow herself, even now, to truly fathom what deep shit they're in, how bad, how truly terribly bad, things actually are.*

## ~ 4 ~

Though he and Stacy had only been dating for a few months, Roger wanted her to meet his family, especially Clare, his sister and only sibling, and Marshall Tuckman, his brother-in-law, both of whom had been so openly sympathetic to him during the trauma of his divorce four years ago. Lately he considered Marshall one of his closest friends, even if he suspected that the feeling wasn't mutual, and that Marshall had at least a few other friends who meant more to him. But that was fine; just knowing Marshall was the sort of benevolent guy he could count on was enough for him. After Allyson had moved in with Warren Whitcomb, it was Marshall who had recommended that Roger consider going back on the antidepressants he'd given up years ago. Marshall wasn't a shrink—he was an orthodontist—but he seemed to have a keen understanding of Roger, a keener understanding, perhaps, than even Roger himself possessed. And so when Marshall had gently suggested that he get himself back into therapy and back on Zoloft, Roger took his advice. But first he'd surfed the Internet and taken a quiz:

"Do you have a persistent empty feeling?" *Check.*

"Do you suffer from insomnia?" *Check.*

"Do you have an inability to enjoy yourself?" *Check.*

"Do you have persistent feelings of hopelessness?" *Check.*

"Worthlessness?" *Check.*

"Helplessness?" *Check.*

His new therapist at the time, Dr. Avalon, a man in his late fifties, took pains to explain to him the obvious: that major life stresses, divorce among them, increased the likelihood of a person falling prey to depression. "Not that you have to be a genius to figure *that* one out," he said, and smiled faintly.

Roger himself dwelled perhaps a bit too long on the subject of Warren Whitcomb and Allyson and the mortification he felt at having been thrown overboard. During one of his appointments those first few months after the divorce, as he talked, he caught Dr. Avalon dozing in his armchair, his ballpoint pen tucked between two fingers of his left hand, his head of dyed orangey-brown hair canted toward one shoulder. Though his initial reaction was one of outrage, Roger immediately began to worry that he'd bored Dr. Avalon to death and would be fired for it. And then what? It was so hard to find a good therapist; just the thought of looking for someone new exhausted him.

*So why did you leave your last therapist?* the new one would ask him.

*Actually . . . I didn't quit; I was fired,* he imagined himself confessing.

As he watched Dr. Avalon snoozing, Roger had amused himself for a few moments by thinking of sarcastic things he might say when the doc awakened.

<u>That</u> *boring, huh?*

*Out partying last night at a strip club with some of your fellow shrinks?*

*Didn't they teach you in med school to at least* <u>pretend</u> *that you're listening?*

He decided to let Dr. Avalon sleep for five minutes and five minutes only; while he waited, he read the *New York Times*, catching up on O. J. Simpson's legal troubles, the Clinton administration's dislike of the word "genocide" to portray the mass killings in Rwanda, and the new finding that heavy usage of Tylenol could lead to serious liver damage. Just as Roger was starting to read about the death threats against Speaker of the House Newt Gingrich, Dr. Avalon's eyes flew open, he straightened up in his seat, and said, "I'm sorry, this obsession with Warren Whitcomb has made you feel *what*?"

"Oh, forget it," Roger said, and steered the subject toward Tylenol and his refusal to believe that just one a day, seven a week, could actually be dangerous. As long as he had his prescription for Zoloft, and could convince Dr. Avalon that he needed to keep taking it, what did it really matter *what* they talked about? He'd come to believe that talk therapy was pretty much bullshit, anyway. Sure it was horrible that Allyson had replaced him with Warren Whitcomb, but the Zoloft was making him feel a hell of a lot better. More optimistic about the future, and not as pissed off at Allyson. He boldly cut back his visits to Dr. Avalon to once every two weeks, and then, a couple of years later, to once a month, which was the schedule they were sticking to now. He appreciated Dr. Avalon's Saturday office hours, and his willingness to conduct sessions over the phone, if necessary.

This afternoon, just hours before the family dinner, when he told Avalon that he'd invited Stacy to meet his family tonight, the doctor merely nodded. And scratched the tip of first one ear and then the other.

"What's on the menu?" Avalon asked, as if he were hungry and interested in talking about food. "Your sister's going to be cooking?"

"Well, Stacy just had a root canal the other day, and has to be very careful chewing until she gets the crown put in. So I think dinner's just going to be something soft, like pasta." Looking around the lower Fifth Avenue office in vain for some pictures of Dr. Avalon's family, Roger thought about the inherent unfairness of their relationship: he was expected to reveal all about *his* family, while Avalon concealed every-thing about his. Shockingly Dr. Avalon had violated his own rules earlier in their session today, and bragged that his wife had, at the surprising age of fifty-six, passed her road test and gotten her driver's license.

"Congratulations," Roger said, "she should be very proud of herself." But the conversation about the road test ended abruptly, and then they were back to discussing the family dinner that would be taking place shortly in his sister's apartment all the way over on East End.

"Root canal," Dr. Avalon was saying grimly. "And yet you feel confident Stacy will be up for this dinner?"

"I do," Roger said. He hoped she'd be wearing one of those short, tight skirts of hers; he always looked admiringly at her shapely hips and legs, and hoped that his brother-in-law, Marshall, would, too. Even though, of course, Marshall was happily married to Clare, and had been for nearly fifteen years.

During the final minutes of his session, Roger began to talk about the new mall in which he and his business pals had invested in suburban Atlanta. There was valet parking, and there were high-end retailers like Neiman Marcus, Vuitton, Burberry, and Williams-Sonoma. There had been some complaints about the food court and its disappointing offerings, but that could be rectified, Roger said.

"You have high hopes, I gather," Dr. Avalon remarked afterward, as Roger rose from his seat to let himself out. "Best of luck to you."

"I'll let you know how it goes," Roger said. He meant Stacy and the family dinner, but then wondered if it had been the mall outside of Atlanta that Avalon was referring to.

*Ah, Fort Lauderdale, spring break capital of the universe, Stacy thinks, navigating a shopping cart up and down the cereal aisle at Publix, the supermarket where she's stocking up on staples before the family settles into her mother-in-law's condo for the week. Will and Olivia argue over tall boxes of Cocoa Krispies and Cocoa Puffs while Roger acts as referee, and Stacy stares at the small*

mob of college students in bikinis and flip-flops, their arms goosebumped in the icy, extravagantly air-conditioned store. She herself is wearing a T-shirt and yoga pants, and absently rubs her hand over her slightly rounded, middle-aged stomach as she tries to ignore the college girls' enviably flat ones. And hears one of them—a teenager with a large Hello Kitty tattoo on her shoulder—say to her friends, "She's, like, nice, and pretty, and she's REALLY popular—so why the hell would anyone want to be with her?"

"I know," another girl says sympathetically. "It so totally makes no sense at all."

When she looks away from the girls, Stacy sees that her family is gone. Without a word to her, they've disappeared and left her here on her own. Her iPhone is in the car, she realizes, and so she will have to roam one long, chilly aisle after another in search of the husband and children who so thoughtlessly left her behind.

She feels a little panic-stricken, as if caught in one of those banal nightmares, the one where you awaken in the wrong bed in the wrong house and can't seem to find your old life, no matter how desperately you search for it.

## ~ 5 ~

Stacy's plan had been to take the subway from Brooklyn to the Upper East Side, and then walk over to Clare and Marshall's apartment on East End. But Roger, who still lived in the same apartment in the city four years after his divorce, told her that was crazy; instead, he drove from the Upper West Side to Park Slope to pick her up, then back into the city to his sister's apartment, leaving his BMW in the building's expensive garage. Which impressed Stacy, because this was something none of her friends or previous boyfriends would ever have done. (They would have circled the neighborhood endlessly, she knew, looking for a parking space out on the street rather than spend money on a garage.)

In the mood to snuggle up to Roger now as they left the car and rode the elevator from the garage to the lobby, Stacy linked her arm in his. Roger was dressed smartly in khakis with an impressively ironed crease down the front, a pale-blue crewneck linen sweater, and, on his big feet, what Stacy guessed were very pricey loafers. Compared to Kurt—the legal aid lawyer she'd been with before she and Roger met— Roger was dressed like a prince. (She almost told him so, but then thought better of it. Mentioning the name of someone you'd slept with to someone you were currently sleeping with was never a good idea, she understood.) In fact, she'd come to realize, Roger was an exceptionally well-dressed guy. His apartment had a walk-in closet the depth of which she'd never seen before: it was really like a room unto itself, and lined with endless suits sporting labels that were mostly unfamiliar to her. Though Brioni and Zegna were names she'd never heard of, she sensed she would be better off not knowing the price tags that had been attached to them. Roger's glossy leather shoes were neatly arranged on fancy wooden racks, and there wasn't a scuffed or comfortably broken-backed pair among them; even his collection of running shoes, on a separate rack, looked nearly immaculate. There was a motorized tie rack that displayed one crisp-looking tie—there were seventy-two in all, he told her—after another; when you pressed a button, they rotated past, arranged by color. Silvery blues and mini-striped lavenders and tiny-checked pale greens drifted by, all of them silky to the touch, and handmade in Italy. And all those Sea Island cotton dress shirts, dozens and dozens of them, tattersall and mini-tattersall, pinstripe and microcheck windowpane, oxford stripe and houndstooth. Each one bespoke, made-to-measure. Once when she'd slept over and she and Roger were getting dressed in the morning to go to work, she saw his index finger stroking, almost lovingly, she thought, one of those silken ties, savoring what, to him, might have been the very texture of his success. When she gently questioned him about the *need* for all this stuff, Roger explained to her how important it was for him to show up at meetings with his investors or when he was closing a deal, dressed like a man who was at the top of his game. It was true, she realized—just peeking into this vast closet you thought, as you were meant to, that all of this belonged to one of those masters of the universe, someone who could, and did, have everything he wanted, all of it top of the line.

She saw, too, that it wasn't that he paid undue, extravagant attention to his stuff, it was simply that he had a taste for fine, expensive things. That wasn't a sin, after all, she told herself. In a way, perhaps she even admired him for it, just a little.

Now she was handing Roger the rather flamboyant bouquet of tulips, roses, orchids, and irises she'd bought for his sister, Clare, at the Korean market near her apartment. She'd spent ten dollars on the flowers, and it felt like a lot of money. Someday, she hoped, that ten dollars would seem like less than nothing to her. But if that day never came, and she spent the rest of her life working for a nonprofit social service agency, well, so be it.

Stacy had decided to listen to her grandmother and forgo both the short skirt and the extremely high heels. But her armfuls of bracelets and their metallic ringing against each other cheered her, as did the long, colorful peacock feather earrings she wore that gently skimmed the sides of her neck.

She and Roger got into the elevator that would take them up to the apartment, along with a child—about the age of Stacy's twin nieces—who held on to the hand of her babysitter, a small, weary-looking Filipino woman dressed all in pink.

"I said," the little girl shrieked, "we're NOT allowed to WHISPER in school!"

"You hush now, Amanda," the babysitter said. "It's time to take a bath and settle down."

"YOU hush now," Amanda said, but her face turned sunny, and Stacy smiled at her. She thought of her nieces, Danielle and Savannah, and how sometimes, her sister had confided, they reduced her to weeping, even though they were only four years old and as well behaved as could be expected. It was just too hard, Lauren said, *too, too hard.* Getting them dressed in the morning in whatever outfits they insisted on, fixing their wispy, tangled hair, their breakfast (strictly Count Chocula on school days, Boo Berry on weekends), the lunches they took to school in their Barbie lunch boxes, because they were obsessed with Barbie, and wanted to know why they couldn't wear their Barbie pj's to school if they felt like it, and no, they didn't want to brush their teeth, not this morning, but maybe tomorrow morning, and why couldn't the hamster sleep under the covers in Danielle's bed, and *Green Eggs and Ham* was boring, and Sam I Am was a dumb, stupid name, and why couldn't Lauren read them something else, something better, like the *Barbie I Can Be a Ballerina* book. Lauren had begun to weep over the phone just reciting the litany of things that sometimes made her life as a mother so difficult, and of course she didn't expect Stacy to feel much sympathy for her because how could she, she who worked with all those damaged, pathetic people out on the filthy streets of the city, people who had nothing, *less* than nothing.

When the elevator drifted to a stop and Amanda and her babysitter got off, the little girl was rubbing her eyes with both hands and crying for her mother, who was apparently still at work, according to the babysitter, who said, "Mommy's a doctor and has sick people to take care of, even on a Saturday, you know that, hon." Which made Amanda cry even harder.

Stacy thought of how grateful she was for her own simple, childless, child-free life—a busy life that was filled with work and friends and, these past few months, Roger— but she could, with some effort, imagine what it would be like to feel otherwise. Suddenly, as they arrived at the apartment and Clare stood in the doorway to greet them, Stacy caught herself grinding her teeth (a nasty habit her dentist had repeatedly warned her against), and felt a spasm of pain deep in her mouth where her poor molar had been cleaned out with cruel instruments just the other day. She closed her eyes and let the pain pass through her, all the way through her cheekbone and up under her eye, and soon she was fine, smiling at Clare, a small woman in her midforties with lovely manicured hands, perfectly straight, light brown hair, and a long, elegant nose—Stacy's future sister-in-law (though who knew at the time?), who hugged and kissed her even though they'd never met before.

They bonded right away; Clare was a psychologist in a public middle school on First Avenue and 100th Street, and she knew plenty about dysfunctional families, plenty about fatherless children of mothers struggling with substance abuse, sexual abuse, child abuse—Clare had heard it all. She took both of Stacy's hands warmly in her own and welcomed her into the family-sized apartment whose floor-to-ceiling windows overlooked the East River and Carl Schurz Park, and where the glass dining-room table was already set for the meal she'd been preparing for half the day, she told Stacy. Marshall appeared, with his thin head of graying hair, and offered his hand, and he was followed by Nathaniel, their eight-year-old son adopted at birth from Colombia, his eyes and hair black as could be, his skin beautifully smooth and dusky. And then there was Beverly, Roger's mother, in her early seventies and still pretty; Stacy knew that she had once been head-turningly so—she'd seen some of the pictures that documented her beauty over the years. Her memory wasn't quite as good as it used to be, Beverly confided in the kitchen, where she and Stacy had gone to help Clare, even though Clare assured them everything was under control, and that she needed absolutely nothing from them.

"My Walter—that was Roger's father—used to say that getting old, and older, was no picnic," Beverly informed Stacy. "He was afraid of it, of getting old and not being able to play a good game of tennis anymore, or parallel park his car like a young person. Maybe that's why he died at seventy, before he was *truly* old," she mused, and popped an hors d'oeuvre into her lipsticked mouth. It was a tiny, bite-sized quiche lorraine, and Beverly declared it "darling." Which wasn't a word Stacy would ever have used to describe a morsel of food. But since this was Roger's mother and she wanted to make a stellar impression, or at least something approaching a stellar impression, Stacy nodded her head in agreement and echoed, *Darling*.

⸿

Clare and Marshall (whose flourishing Upper East Side orthodontics practice catered mostly to private school kids in the neighborhood) seemed enviably cozy in their marriage. Stacy could tell by the affectionate way Marshall touched Clare's wrist from time to time as they sat at the dinner table enjoying the gourmet mushroom-and-asparagus ravioli Clare had made from scratch with the help of a pasta machine she'd seen on an episode of *Martha Stewart Living.*

"Did you know Martha used to babysit for Mickey Mantle and Yogi Berra?" Clare asked.

"You mean for the *kids* of Mickey Mantle and Yogi Berra," Roger corrected her as he helped himself to some garlic bread that sat fragrantly in a wicker basket at the center of the table. Stacy took a small piece from the basket, figuring that if Roger was going to reek from garlic tonight, she might as well join him.

"The man was a drunk," Beverly said. She was having trouble transferring red leaf lettuce and croutons from the salad bowl to her plate, and Clare reached over to help her mother, adding a few cherry tomatoes. "You *know* I don't like tomatoes and never have," Beverly said sharply, and Stacy took note of the worried look Clare and Roger exchanged between them.

"Mom, you *love* tomatoes," Clare reminded her.

"Not only was Mickey Mantle a drunk, he was also a born-again Christian," Beverly reported. She speared a tomato with her salad fork. "Yogi Berra I don't know a thing about."

Nathaniel, the eight-year-old, announced that he didn't like the pasta *or* the salad, and he ate one piece of garlic bread after another until there was nothing left in the basket. And then he washed down all of it with a liter of Pepsi, which he carried to the table from the kitchen and drank straight from the bottle. Stacy wondered—not that it was any of her business, and not that she knew anything at all about the current theories of child-raising—if his parents might have reined him in a little if he'd been their biological son.

"Can I be excused?" Nathaniel asked quietly, but no one paid any attention. Stacy had heard from Roger how desperately Clare had wanted to give birth to a child of her own, and all about the costly IVF treatments she'd had, not one of which resulted in a pregnancy that lasted longer than nine or ten weeks. Then when Clare turned thirty-six, she and Marshall threw in the towel; after a three-month wait, they found themselves on a Boeing 727 to an orphanage in Colombia. Nathaniel was in third grade now in a high-profile private school where he was struggling, both socially and academically, and Roger had mentioned that his sister and Marshall were considering a different sort of school for him, perhaps one where the bar wasn't set quite so high.

Nathaniel was handsome but sullen, Stacy thought. She'd never seen an eight-year-old so lacking in joyousness, though perhaps he was just tired; after he'd finished gobbling and gulping his ill-advised dinner of garlic bread and Pepsi, he put his head down on the linen tablecloth, dangerously close to his mother's wine glass, and walked his fingers up the stem of the glass and back down, over and over again.

"Can I PLEASE be excused?" he yelled now, and this time, Clare said *Yes, of course, sweet pea,* and Stacy found herself relieved by the swiftness with which Nathaniel bolted from the table. Hate to say it, but the kid was sort of charmless, she thought. She couldn't imagine tucking him in every night as his parents did, kissing him lovingly on his smooth dark cheek, but maybe the fault was hers and not the little boy's, this child who'd spent the first few months of his life in an orphanage before being rescued by these good-hearted, desperate wanna-be parents. Maybe she just wasn't the kind of person to readily appreciate whatever there was to raising a child from infancy to near adulthood; maybe she just wasn't one of those natural-born mothers, the sort who didn't need to be reminded to savor every last bit of her child's growing up; the kind of mother who would nurture endless hopes for her son's future, even if she might have been fooling herself and it had been clear all along that her child was going nowhere fast. Or maybe it was simply that Stacy wasn't yet ready at this moment to transform herself from a relatively serious-minded thirty-something *career woman* (a phrase she hated—how come there weren't *career men?*) to a woman willing to put her own life on hold for a bit while she nurtured someone else's.

She took another look at Nathaniel, who was sitting upright on the living-room couch, holding one of those Nintendo Game Boys in his hands, frantically pressing two red plastic buttons with his thumbs, grunting in concentration, and, occasionally, whooping with pleasure when he scored a victory of some sort or another.

"What's going on, Nat?" Clare asked. "Did you defeat Tatonga, the Mysterious Spaceman, and save Princess Daisy?"

"Yesss!" Nathaniel said, and you could hear in that jubilant voice what it was he lived for, Stacy thought. She felt her view of him softening; he was just a little boy enthralled by a dopey, hand-held video game. Why had she been so hard on him? *Sorry*, she said silently, and as Roger dropped his hand into her lap and absently rubbed his fingers across the small, bumpy field of her knuckles, she found herself hoping to fall deeper and deeper in love with him, wherever that might lead. Her parents were gone, her grandmother was old, her sister was fixed firmly in her split-level home in Connecticut with her husband and the twins; sadly, Stacy's life and Lauren's no longer intersected much. The truth was, she didn't have much of a family to claim as her own.

"Dessert?" she heard Clare say. "There's chocolate mousse, nice and soft for *you*, Stacy. So the root canal went okay?"

Yes, and while Stacy had been relaxing in the dental chair waiting for the Novocain to take effect, she'd overheard the endodontist's assistant whispering to another assistant about the conspiracy charges that had been brought against the endodontist's wife, who'd allegedly been part of a suburban drug ring specializing in the distribution of coke and amphetamines.

"No kidding!" said Marshall. "An endodontist married to a drug dealer! You know, I briefly considered specializing in endodontistry myself, but then the thought of spending my work life removing damaged pulp and cleaning and sealing the insides of one tooth after another seemed just a little too depressing, if you know what I mean. Orthodontics, however, well, that's another story altogether!" he said cheerfully. "Though there's nothing harder than trying to get kids with braces to floss their teeth."

*Nothing?* Actually, Stacy could think of a great many things, starting with the trauma of losing your mother in a plane crash en route to the flashy casinos of Atlantic City in the company of a guy who had only just become her boyfriend.

She liked Marshall, though, and so she said nothing, and instead, nodded and smiled, as if she knew all about those intractable kids who refused to floss. Raising her wrists to her shoulders to flip back her freshly cut and blow-dried hair with both hands—an old, old habit of hers—she set her dozens of silver bracelets ringing.

A couple of hours later, as she and Roger made out like teenagers in the front seats of the BMW he'd parked on her street in a darkened Park Slope, Stacy suspected that she would be seeing his family again. And again.

∽

*Now that he's gotten official approval from the Florida Department of Law Enforcement, Roger can take possession of the secondhand 9 mm Glock 26, for which he's already paid $385 plus tax. He's sweating here in this air-conditioned shooting range, and his heart seems to be working harder than usual. His mouth is dry as he offers the simple word "thanks" to the guy behind the counter who hands the pistol over to him; it's been placed into a brown paper bag, the size he would get at Starbucks to take home his iced coffee and a single multigrain bagel.*

*The ammo is in a separate bag; both of these he stashes inside the glove compartment of the rented Toyota, which he left baking in the Florida sun.*

On the way back to the condo, he stops off at a Walgreen's and buys three souvenir T-shirts: two child-size, one adult. They are white shirts with a pink-eared rabbit on them, and underneath the rabbit are the words "Some Bunny in Fort Lauderdale Loves Me."

The children will like them so much, they'll throw them on over their sopping wet bathing suits the instant they climb out of the pool. Stacy will smile and say she'll wear hers to bed tonight.

They haven't had sex in about a month, he realizes, and it's entirely his fault.

Roger was determined to ask Stacy to marry him, though he understood that she might say no, pointing out that they'd only known one another for five months or so, and that she was in no particular hurry to settle down. There was some competition for him to worry about as well: a guy named Rocco Bassani, who, despite his name, Stacy told him, was 100 percent Jewish. Rocco happened to call while Stacy was busy making Roger her version of Buffalo wings for dinner; when she hadn't managed to get to the phone in time the other night, Rocco left a short but playful message on the answering machine in her modest-sized living room, a message which Roger wasn't, of course, meant to hear. It was painfully transparent to him then that Stacy and Rocco were more than just friends; hearing his message *(Say hey, good-lookin', What ya got cookin?)*, Roger instantly lost his appetite, and the scent of those Buffalo wings in the oven suddenly went from mouthwatering to repellent.

"I'm *so* sorry," Stacy said. Armed with a black rubber pot holder in each hand, she bent to remove the tray of wings from the oven. She dumped the tray in a hurry onto the top of the stove, her face flushed, Roger thought, with both the heat from the oven and her embarrassment at having been caught two-timing him. With someone named Rocco, for Christ's sake. For an instant or two, he convinced himself that Rocco was a plumber, someone whose hands went down your toilet or sink or the drain in your shower, searching for whatever was clogging things up. Or, if he wasn't a plumber, perhaps a contractor instead, a rough-hewn guy with lousy grammar, not to mention plenty of gray-green crusts of dirt under the nails of his blunt-tipped fingers. (Roger himself had dealt with many such guys in his real estate development business, and, in truth, he actually admired what they could do with their hands.)

But Rocco, it turned out, was an ophthalmologist, specializing in the treatment of glaucoma. He and Stacy had met in college back in the eighties, lived together for a few years while he was in med school at Cornell here in the city, and then split up. Afterward Rocco had fallen for someone named Isabella, a pediatric nurse with a high-pitched voice and wild, curly red hair, Stacy said.

"Isabella had a long, sad face, which probably wasn't the best kind of face for all those sick children she was dealing with every day . . ."

Roger wasn't the least bit interested in the nurse Rocco had fallen for after med school. Despite himself, he put his fingertip to one of the still-sizzling wings on the tray, then slipped his finger into his mouth. Excellent sauce; a little tangy, but not too hot, he thought. *Just perfect.*

"Well, listen, 'Women have died from time to time, and worms have eaten them, but not for love,'" he heard Stacy saying now. "And that goes for men, too."

"Says who? In any case, that's very cynical, don't you think?" Roger said.

"That's Shakespeare, buddy. Or, more accurately, *my* version of Shakespeare."

Even though his appetite was gone, Roger's stomach grumbled crossly, trying to tell him something. "You're sleeping with him?" he asked. Like a child, he clapped his hands over his ears so he wouldn't have to hear her answer.

"Rocco? Umm, not really."

Stacy set the table with shiny pink plastic place mats, salad-size plates rimmed with pink, and plain white dinner napkins. "The thing is, I did love him, but not, um, what I would call a full 100 percent."

She seemed to be speaking an utterly foreign language; honestly, could you love someone 90 percent? Or 75 percent? If you loved someone, say, 45 percent, was there any hope at all for the relationship? Roger thought of his mother assuring him, when he was a child, *I love you with a full heart.* What if she'd said, instead, *I love you with 75 percent of my heart?* Would he have been smart enough to have been insulted?

Never mind about Rocco: what about Roger himself? Did Stacy love *him* with a full heart, i.e., 100 percent? From time to time, when she woke up in his bed, or he woke up in hers, she'd leaned toward him and murmured something about love, her face turned slightly away from his because of her morning breath, not that he would have minded.

She'd never said what, exactly, it was that she loved about Roger; he would have to ask her sometime, but not now, not when Rocco's voice was fresh in both their minds. And what did he love about *her*? Well, just about everything, starting with her youth (thirty-three was, by his standards, refreshingly young), and her lively hopefulness that took him by surprise now that he had passed forty and was all-too-aware that he'd already lived out half his life—if he were lucky, that is. He loved her full (but not too-full), pretty face, her slightly pointed chin, the arch of her dark eyebrows, and the way she could illuminate a room with her passion for the clients she worked with.

"I need for you to stop seeing Rocco," Roger said. He went to Stacy's banged-up, mustard-colored refrigerator and poured himself a glass of OJ. "You think that no one ever died for love, but guess what, that's just wrong," he told her. He guzzled a mouthful of juice, but then had to spit it into the sink. "This stuff is spoiled—it's fizzy!" he said, a little outraged. He took a look at the expiration date on the container and saw that it had come and gone nearly four weeks earlier. *Oh, this girlfriend of his desperately needed someone to show her the way.*

"Sorry," Stacy said. "I guess I should have checked the date, huh?" She fooled with the napkin at his place setting, folding it back and forth until she'd made a fan.

"Come on over here, you," Roger said, and summoned her into the galley kitchen where there was barely room for two people to stand side by side. But instead of waiting for her to come to him, he rushed to meet her at the table, and arranged his arms around her beautifully straight back. "I don't want to know anything at all about Rocco," he said. "Not a thing. I just want to know that he's gone from your life. And by that I mean *100 percent* gone." There was an outline of a tiny purple heart tattooed on the underside of Stacy's wrist, and Roger raised it to his mouth and kissed it. *One hundred percent,* he murmured.

He saw something pass fleetingly across her face, a look of what he believed to be a lovely pure empathy, and that, at least for the moment, was enough to fill him with hope.

*Roger has returned from doing some errands, but even though he's vague about where he went, she doesn't press him because Will and Olivia are so happy with those new T-shirts of theirs. After microwaved chicken nuggets are served for the kids' lunch, they drive a half hour to Butterfly World in Coconut Creek. Southern monarchs and Emerald Swallowtails and Sara Longwings land delicately on the kids' shoulders and on their fingertips in the Paradise Adventure Aviary, but Olivia and Will get a bigger kick from the Bug Zoo, where they're fascinated by the exhibits of live spiders, walking sticks, and mantises, praying and otherwise. As they earnestly study a walking stick almost completely camouflaged by the branches it rests upon, Stacy can't help but notice that Roger resembles, as he has so often these days, one of those disengaged fathers who's cemented to his BlackBerry. She hates to see*

him like this, hunched against the wall in a corner of the Bug Zoo, scrolling through his e-mails and text messages so anxiously.

"It makes my stomach hurt to see you like this," she says, whispering into his ear now.

"What?" he says, and continues to scroll.

"My stomach," she says. She takes two caplets of Pepto-Bismol from the pink plastic bottle she carries with her everywhere these days. "Indigestion, heartburn, I don't know. I worry about you and then my stomach hurts."

"Don't worry," he breathes, but he can't turn his head even for an instant to look at her as she swallows down those pink caplets with a quiet sip from a bottle of Aquafina.

Isn't he supposed to be on vacation? A family vacation, as a matter of fact, all four of them free to savor each other's company unfettered by the responsibilities of home and work and school.

It's going to be a long week, she fears, and though she hates to admit it, even to herself, a small, selfish part of her is already guiltily looking forward to the moment school starts up again a week from next Monday.

## ~ 7 ~

The night she went over to Rocco's apartment to have a discussion with him about their future together (or the lack thereof), Stacy slept with him one last time. He had just finished telling her a terribly sad story about a middle-aged patient of his, who, in addition to suffering from deteriorating vision, had recently been given a devastating cancer diagnosis, one that held out little hope for the guy's future. Stacy's eyes brimmed as she listened to Rocco talk about his patient; somehow, though she hadn't meant for it to happen, they ended up in his bedroom, and then onto the bed itself. Rocco was an attending physician at New York Hospital, and had been making a pretty nice salary for a while now, but you'd never know it by the look of his apartment, a one-bedroom co-op in a doorman building near the hospital, on a leafy side street off First Avenue. The apartment had very little furniture in it, as if Rocco had just moved in, though he'd actually been there for several years. There was a big, expensive-looking forest-green leather couch in the living room and also a coffee table, but no chairs or dining table, and neither carpeting nor a rug on the scratched and stain-spotted parquet floor. The bedroom was no better. All four corners of the nearly empty room were occupied by tall, sloppy piles of books and medical journals. Here, too, as in the living room, Rocco hadn't even bothered to put up new window treatments; the windows were covered by nothing more than dusty, yellowing venetian blinds left behind by the previous owner.

"What you need, Rocco, is a woman or two in your life," Stacy told him sternly after he rolled off her and lit up a joint in his bedroom. "Not to mention some nice Levolors."

Both of them were naked, except that Rocco had, in the heat of the moment, neglected to take off one of his socks. "I mean this apartment is ridiculous. How lazy can you get? How much energy does it take to buy a rug, or some carpeting? What's wrong with you, you lazy bastard?" Stacy took a hit from the joint and smacked him lightly over the head with the current issue of the *Journal of Cataract and Refractive Surgery* that she'd picked up off the night table.

"Ow," said Rocco, pretending she'd hurt him. A line of curly dark-blond hair bisected his stomach and groin; idly, Stacy tugged at it, but so gently that Rocco seemed not to notice. She was going to miss him, she realized—their history went back a long way, all the way to Cambridge, where he had, freshman year, been dating her dearest friend Jefrie-Ann Miller, one of the pals Stacy had gone shopping with at the Harvard Coop in June. Remembering the reunion now, she thought of Roger, and how everything that had passed between the two of them stemmed from the wallet and key ring she'd dropped on the floor of the muffin shop. Or *shoppe*. What if she'd been paying attention and the wallet and keys hadn't fallen from her hands? Would she and Rocco be in a different sort of relationship now? They'd been friends first, then live-in lovers for three years, then exes, and then friends again, albeit friends who'd once seriously considered marriage; if not for Rocco's adamant refusal to even contemplate the possibility of having children someday—he'd sealed the deal with a vasectomy in his final year of med school—Stacy might have married him, she believed. He'd been the very first love of her life, and now she was here to tell him that seeing each other again, even as old friends, just wasn't a great idea.

"I'm going to marry Roger," she heard herself say. She took another hit from the joint before handing it back to Rocco.

"Whoa! Are you guys engaged or something?"

On the clock radio next to her side of the bed, Aerosmith's "I Don't Want to Miss a Thing" was playing now; its extravagant sentimentality was too much for Stacy, and she had to turn it off. "Nope, I just have a feeling—a pretty strong one, actually—that it's going to happen, that's all," she told Rocco. "He's forty-two, going on forty-three; I think he wants to get moving, you know? And you know what, so do I," she heard herself say.

"You wanna marry a guy in his forties?" Rocco said. He offered the joint to Stacy again, but she'd had enough.

"You sort of sound like an ageist idiot," she said. "Never mind those Ivy League degrees of yours."

"Forty-two, man . . . any way you look at it, it's not young."

"Trust me," Stacy said, "it's not a problem. Someday, when Roger's ninety-five and I'm a mere eighty-six, I may think of him as extremely old, but, until then, I predict it's all going to be fine. Better than fine. And he's kind of a great guy, by the way—smart, successful, self-assured, and there's this generosity I keep seeing in him; he's someone who really just wants to take care of me . . ."

Rocco looked at her sadly; or maybe, Stacy thought, he was just goofy and stoned. "I'm never going to meet him, am I?" he said. He pulled off the one sock he was still wearing and pitched it across the room.

"What? Isn't it bad enough he had to hear your message on my answering machine?" Stacy said. That look of shock and confusion and melancholy on Roger's face, the way he'd cringed at the sound of Rocco's voice; it was almost as if she could feel the muscles in his body contracting in horror. If she'd been just the slightest bit uncertain about whether she loved Roger, she'd known, at that uneasy moment in her apartment the other night, that she could never stand to see him hurt like that. Surely that was love, wasn't it? Roger was more generous—or at least more open—about his love for her, but she could already feel herself swiftly catching up.

She untangled her legs from Rocco's now, more than a little queasy at having allowed herself to fall so effortlessly into his bed.

"Actually . . . I came over here to break the news to you that we can't see each other again," she confessed. She had some trouble finding her bra, which had somehow disappeared behind Rocco's bed; brushing off a dust bunny or two that clung to it, she got back into the bra and then her jeans.

"Not even as friends?" Rocco asked, and casually adjusted an errant bra strap for her before she slipped on her sweater.

"Friends don't fix friends' bra straps for them, at least not when one of those friends happens to be a guy."

"And whose rule is that?" Rocco said. The joint had burned down to almost nothing, but he took one last hit before putting it out and unwrapping a root beer-colored lollipop that he discovered under his pillow, and which he immediately began to crunch on.

"You're going to break a tooth," Stacy warned him. "It's *my* rule, and it's a sensible one, don't you think?" She wondered if having lost her parents while she was still in her twenties had somehow made her selfish, more inclined to look out for her own best interests than she might otherwise have been. If so, she regretted it. But listen, you could get behind the wheel of your own life but steer it only so far. Sometimes it happened that you were screwed by forces beyond your control—a force like that reckless fool of a middle-aged guy who insisted on taking your mother flying on an especially windy afternoon.

"After all these years, we're going to miss each other too much," Rocco pointed out. "I can't agree to this craziness of yours. You're telling me that we can't even meet for a coffee every now and then? I mean, where's the harm in that?"

Sitting at the edge of Rocco's bed, Stacy had zipped up her high-heeled boots, and was now out of the room and looking for her leather jacket, which she could have sworn she'd slung over the coat rack. From the foyer, she called out to Rocco to come and help her, and when he appeared, entirely naked, she made a visor of her hand to shield her eyes. "No more," she said. "Don't."

"Oh, I know you don't mean that," said Rocco, but began heading back toward the bedroom to get dressed after he handed her the leather jacket, which had been hidden directly under his trench coat on the rack.

"Oh, I *do* mean that!" yelled Stacy. "You're no longer the ex-love of my life, buddy. I'm officially not thinking about us ever again. Ever!"

A jean jacket had fallen to the floor and was stamped with a dusty footprint, Stacy noted. She expected a couple of tears to spring to her eyes as she hugged Rocco one last time, but they didn't; there was only the sight of his downcast face as he stood in gray-and-black striped pajama bottoms in the open doorway and watched her walk down the hall toward the elevator.

*The kids are asleep at the other end of the apartment, on the corduroy futon that opens up neatly into a double bed in the den. When Stacy tiptoes down the hallway to check on them, she sees that Olivia is flat on her back with a leg hanging off the side of the futon, the heel of one tiny foot nearly touching the carpet; Will is in a fetal position, his thumb stuck comfortingly into his mouth. Stacy considers unplugging it, but doesn't want to risk waking him. She kisses both of her children on the tops of their slightly sweaty heads, and walks out of the room on her bare toes.*

*Roger is waiting for her in his parents' bed, sitting up in his boxers against the upholstered headboard, his ever-present BlackBerry in hand, inspecting his e-mails with a frown. He is fifty-two years old and looks it; his hair is almost completely gray now, which takes Stacy by surprise from time to time. When she studies photographs from* their wedding and honeymoon, or even those taken from her hospital bed in the maternity ward at Mount Sinai, where Will was born three years ago, she sees a different Roger, younger, of course, but also happier, clearly possessing a sheen of confidence and well-being that she hasn't been aware of for months now.

She knows exactly how long it's been since they've slept together—thirty-four days—and feels a little sickened by that fact, as if it suggests she and Roger may have lost the easy familiarity with each other's bodies that they've savored for all the years of their marriage.

Climbing up onto her side of the bed, dressed in her "Some Bunny Loves Me" T-shirt and not much else, she waits for Roger to put down his BlackBerry. She runs her fingertip along the inside of his arm, then down his leg, all the way down to his sturdy ankle.

"You're tickling me," he says. "Please stop."

Humiliated, she rolls over onto her other side, facing away from him and his damn BlackBerry.

"Wait, I'm sorry, just one more e-mail," he says, but why should she believe him?

She who can probably count on one hand the number of soulful kisses exchanged between them during those thirty-four days.

ॐ

She has no idea what time it is when he wakes her, but it's still pitch-dark in the room, and he raises her T-shirt up and over her head in a hurry. He's hard, though not hard enough, and that's because it's his parents' bed they're sleeping in, and maybe it's just too creepy, he explains.

"Just tell me you love me," he says. He sounds exhausted and his voice is full of all kinds of disappointment.

"Of course I do," she says. "<u>Of course</u> I do!" But it's not enough; he asks her to say the whole thing this time.

"I . . . love . . . <u>you</u>," she says, hoping she sounds as adamant as she means to, and then she hears him weeping, something she has witnessed so painfully more than a couple of times since his poor, poor, deeply unlucky sister died two months ago.

You can't listen to a man sobbing in bed beside you and do nothing; you can't stop the fine hairs at the back of your neck from stiffening, or the muscles in your stomach from contracting in sympathy. You can take all the Pepto-Bismol you want, and kiss your husband's tears so delicately and lovingly, but, in the end, none of it, Stacy understands, is going to make a bit of difference tonight.

# ~ 8 ~

On a Sunday afternoon, the day after Halloween, Roger went downtown to the diamond district on Forty-Seventh Street, to shop for a ring for Stacy. He would have preferred to do his shopping at Cartier or Tiffany, but his mother had a cousin named Zlata, a Holocaust survivor from Hungary, who was in the diamond business, and this was where everyone in Roger's family had always gone. He walked past one small jewelry shop after another, many of them owned by Orthodox Jewish guys who spoke Yiddish-accented English and who all looked the same to Roger in their black suits and plain white shirts, their pallor, their near-sighted brown eyes corrected by what appeared to be identical black-framed glasses. Looking through the shop windows at these guys and what he perceived to be their melancholy faces, Roger could swear he saw the tragic history of all of European Jewry reflected in them. Just before entering Zlata's store, Forever Diamonds, he watched as what looked like gallons of popcorn mysteriously appeared out of nowhere and blew across the sidewalk, scattered by the chilly November wind. It was two o'clock now; he was hungry for lunch, his hands were cold, and the jacket he wore wasn't heavy enough for the surprisingly brisk weather.

From behind the counter of Forever Diamonds, a fifty-ish man said, "*Velcome.*" The store was empty of customers, and Zlata wasn't around; she'd been called away to New Jersey to help take care of her grandchildren, the man said, after Roger explained who he was. There was a color photograph of the beloved leader of the Lubavitch Hasidim, Rebbe Menachem Mendel Schneerson, taped to the wall, the same portrait Roger had seen in the window of nearly every shop he'd passed on Forty-Seventh Street today. He stared at the Rebbe's blue eyes, his gentle, smiling face, this guy who was regarded by many of his followers to be the messiah.

The man behind the counter, who was named Shmuli, introduced himself as Zlata's business partner and smiled at Roger agreeably. "You know who the Rebbe is? He *vill* help you even from beyond the grave," Shmuli promised.

Would the Rebbe help him pick out a diamond ring for Stacy? Roger joked, though he knew, even as he said it, that Shmuli might think it was sacrilege to joke about the saintly Rebbe.

But Shmuli only shrugged. "You're looking for . . . ? Round-cut? Marquise? Emerald? Princess? Pear? *Vat* can I help you *vit?*"

*Vell, let's see.* Beyond the cut of the diamond, there was also clarity and color to consider. So much to worry about: Roger had looked at endless photos of diamonds on the Internet over the past few days but hadn't been able to make a decision about any of it.

Shmuli was patient; in addition to his expertise, he offered tea and a small ceramic bowl of shelled walnuts and almonds as Roger examined the stones that had been arranged for him against a piece of maroon velvet spread across the top of the glass counter.

Did he know *vat* size finger the bride-to-be had?

Her fingers were long and thin, Roger said, and blushed, thinking of the smooth, pale slice of knee visible through the rip in Stacy's favorite jeans, and how the sight of it, just last night, filled him with lust, and also love, as he slid his own finger into the hole in her jeans and stroked her bare knee.

*Vell,* long and thin *vasn't* a size, Shmuli said, but not to *vorry,* later they could size the ring for the round-cut dia-mond Roger had finally chosen—for its brilliance and fire—after Stacy saw the ring. Which, Shmuli promised, would be ready for Roger to pick up by, let's see, Thursday or Friday.

Roger forked over his credit card, and gazed directly into the Rebbe's clear blue eyes, looking for his approval, never mind that the old man had died in 1994 and Roger the faithless had never once made a pilgrimage to his final resting place in Queens—where thousands of the Rebbe's followers from all around the world, Jew and non-Jew alike, flocked every day of the year, except on the Sabbath, according to Shmuli.

Shmuli was from Berlin, Roger discovered, though he'd been born in a displaced persons' camp in Poland directly after the war. And he was certain, he told Roger as he handed him his credit card receipt, that the Rebbe was indeed the messiah. "You and your family should come to his grave for blessings and spiritual guidance," he advised Roger. "*Vat* can it hurt to go?" He tapped Roger's wrist lightly with his index finger. "By the *vey*, that's a beautiful *vatch* you got there. *Vat* you pay for that Rolex?"

"A lot," Roger said vaguely. He folded the receipt into a tiny square, and slipped it into the pocket of his khakis. He had just spent more than $8,000 on an engagement ring for Stacy, who, for all he knew, wasn't quite ready to take the plunge, to upgrade from girlfriend to fiancée. It had been five months since she'd dropped her wallet and keys; wasn't that enough time? He was eager to get a move on, to settle into a life embellished by a wife and children, that hectic life, filled to the brim, that most of his friends had been living for ten or fifteen years by now. His fortieth birthday was behind him, and he didn't want to wait any longer, didn't want to be robbed of the life he'd been patiently waiting to make his own.

Sauntering along Forty-Seventh Street toward Fifth Avenue now, he saw, the day after Halloween, some nut dressed as the killer in the movie *Scream*, wearing a black hood and cloak, his white rubber mask mimicking the figure in Edvard Munch's *The Scream*. As they passed each other, the nutjob behind the mask politely put up a hand in greeting.

∽

He's been in Florida long enough that his children are now the color of Melba toast. He's been trying to spend as much time with his family as he can, though sitting around the pool every morning while Stacy plays with Olivia and Will in the shallow end bores him. Roger doesn't like the water very much, and never has, not since he was a child and his parents belonged to a beach club on the south shore of Long Island; his mother and father had a hard time getting him into the water—chlorinated or salt, he wasn't fond of either—just as Stacy has a hard time getting him into the pool now. The smell of chlorine is vaguely unpleasant to him, and the stickiness of dried salt water annoying, along with the gritty feel of leftover sand between his toes and his teeth and inside his ears. Stacy insisted that the kids see the ocean, though, and so all four of them spent a couple of hours yesterday at the beach, where they rented striped canvas chairs and Roger and Stacy escorted Will and Olivia to the water's edge so they could get their tootsies wet.

Sitting on a chaise longue at the pool, Roger watches a young guy towing his toddler on a Styrofoam float; the little boy is sitting upright, his mother's arm supporting him around his waist, and he looks terrified. The mother is saying, comfortingly, in a sing-songy voice, "Mommy loves you and Daddy loves you, everyone loves little Cooper, it's true." But Cooper is in tears now, and wants to be returned to dry land. And he has Roger's sympathy.

The truth is, Roger's got a lot to do before this vacation comes to an end.

For one thing, he has a note to write. Actually it may end up considerably longer than a note; he will have a lot of explaining to do and that may take up a couple of pages. Or not.

He brought a yellow legal pad with him from home, for that very purpose. Of course he could type it all out on his laptop, but that seems awfully impersonal, doesn't it? The things he has to say are enormously important and intensely felt, and handwritten is the way to go, he's sure of it. Line after line of neatly typed, perfectly formed words just won't cut it.

He checked on the pistol last night after he and his family returned from dinner at Outback Steakhouse; the kids were dozing off and Stacy was in the back of the Toyota, tenderly rousing Will and Olivia out of their car seats and along the parking lot to the locked front doors of the condo. Opening the glove compartment, running his hand across first one brown paper bag and then the other, Roger felt reassured. But just a moment later, his pulse quickened, and he began to feel more than a little queasy, more than a little light-headed. He thought he was going to vomit up his no-better-than-mediocre steak dinner, but when he pushed open the door on the driver's side and leaned out, nothing but a thin string of bile fell from his mouth.

Stacy, who was already upstairs with the kids, looked at him anxiously when he walked through the door. "What happened to you?" she said. "What's wrong? Are you sick, baby?" She put her cool hand on his moist forehead and kept it there.

"It's nothing," he said. "Nada. Or nothing that a glass of water and an after-dinner nap wouldn't fix." He knew how to lie, and was, in fact, getting good at it.

His kids are waving to him from the pool now, each of them outfitted with inflatable water wings, Will's imprinted with images of Spider-Man, Olivia's with smiley faces. Leaning back against the aqua-blue concrete wall of the pool, her arms crossed behind her head, Stacy smiles at Roger in his vinyl chaise longue.

Smiling back, he aims his BlackBerry in his family's direction, and snaps their picture.

# ~ 9 ~

Stacy and Roger were in his living room watching *Frasier*—which occupied a place of honor in her pantheon of TV shows—when, during a commercial, and without fanfare, Roger handed her a small, satiny, black drawstring bag.

Her hand was deep inside a bag of gourmet pumpernickel pretzels, and she withdrew it to accept the gift Roger held out to her. "What's this?" she asked, brushing salt crystals from her fingers.

"Well, why don't we find out?" Roger said. The neutral expression on his face told her nothing, but he was rubbing his hands together impatiently, and she sensed a bit of apprehensiveness. He had been generous to her all along, having given her, on their three-month anniversary, a trio of thick, interconnected sterling silver bangle bracelets to complement the armfuls of skinny ones she wore every day, and on their four-month, a pair of gold-and-sapphire earrings from Cartier. The gifts had taken her by surprise, and both times she had nothing on hand to give him in return. She was greatly touched by his generosity, and the sweetness of his sensibility, and ran out to a bookstore the day after each of the anniversaries to pick out a paperback for him—short story collections by John Updike and Flannery O'Connor, two writers whose work she loved.

Turning away from the TV now, Stacy eased the fingers of one hand into the opening of the velvet bag, flipped it upside down, and watched as a diamond ring slid into her waiting palm. "*Whoa*, is that what I think it is?" she said, and feigned astonishment, when, in truth, she'd sensed, over the past few weeks, that this was what Roger had been contemplating.

She hugged him, exuberant—because this promise of a shared life was what they both so ardently wanted—and started to slip the ring over her finger, but stopped at the first joint, allowing Roger to finish the job. They admired the ring together, switching on the halogen reading lamp at the side of the couch so that the diamond could show itself off, then Stacy, smiling, listened carefully as Roger said, *I love you.*

*Frasier's* live audience roared with laughter, but Stacy hadn't, of course, been paying the slightest attention, and she allowed herself, for a split-second, to wonder what was so funny.

Her cheek was against Roger's shoulder, and she could feel the warmth of his skin through his thin shirt. "I love you so much," she said easily, understanding in that instant that her affection for Roger had ripened into what was surely the deepest sort of love.

She thought immediately of calling her parents; it was one of those times when, even now, years after their deaths, she couldn't quite believe that a phone call to them wasn't within the realm of what was possible. Neither of her parents had lived long enough to see her in any way settled; her father hadn't even made it to her college graduation. She could borrow Roger's BMW, drive out to visit their graves, far away in Suffolk County on Long Island, and share the news with them . . . But that was just a little creepy, wasn't it? It was one thing, she supposed, if you believed in an afterlife, but frankly, the very notion of one was, to her, no more than wishful thinking at its silliest.

She picked up the phone in Roger's kitchen and called her grandmother, apologizing for awakening her, even though it was barely nine o'clock.

"This better be good," Juliette said. "Just a minute, let me find my glasses."

Stacy studied her ring as Juliette took her time. It was a beauty; she could see all the way through the center of the diamond to the platinum band beneath it.

Following her into the kitchen, Roger snuck up behind her, and laced his arms around her waist. "Let me talk to Gram," he said, and took the phone from Stacy.

She listened as he sweet-talked her grandmother, saying, "I will . . . I will . . . I will, don't worry . . . Of course I do. Sure . . . you bet."

When Stacy got the phone back, Juliette said, "Mazel tov, baby-doll! But I have to tell you that I'm not in love with the fact that he's a man in his forties. On the other hand, I believe him when he says of course he's going to take very good care of you."

"Oh, he absolutely will," Stacy assured her.

Roger had poked his head inside the refrigerator, and he withdrew a bottle of Cristal with a noticeably shiny gold bow attached to it. "Come on, hang up," he mouthed, and rolled his eyes exaggeratedly, but Stacy shook her head.

She let her grandmother go on and on, mostly about how sad it was that Stacy's mother had missed out on the opportunity to shop for a wedding dress with her. Then Juliette moved on to the subject of "your mother's idiot boyfriend who we'll always hold personally responsible for the death of my beloved child and your beloved mother." There were tears in Stacy's eyes as she held the receiver away from her ear and tried her best to ignore her grandmother's rant. She watched as Roger busied himself opening the bottle of Cristal, which Stacy would later learn—to her amazement—had cost him more than a hundred dollars. How could she tell him that she preferred Diet Coke, nectar of the gods, to the taste of champagne? It seemed embarrassing to admit, and might even be seen by him as a flaw in her character. She had plenty of other flaws, she thought, that, in the five months they'd been together, Roger had yet to discover. The one she'd worked hardest to hide from him was the shameful fact that, unlike Grace, her mother, Stacy wasn't much of a housekeeper. Her mother had rules: always make your bed first thing in the morning; never leave home with dirty dishes or silverware sitting in the sink; clean the bathroom thoroughly every day with Ajax, Windex, and bleach; dust the top of your dresser once in the morning and again at night before you went to sleep—these rules of hers were exhausting just to contemplate, Stacy thought. And the truth was, the one thing she'd always believed about rules was that they were meant to be broken. Thus the less-than-pristine condition of her bathroom and kitchen when there was no one around to check up on her; Roger, for example, or her sister, who'd inherited her mother's respect for neat and clean. In Stacy's view, life was all too brief (hadn't the random cruelty with which her parents' lives were extinguished shown that to her?). And after she was finished with work for the day, there were just too many books to read, too many movies to see, TV shows to watch, and music to listen to; given these abundant pleasures, why would she bother to agonize over the sink she'd scrubbed only half-heartedly?

As Roger poured champagne for them into a pair of polished-looking flutes, and signaled comically one more time for her to get off the phone, she thought of what a comfort it was to know that, in all the world, it was Roger who wanted to take care of her; this was, she recognized now, at the very foundation of her love for him—this need and desire of his to watch over her and keep her happy. Though perhaps they weren't perfect soul mates—they were, after all, a social worker and a real estate developer inhabiting sharply different worlds that had barely a note in common—it was still possible, wasn't it, to find yourself free-falling toward love nonetheless.

⁂

After Roger called his mother and sister, both of whom asked to speak to Stacy and welcomed her happily into the family (*Thrilled to death!* Clare shrieked into the phone), Stacy dialed her sister's number in Connecticut. Her brother-in-law, who was named Chuck, answered the phone. He was a modestly successful woodworker and cabinetmaker, and Stacy had always wished they'd liked each other more. She'd sensed almost immediately that Chuck was not a fan of hers, and she never quite understood why; she always worked perhaps a bit too hard to try and win him over, even though she knew full well that it was a losing battle.

"Hey, Chuck," she said, and took a sip of champagne. Why was it always so hard to talk to him? Because she had gone to Harvard and he hadn't gone to any college at all, not even for a single semester? Could that simple fact really have been the reason? She'd always worried that it was her own fault Chuck didn't like her, but maybe, as Roger had delicately suggested, she was being too hard on herself. She had, more than once, tried to find out from Lauren if she'd ever offended Chuck in any way, but Lauren's response had always been, *Come on, that's insane!*

She asked now about the twins, who'd just gone to sleep, one of them with an ear infection and a fever of 104. "Oh, that's awful," Stacy said, and after hearing about a couple of trips to the pediatrician, wanted to know if her sister was around.

"She's in the shower," Chuck reported, but Stacy didn't believe him. She told him why she was calling, and was glad to hear the word "congratulations" in his response, even though it was a word uttered without much animation. She hated it that his indifference pained her, and then she was shocked to hear Chuck say, "He's in commercial real estate, right? So is he rich?"

She looked over at Roger, who was sipping his champagne and paging through some magazine—*duPont Registry: A Buyer's Gallery of Fine Automobiles*—she'd never seen anywhere except in his apartment. She wanted to tell her brother-in-law to mind his own business, but instead she murmured, "I honestly don't know." But how could she not? There was this spacious apartment of his here on West End, his top-of-the-line BMW, all the lovely, expensive restaurants he took her to every weekend, the vacation he'd treated her to in Acapulco. She was a caseworker for a nonprofit; she spent her workdays helping the poor and the fucked-up, the disenfranchised and the voiceless; she didn't keep track of other people's money and how they spent it. To be honest, she just didn't care. Nor did she worry too much about how Roger earned his living—he was, he'd explained, someone who helped to build places where retail companies could create jobs for those who needed them. Every time a mall of his went up, he was helping to stimulate the economy, wasn't he? Why should she have moral reservations about that? Not everyone was suited for the sort of sometimes-emotionally draining, ill-paid work she'd been drawn to; she'd have to be an idiot not to recognize that. And, too, she recognized that Roger did have a social conscience—she'd once seen, on his desk here in the apartment, resting carelessly on top of a layer of magazines, a $5,000 check he'd written out to the Make-A-Wish Foundation, the sight of which caused her eyes to fill.

*So is he rich?* "I don't know," she repeated to Chuck, and a moment or two later, Lauren picked up the phone.

Her congratulations sounded genuine, but then, immediately afterward, she began to limn the details of Danielle's ear infection. "I had to keep her out of school all week. If you think babysitters come cheap out here in the 'burbs, well, you're wrong," she finished, the sound of her voice marred by a trace of self-pity.

"So you'll be able to come to the, um, engagement brunch Roger's mother decided to have for us next weekend?" Stacy asked. How pathetic would it be if, except for her grandmother, no one at all from her side of the family showed up?

"I'll have to ask Chuck," Lauren said, "but I kinda think we'll be there, don't worry."

Before the conversation ended, Stacy waited for her sister to offer a little more on the subject of her congratulations—to elaborate, perhaps, on how happy she was that Stacy was finally settling down with one of those good guys, thoroughly steady and solid, someone you'd choose to be the father of your children when, in fact, you were ready to have them. The only time Lauren and Chuck had met Roger was at dinner one night toward the end of the summer, and it hadn't gone as well as Stacy had hoped. Le Bernardin, the restaurant Roger had chosen, was among the most expensive in the city, and Stacy could see how uncomfortable her sister and Chuck were when it came time for them to make their selections from the menu. Even though Roger had quietly mentioned that he was treating them to dinner, Stacy was pained to see the resentment in Chuck's face as he ordered the very pricey calamari filled with prawns and shiitake mushrooms, and for Lauren, the equally expensive peekytoe crab. She realized it had been a mistake to take them to this restaurant they could never have afforded on their own, and Stacy had wanted to kick herself afterward for having been so dense. But she understood, too, that for reasons she couldn't quite fathom, it was important to Roger to be able to treat family and friends to an extravagant meal—to announce to them in this way, perhaps, that he was doing very well.

She could wait all night now for Lauren to reassure her that she had chosen wisely, that Roger was a prince, a prize, a keeper. She could wait all night, all the way through to tomorrow, but it wasn't going to happen.

"Gotta go, one of the twins is crying," Lauren was saying, but for the second time tonight, Stacy told herself that she knew a lie when she heard one.

"Okay, bye, love you," she said to Lauren. Of all the different kinds of unrequited love, this was hardly the worst, she thought. Still, it would have been nice . . .

∽

*They're lunching at a plastic table at Burger King when her phone, positioned next to a tall, waxy cup of Diet Coke, begins to ring. She sees that it's Marshall, and also that there's ketchup smeared above Will's brow and under his nose, a vividly red purée which she wipes off with the flimsiest of paper napkins as she talks to her brother-in-law, who is very distressed about something to do with Beverly.*

*She thinks of her mother-in-law and the assisted-living center overlooking the East River where Beverly is doomed to spend the last years of her life on the single floor reserved for those residents with Alzheimer's.*

*The one piece of jewelry Beverly took with her when she moved into her room at Renaissance Living Center was her engagement ring, a small marquise-cut diamond that, Clare had hoped, would serve to remind Beverly of who she was.*

*This proved to be a mistakenly optimistic notion, as, before too long, Beverly ceased to remember much of anything. She has been inhabiting another planet, one of her own creation, ever since moving to Renaissance two years ago.*

*Now her diamond ring is gone.*

*And Clare.*

*According to Marshall, who heard it yesterday—during one of his occasional visits to Renaissance—from someone who works security there, in all likelihood the ring was slipped off Beverly's wizened finger the other night when no one was looking, then pocketed by one of the women who was subbing for Starquasia, Beverly's regular caregiver. Someone whose job it is to escort Beverly to the bathroom whenever necessary, give her a shower every day, and wash and condition her hair on Tuesdays and Fridays.*

*"Oh, Marshall, I'm so sorry about the ring," Stacy says. The cuticles of two of her fingers are rimmed with the*

ketchup she wiped off Will, and she needs to get up and wash her hands. After that she will have to tell Roger all about his mother's diamond.

"My mother?" Roger mouths. "Does he want to talk to me?"

Marshall says, "At least Clare's not here to see this, to see how people are all too eager and willing to take advantage of a pathetic old lady with dementia."

Yes, at least there's that.

"You know, I still haven't given away Clare's clothing," Marshall says. "I just can't bring myself to go into her closet and do what has to be done."

"I know," Stacy says. "I know." She offers to help him, as she has once or twice before, and this time Marshall says yes, as soon as Stacy's back from Florida they should make a date to go through Clare's stuff.

"She would have wanted you to have her mink bomber jacket," Marshall tells her. "It's a beautiful jacket, just a couple of years old. Promise me you'll take it?"

It's eighty-four degrees today in Fort Lauderdale, and the very idea of a mink jacket seems sort of repellent on any number of levels, Stacy is thinking, but she wouldn't dream of turning Marshall down. Because if he's convinced that Clare would have wanted her to have it, she can't and won't disappoint him. She'll never wear it, but Marshall doesn't have to know that, doesn't have to know that a temporarily retired social worker whose specialty was arranging services for the homeless can't possibly fit comfortably into a mink jacket, no matter what the size.

"Yeah, sure, I'd be honored to have it," Stacy says, and promises, before hanging up, that she will absolutely, positively, go through Clare's closet with him when she gets back to the city.

"Kisses for the kids," Marshall says, instead of good-bye.

Olivia, who is sitting next to Roger, scoots under the table and emerges on the other side, climbing into Stacy's lap now, pressing her face against Stacy's, her pale hair smelling of french fries, her cheek nearly as satiny as a baby's.

"What is it, sweetie pie?" Stacy says. She plays with her daughter's hair, traces the rim of her ear, as Will ducks beneath the table and cozies up next to Roger.

"Marshall didn't need to speak to me?" Roger says. "Not that I'm complaining."

"We'll talk later, okay?"

"Can I get my ears pierced?" Olivia asks.

"What?" Stacy says. "You're five years old, sweetie pie. What's the rush?"

From across the table, Roger is eyeing them in a melancholy way.

"Hey, lighten up, big guy!" Stacy says. He must be thinking about his sister, she guesses, and imagines just how hard it is for him to talk to Marshall on the phone, let alone visit with him at the apartment on East End where Marshall and eighteen-year-old Nathaniel are doing their best to stay afloat.

She and Roger don't talk about those things, not that Stacy hasn't tried. Lately he just doesn't seem to want to talk to her about anything at all.

It's worrisome, no question, but things are bound to get better, aren't they? If not today, she thinks, then surely some other day. Taking out her bottle of Pepto-Bismol, she unscrews its child-proof cap with the center of her palm. She shakes out three caplets, even though the label says that two at a time is enough. Enough for some people, maybe, but not for her. She whose husband seems to have lost the desire to share even the smallest shred of information with her, preferring, instead, to sit in silence contemplating his BlackBerry, as if all the wisdom in the world were visible on its 2" x 2" screen.

## 10

Stacy had never had a manicure in her life and she never would; though her fingers were long and quite thin, her nails were small and a little wide, and she hated drawing attention to them. And so when Roger's mother suggested she get a manicure to show off her ring, Stacy had to say no.

The Sunday brunch on Long Island that Beverly had arranged so attractively across her French provincial dining-room table wasn't the standard bagels and lox that Stacy had been expecting; it was, instead, a lovely selection of sushi, avocado rolls, yellow tail-and-scallion rolls, and shrimp tempura, along with bowls of edamame, plates of shrimp gyoza, seaweed salad, and tuna tataki.

"And I never even thought to ask if you liked Japanese food," Beverly said as she cupped Stacy's face in her own small manicured hands. "It could have been a disaster!"

"No, no, we love Japanese food," Stacy reassured her; by "we," she meant Roger and herself; as for Lauren and Chuck and their family, well, they would just have to get with the program.

"What was she *thinking*?" Lauren whispered in Stacy's ear. "Does she really think four-year-olds are big fans of seaweed salad? I mean, come on, this mother-in-law of yours needs a reality check."

Mother-in-law-to-be.

Juliette, her grandmother, sidled over to them; unlike Lauren—and the twins—all three of whom were wearing jeans, sneakers, and souvenir sweatshirts from the San Diego Zoo, Juliette was more formally dressed in a dark pantsuit with a gold starburst pin on the lapel. On her feet were ankle-length, square-toed black boots; a silver cane hung from her wrist. "The big news is that my surgeon says I need a knee replacement," she announced, "but I can tell you right now that it's not happening. Ever. My personal goal in life is to avoid hospitalization at all costs. The last time I was in the hospital was in 1964, and that was for gall bladder surgery, because in those years you—"

"*I* was in the hospital in 1964!" Beverly said excitedly. "I was thirty-eight years old and had to have an appendectomy, which—"

"Maybe I can find some peanut butter for the twins," said Stacy. "Let's go take a look," she instructed her sister. Roger's mother and Juliette were in a senior citizen huddle, their helmets of silver hair shining in the track lighting overhead as Stacy and her sister left them and went off to the kitchen. Stacy was wearing her highest heels and tightest black leather skirt; standing next to Lauren in her jeans and sneakers, she felt too tall and considerably overdressed. But really, couldn't her sister have found something more suitable to put on than those clunky cross-trainers and that sweatshirt advertising a zoo? And why was her sister dressed exactly like the twins? It seemed kind of juvenile, a grown woman dressed like her four-year-olds.

Stacy and Lauren were three and a half years apart; her sister was born in 1968, that terrible year in which both Martin Luther King and Robert Kennedy were assassinated, but also the year Stacy started preschool and had become what everyone called—their voices invariably rising in pitch and enthusiasm—*the big sister.* Though her parents never believed her, she had sworn, years later, that she vividly remembered seeing the newborn Lauren for the very first time in one of those see-through plastic bassinets in the hospital, her father in his full-length tweed coat holding Stacy up to the glass wall of the nursery and pointing out her sister, who'd been born with so much hair on her head that the nurses had clipped a ribbon to it. Never mind her parents' disbelief; Stacy remembered the red ribbon that distinguished her sister from every other newborn in the hospital's nursery. She remembered, too, standing outside a small store (the Butterworth Bakery?) in a strip mall in their Long Island town, carefully guarding Lauren in her stroller while their mother went in to buy something—a peach pie? A loaf of bread adorned with the caraway seeds her father liked? So far so good, except that Stacy had grown tired of watching over the baby, and, in a moment that was tainted by impatience, boredom, and probably more than a whiff of jealousy, her four-year-old self tipped the stroller back so that Lauren would fall out onto the hard, hard sidewalk and maybe even crack her head open the smallest bit. And just as Stacy tipped the stroller and the baby began to slide down toward the pavement, two women happened to walk by. *Young lady!* one of them called out to her while the other one righted the stroller. *If you're going to be naughty like that, we're going to take that baby away from you!* A plan which, at that moment, would have suited the four-year-old Stacy just fine. Actually . . . better than fine. The baby merely turned her head to stare at her, while one of the women stepped into the bakery to get Stacy's mother, and Stacy herself must have felt something like remorse, because except when it came to that baby, she'd always, it seemed, done everything right. Her parents rarely raised their voices to her; she was, they always said, *such a good girl.*

She wanted her sister to be happy for her now, at this little brunch in honor of her engagement, but it was asking too much; her sister had other things on her mind. She hadn't even asked to see Stacy's ring; instead, unbidden, Stacy shyly extended her hand—as she had for Beverly and Clare, both of whom had said they were *dying to see it*—so that her sister could get a good look whether she wanted one or not. *Very nice,* Lauren said, so perfunctory, when what she should have said was *beautiful* or *gorgeous*; at least she'd kissed Stacy's cheek, though without the hug that might have accompanied it. It hit Stacy then that her sister didn't have an engagement ring of her own, that Chuck hadn't had the money for one and that Lauren had insisted years ago that she honestly didn't care, that it was petty to care—what did she need a ring for when she knew perfectly well how much Chuck adored her? And Stacy was mortified at having insisted Lauren take a nice long look at something she probably didn't want to see.

Searching through Beverly's pantry now, Stacy found a jar of extra-crunchy peanut butter, which, wouldn't you know it, the twins wouldn't touch, wouldn't even look at, because of course they only liked the plain creamy kind, Lauren explained apologetically. She took the jar from Stacy, asked for some bread (no, the twins didn't like raisin bread, but they'd take the seven-grain if nothing else was available), and, to Stacy's astonishment, after making the sandwiches at the kitchen counter, proceeded to pick out the nuts from the peanut butter with the tines of a salad fork. *Not to be believed*, Stacy thought, as her sister went at it with the concentration and precision of a surgeon, tossing minuscule bits of peanut into the sink.

"I'm just kind of blown away by what I'm seeing here," Stacy said, but Lauren misunderstood her.

"You mean my kids are spoiled brats because they won't eat what's on the table like everyone else?"

"No, of course not, it's not that. It's that . . ." It was hard to talk about love with her sister, even that extravagant, over-the-top maternal sort that compelled Lauren to patiently extract every last speck of peanut from her children's lunch. "You're such an incredibly devoted mother," Stacy said, "that's all."

"Yeah, yeah, I kind of go a little crazy sometimes when it comes to them, but, hey, they're my kids; it's my job, you know?"

Stacy nodded, but she *didn't* know, and would, if pressed, admit that she didn't fully understand, though she suspected that someday she would.

Lauren's husband, Chuck, came looking for them in the kitchen. He was burly and bearded, and dressed in jeans and a linty black T-shirt. There was a crucifix around his neck; Stacy couldn't help but stare at Jesus's long, pitifully thin outstretched arms nailed to the cross. Usually the sight of a crucifix meant nothing to her, but this one, lying against her brother-in-law's chest, seemed terribly poignant.

"Hey, Savannah and Danielle are hungry," Chuck announced. Even though he wasn't much more than thirty, Stacy noted, with surprise, a few strands of silver glinting in his hair.

"How are your parents?" she asked him. She knew that his father had recently lost his job as a manager at a Chrysler Plymouth dealership, and that his mother had been obligated to look for work after decades at home. The only time Stacy saw them was at the twins' birthday party every year.

"My parents? Well, both their parakeets died, one after the other," Chuck said. "And my mother was actually kind of heartsick. She and my father decided to open a small bird shelter to honor their lives. The parakeets', that is. Listen, dogs and cats I get, but parakeets? I think my parents need to move on." He put one arm around Lauren, and the other around Stacy. "You two girls need to spend more time together," he said. "Just a suggestion, you know?"

Stacy reached over and touched the small gold crucifix that hung from the chain around her brother-in-law's neck. "You're right," she said, and waited for her sister to agree with her.

Lauren said something that sounded like *mmm*; Stacy decided to interpret that as a *yes*.

"You could come wedding-dress shopping with me," Stacy said.

Her sister nodded soberly. "Sounds like fun."

Watching Savannah and Danielle as they devoured their peanut butter sandwiches at the table that held the Japanese buffet, Stacy was embarrassed to admit that four years after their birth, she still had trouble telling them apart. They dressed exactly alike, but today, at least, one of them (Danielle?) had a pink satin headband in her dark hair, and the other twin, a purple one. And each of them had a Beatrix Potter stuffed animal resting in her lap—Peter Rabbit sporting a royal blue jacket, and Pigling Bland in a striped vest and yellow shorts.

Clare had joined them at the table now; she stood beside Stacy and Lauren and sighed at the sight of the twins. Stacy understood that this was the sigh of a woman who would have chosen a daughter for herself in that Colombian orphanage if only that had been possible.

"So, girls, which one of you is Savannah and which one is Danielle?" Clare asked. She loaded up her plate with seaweed salad and gyoza and used the lacquered chopsticks that Beverly had brought back from a trip to Beijing with her husband back in the eighties.

"I'm Savannah," the twin with the pink ribbon said, and the other one snickered.

"She's lying—*I'm* Savannah."

Though Stacy would never admit it to her sister, she had no idea who was telling the truth. She wasn't the greatest aunt, she thought regretfully. She only had two nieces to keep track of, and she couldn't even tell who was who. Her impressive SAT scores were of no value here, nor was her prodigious memory. When it came to anything that had to do with her sister or her sister's family, she just wasn't up to snuff.

"Cut it out, girls, you're confusing everyone," Lauren said, but you could hear the affection in her voice. "I can't even begin to tell you how many times Chuck used to mess me up just for fun," she addressed Stacy and Clare. "This was when the girls were newborns, and the only way I could tell them apart was by the red nail polish I painted on Savannah's tiny little big toe. I would change Danielle's diaper, put her back in the bassinet and ask Chuck to hand over Savannah. And he would hand me back Danielle, just to drive me crazy!"

"You're so lucky," Clare said, and her voice sounded so wistful, Stacy put a hand on her shoulder.

"Lucky?" Lauren said. "It was a barrel of laughs, believe me, especially at three in the morning, when all I wanted was to put my head back down on that pillow."

"I meant lucky to have two daughters."

"They were a huge surprise, actually. There were no twins in either of our families."

Stacy helped herself to a couple of gyoza; too lazy to use chopsticks, she ate with her fingers. "Not exactly true," she said. "Mom had those cousins of hers, Marlene and Janet Something, who never married, lived together their whole lives, and dressed identically, even when they were in their seventies."

"That's so creepy," Lauren said. "I mean, what the hell was wrong with those two?"

"Savannah and I are going to live together when we're grown-ups," Danielle informed them casually. "We're going to live next door to you and Daddy our whole lives."

"Is that the sweetest thing you've ever heard!" Clare said.

"Oh my god, are you kidding me?" said Lauren. "Girls, you need to set higher standards for yourselves. You don't want to live next door, trust me."

Though Savannah continued, contentedly, to eat her sandwich, Danielle burst into tears, and Stacy watched as Lauren calmed her, lifting Danielle into her arms, smooching her all over.

"Mommy's so sorry," Lauren said. "But you need to stop crying and finish your lunch, okay?"

"We DO want to live next door," Danielle insisted. "And we'll bring our husbands with us."

Stacy had to smile. "Sounds like a plan," she said. "A carefully considered one, apparently."

"Just wait till *you're* a mother, big shot," her sister teased.

Roger's mother and Stacy's grandmother, who'd briefly disappeared, were back again, still talking about their health. "Every time I go to my internist, I have to make a list of all the medications I'm on, otherwise I forget one or two when he asks me," Juliette was saying. "And I'm someone with an excellent memory, as it happens."

"I'm not," Beverly confessed. "I used to be, but I'm not anymore. For example, those two little girls over there? They're your great-granddaughters, of course, but I can't seem to remember their names . . ."

For a moment, Clare looked distraught, and then she said, "Danielle and Savannah, Mom."

"Such sweet little girls," Beverly said. "How old are they?"

Wiping away her tears with the palms of both hands, Danielle said, "We're four. How old are *you*?"

"Hmm, seventy-two, going on seventy-three, I believe."

"You're old," Savannah pointed out.

"Well, I'm certainly not young," said Beverly. "Calvin Coolidge was president the year I was born. Did you know that he couldn't stand his mother-in-law and she returned the compliment?"

Stacy reminded herself that this was the woman who was going to be her mother-in-law. "Fascinating!" she said.

"Does anyone want to know who was president when *I* was born?" Juliette asked. "Woodrow Wilson, for those of you who might be interested."

"Ah, former president of Princeton University, and son of a slave owner," Beverly said. "Also, the only US president who had a PhD. Actually from time to time I find myself wondering if I'm what they call an idiot savant. I know so much presidential history, it's almost frightening. But ask me what I had for dinner last night, and, well, that's a little frightening, too. I'm guessing pork chops baked with cinnamon apples, but it's entirely possible that was two nights ago rather than last night."

"Frankly," Juliette said, "Jews—even secular, non-practicing ones—shouldn't be cooking up pork chops in their kitchens, no matter how delicious the recipe might be."

Everyone fell silent. "I wonder where the guys are," Clare said a few moments later, and just as Stacy offered to go find them, Roger showed up, trailed by Marshall and Nathaniel, the little boy carrying a weird-looking stuffed animal resembling an owl, with jumbo-size pink ears and small white feet.

"A Furby!" the twins cried.

None of the women except Clare had any idea what they were looking at, and Marshall had to explain that this Furby thing was an interactive electronic robot capable of learning English—though because Nathaniel's was brand new, at the moment it could only speak its own language.

"Let's hear him talk!" Savannah said. She and her sister were out of their seats, rushing at Nathaniel with such enthusiasm, they nearly knocked the kid over onto the floor.

Narrowing his eyes at the twins, Nathaniel pressed the Furby close to his chest. "He doesn't want to talk to you," he said. "Maybe later."

"Come on, Nat," Roger said. "They're just little girls; can't you give them a break?"

Apparently he could, even if he didn't want to: with a sigh, Nathaniel rubbed the robot's belly; instantly it responded, in a childish, cartoony voice, "You-nye-boh-doo."

The twins shrieked with pleasure.

"It means 'how are you?' in Furbish," Nathaniel interpreted for them.

He patted the creature's belly again, and this time it said, "Wee-tah-kah-wee-loo."

" 'Tell me a story,' " Nathaniel translated proudly.

The twins had fallen in love with him and his interactive robot; anyone could see that. When Nathaniel left the room with his Furby, it was no surprise that the girls ran after him, begging for a chance to rub the magic belly.

The annoying sound of the Mister Softee jingle suddenly flowed from the cell phone in the back pocket of Marshall's jeans. "How are ya?" he said, answering it immediately. "Yeah, yeah, I already told her—and also your, uh, ex-husband—that the bite plate should stay in her mouth twenty-four/seven, except when she brushes . . . I know it's uncomfortable, but she'll get used to it, trust me. And between now and then, she can try some Advil or Tylenol . . . Not to worry, no problem at all." Snapping the phone shut, Marshall said, "Sorry, everyone. Had to do a little hand-holding there."

Stacy liked the soothing way he'd spoken to the patient's mother, the way he hadn't allowed himself to sound even a trifle bored or patronizing. She felt affection for Marshall, and even more of it for Clare. Soon she would officially be a part of the family; they would introduce her as their sister-in-law, and she already liked the sound of it. She and Chuck had never had much to say to one another, but it was different with Clare and Marshall; they were more her kind of people, she felt, more likely, perhaps, to understand the value of the work she did, and to appreciate the opportunities she'd given up, the opportunities her Harvard diploma would inevitably have afforded her had she chosen another route instead of the nonprofit one. (Not that she had a single regret—she didn't.)

Her mother and father were gone, but, thanks to Roger, she could attach herself to this family of his and render it her own; thanks to Roger, she thought, she had found her way in the world.

She filled up a plate of food for him now, and standing together in the midst of his family, they both ate from it, Roger expertly lifting the chopsticks first to her mouth, then to his, back and forth, again and again, until the plate was empty.

∽

*After a long, hot afternoon at Puttin' Around—a minia-*
*ture golf course Stacy found for the kids—everyone except*
*Roger votes for a late swim. While Stacy plays with their*
*kids in the water, he falls asleep poolside and dreams of*
*a run-in with Dr. Avalon, who claims he's seen Roger at*
*the shooting range and can't believe what he's planning.*

*"I mean, are you out of your fucking mind?" Dr. Avalon*
*barks at him. The two of them are in line at a 7-Eleven,*
*and people are turning to stare.*

*"Don't talk to me like that," Roger says. "And what*
*the hell are you so angry about?"*

*Dr. Avalon is staring at him with such contempt, Roger*
*just can't believe it.*

*"What is wrong with YOU, you lunatic?" Avalon says,*
*sipping on his Slurpee now and looking very undignified.*
*"I'd hate to think that all the time we put in together over*
*the years didn't do you an ounce of good, you fucking*
*head case."*

*"Daddy?" Roger hears someone say; squinting into the*
*sun, he sees that it's Will standing at the foot of the chaise*
*longue. "IHOP or Applebee's, Daddy?"*

*"What?"*

*"We're hungry."*

*Will's bathing trunks are patterned with palm trees and*
*laughing starfish, and reach all the way down to his knees.*
*His belly button protrudes from his stomach; it is, in fact,*
*an umbilical hernia, and the pediatrician has already told*
*them Will's going to need corrective surgery in a year or so.*

*"C'mere and talk to me, baby boy," Roger says, trying*
*so hard to dismiss Dr. Avalon's anger, even as he reminds*
*himself it was only something he'd dreamt. He's disap-*
*pointed with Avalon all the same, and bewildered by the*
*guy's failure to understand. Come to think of it, Avalon*
*hasn't been particularly helpful these past few months,*
*tossing off questions that have only led to darker and*
*darker places.*

*Will has declined Roger's invitation to sit down and talk; he's still standing there in his soggy bathing trunks and damp little feet, waiting for Roger to make up his mind about dinner. Finally he positions his pocket-sized hand on his hip and says, "Applebee's or IHOP, Daddy, you hafta choose."*

*Why does everything seem so impossibly difficult, even a question as simple as this one?*

*"Can you help me, please?" Roger asks his three-year-old. "Help me decide."*

*His baby boy nods solemnly; Roger's never seen a child look so worried before.*

## 11

When Stacy moved into Roger's apartment not long after their engagement, she brought with her three suitcases of clothing, hundreds of books, and two dark-gray Persian cats: a subdued, none-too-bright male named Keats, and a neurotic female named Shelley. Roger didn't have the heart to tell Stacy that cats were not his favorite creatures; though there'd been no dogs in his life since he left home for college years ago, he'd grown up with Shetland sheepdogs and a trinity of funny-faced Brussels griffons. He wasn't happy ceding one of his two bathrooms to Keats and Shelley and installing the big plastic litter box that sat squarely in it; was annoyed by the swirls of cat hair that attached themselves to the black-and-white comforter on his bed; and hated the bits of litter that were sometimes kicked out into the hallway and then crunched under his bare feet. But he loved Stacy, and tried his best to warm to her pets, who generally ignored him but from time to time sat on his head just as he felt himself falling asleep. Love always entailed some sort of sacrifice, he figured, and if surrendering a bathroom to a couple of cats was the worst he had to endure, well, he could handle it.

He and Stacy discussed possible wedding venues every night at dinnertime, studied endless wedding-related websites together, and kept up the conversation as they watched TV before they went to sleep, but they didn't seem to be making much headway, Roger thought. Several times Stacy and her sister had plans to go shopping for a wedding dress, but at the last minute something always seemed to go wrong on Lauren's end—one of the twins developed conjunctivitis, or a strep throat, or a twenty-four-hour stomach virus, courtesy of a classmate at the Kiddie Kollege—and Stacy was left to go it alone. She and her grandmother met in the bridal departments of Bergdorf Goodman, Bloomingdale's, and Saks, but Juliette's bad knee—the one that her orthopedist was still trying to convince her needed to be replaced—slowed them down so much that Stacy was relieved when her grandmother decided to call it quits after a single shopping excursion. ("I'll be there with you in spirit," Juliette told her over the phone, then mailed her a check for $4,000. Which Stacy immediately threatened to mail right back to her, because how could they take money from an old lady when the happy truth was, they clearly didn't need it, thanks to Roger's booming business. *You send that check back to me, I'll cut you out of my will, sweetheart*, Juliette warned her.)

"I'm thirty-three years old and I miss my mother," Stacy said one night when they were at Roger's desk perusing caterers' websites on his computer in the den. She sank her face into her palms, and Roger was surprised to see that her eyes were actually shiny with tears. "I know I sound like a big baby," she said, "but there you have it."

Roger had friends who didn't get along with their parents, who stopped talking to them because of furious arguments over money or what sounded like imagined slights, friends who insisted that if they didn't speak to their mother or father ever again, well, guess what, they just didn't give a shit. Stacy couldn't stand to hear this; once, when she and Roger were out with one of his fraternity brothers from college, a guy named Phil who was enraged by his parents because they refused to lend him and his girlfriend money for a down payment on a house, Stacy got up from her seat in the Thai restaurant, and fled to the ladies' room, where she remained until Phil's girlfriend finally came looking for her. *Stop talking trash about your parents*, Stacy told Phil when she got back to the table. It was none of her business, but there wasn't even a hint of apology in her voice; apparently she just couldn't keep quiet when it came to this particular subject. So Roger apologized for her, which only made her even more upset. And they hadn't seen Phil again since that night last summer.

"And who's going to walk me down the aisle in place of my parents?" Stacy asked now. "Lauren and Chuck? How pathetic would that be?" she said crossly. "I mean, *come on*."

Keats and Shelley, who had an annoying habit of following Stacy everywhere, were on the floor next to the desk; their arms were folded around each other and each was licking the other's face industriously. Roger studied the cats for a moment, trying to summon up some tender feelings for them. "I bet Marshall would be honored to walk you down the aisle," he said, "and why don't you ask Clare to help you find a wedding dress?"

"Hey, sounds good," Stacy said, and it was gratifying to see how swiftly he'd been able to get to her, to shift her mood, just like that, from dark to light. She was, he knew, an optimist, who occasionally had to work at getting him to see things her way, but this time, he was the one who had turned things around.

Mimicking the cats, they embraced, and, as Roger would overhear Stacy say laughingly to her friend Jefrie Miller a few days later about something entirely unrelated, *one thing led to another*, as it often did. Afterward Roger found himself thinking of Allyson, his ex-wife, and how, never, not in a million years, would she have allowed him to undress her on the floor of the den, or made love to him without a comfy pillow under her head. She wasn't a spontaneous person; if anything, she was someone—like Roger—who had to have everything just so, just the way she liked it. And rolling around on the floor like two animals in heat wasn't the way she liked it. Roger thought then of how lucky he was that Allyson had fallen for that loser Warren Whitcomb, the geometry teacher, freeing Roger himself to go after the one true love of his life, which, he recognized, Stacy surely was. Oh, he knew the score, knew that she was the one he simply couldn't live without.

∽

*Roger is perched on the closed lid of the toilet seat reading aloud to the kids as Stacy gives Olivia and Will a bath together. They never share a bath anymore, mostly because Olivia has recently grown shy about her body, but tonight, following an endless day at the Museum of Discovery and Science, Stacy is so beat, she just wants to get both kids in and out of the tub as quickly and painlessly as possible. But what's wrong with Roger? He's reading Doctor De Soto (Stacy's all-time favorite children's book— about a rodent dentist and a fox with an extremely bad toothache) and doing a shockingly poor job of it. His voice is scarily without affect and his eyes are half-closed; it's as if finding the vigor to move from one word to the next is just too strenuous an effort for him. Normally he's a terrifically expressive reader, skillful at doing every sort of voice, from meek to arrogant, squeaky to roaring, and the kids are always an appreciative audience.*

*Today, however, is another story.*

*"Hey, wake up!" Stacy says, snapping her fingers briskly in front of Roger's face before turning back to her naked kiddies.*

*"Daddy's a terrible reader tonight," Olivia offers matter-of-factly, and no one disagrees with her, not even Roger.*

*"Is he sick?" Will asks. He fills a plastic cup with bathwater and raises it to his mouth. "Yum yum yum," he says, smacking his juicy, rosebud lips.*

*"No, he's not sick, but you might be after drinking that dirty, soapy water, mister. As I believe you've been told a thousand times."*

"Will might get sick enough to go to the hospital?" Olivia asks, and there's no mistaking her enthusiasm. "What kind of bacterium is in the water?"

"What?" Stacy and Roger say in unison; Roger, she is glad to see, suddenly seems to have been lifted from his lethargy and indifference.

" 'Bacterium' is one, 'bacteria' is more than one," Olivia instructs them. "Didn't you guys know that?"

Stacy finds it amusing that "you guys" has become part of Olivia's lexicon. "We did," she tells her daughter, "though we didn't know it in kindergarten, did we, Roger?"

Roger sighs. "That's because unlike Olivia, we didn't grow up in the big city."

"Just one little sip," Will says, then deliberately spills the rest of the cup over his sister's head.

After Olivia stops shrieking, Roger announces that he's going to sleep.

"For the night?" Stacy says, shocked. After all, it's not even eight o'clock. "The kids are still up," she points out. "And I could use some help getting them to bed," she adds uselessly.

Help? Not gonna happen; not today, not tomorrow, either.

She contemplates calling Dr. Avalon again, even though she knows, from the last time she called him, just a few weeks ago, that he will immediately cite patient confidentiality and refuse to speak to her—about Roger, anyway. But even if she could convince him to listen to her litany of worries, what would she say? That Roger, a grown man, is too depressed to stay up past eight P.M.? That her fears about him are escalating by the day? That he barely speaks to her, that she's not a mind reader and can't figure out what he's thinking? All she knows is that he carries himself like a profoundly unhappy guy, someone who's so bummed out, he's no longer able to recall the simple meaning of the word "hope."

*There's a burning in her chest as she considers these things, and it worsens now as she bends over to lift Will, and then Olivia, out of the tub. If it's only acid backing up into her esophagus, why do they insist on calling it heartburn—something that actually sounds pretty terrifying when you think about it.*

## 12

Stacy's client, Kim Sutherland, was a diminutive twenty-something in filthy, child-sized saddle shoes, and a black sweatshirt that said, "EVERYTHING I NEEDED TO KNOW, I LEARNED FROM SATAN!" Stacy wasn't at all surprised to hear that Kim had found it in a Dumpster. Kim had the wildest, frizziest hair Stacy had ever seen, and it was held in check by a clean white ribbon tied in a bow at the top of her head. Her face was ruddy, and there was a smear of neon-pink lipstick across her mouth. Formerly of Holly Hill Lane, Greenwich, Connecticut, Kim was a onetime heroin addict who suffered from schizoaffective disorder, and she was, at this moment, coming down from a busy weekend of crack smoking and seated in the rear of a 1996 Chevy Lumina, the agency vehicle Stacy was driving. Up front was one of Stacy's coworkers, a kind-hearted, middle-aged psychologist named Barbara Armstrong, whom she was very fond of. The three of them were en route to a Goodwill thrift shop, where they were going to stock up on a few essentials for Kim before ferrying her to the shelter on the Lower East Side where she'd promised to stay for the night. When they'd found her a couple of days ago, she was slumped on the sidewalk on a large sheet of cardboard in front of a children's store called Goody Two-Shoes. Next to her, suspended from the side of a supermarket shopping cart she'd co-opted, was an opened, empty pizza delivery box she'd scrawled her message across. She'd made it known, in blue Magic Marker along the red-and-white box, that she was "broke, homeless, and shit out of luck." And, Stacy had noted, surprisingly clean, except for those begrimed black-and-white saddle shoes. Kim was a veteran Dumpster diver, and she enthusiastically recommended it as a way of life.

"Yeah, you wouldn't believe all the cool shit I've gotten from those Dumpsters," she was saying as they pulled up to the Goodwill. "Great food, obviously, but once I even found a computer monitor in perfect condition. I tried to give it to my fiancé for his birthday, but he wouldn't take it."

The fiancé seemed highly unlikely, but Stacy had learned that when it came to her clients, often the unlikeliest things proved to be true. "Oh, really?" she said nonchalantly to Kim. "So when was this? You never mentioned that you were engaged." She glanced down at her own engagement ring, which, during the workday, she wore turned around so that you couldn't see the diamond.

"Oh, yeah yeah, Brent and I were going to get married at the New York Botanical Garden, the one in the Bronx, not Brooklyn. We had an event manager and everything, and we booked the Garden Terrace Room. There was a beautiful patio where you could see the Bronx River, and that's where we were going to have the actual wedding ceremony if the weather cooperated. And the menu, let me tell you, was unfucking-believable." Closing her eyes, as if in a trance, Kim recited, "Angel hair with lobster, pumpkin pie soup, endive salad . . ." This last she pronounced "ahn-deev"; hearing that, Stacy no longer needed convincing—she somehow knew for certain that there'd been a fiancé in the picture.

"My parents loved Brent," Kim said, her eyes open now. "They fucking adored him. He was an i-banker, made tons of money straight out of Wharton, but so what, you go to Wharton, that's what's waiting for you out there, right? But then he got his old girlfriend pregnant, and guess who suddenly gets all sentimental and shit about this *baby* of his, and decides, guess what, that he's going to 'do the right thing' and marry the bitch?"

"That must have been incredibly hard for you," Stacy said to Kim, as Barbara murmured her sympathies.

"Totally, I mean, what kinda guy fucks his ex-girlfriend when he's got a fiancée waiting for him at home? Tell me, girls, WHAT KIND?" Kim shrieked.

Kim was so petite (and almost pretty, actually, despite her crazy hair and chapped, wind-burned face), and the words that were coming out of her mouth so fierce, Stacy could hardly believe it. "I think you need to take a deep breath, Kim," she said. She scored a parking space on Second Avenue—a miracle, really—and she and Barbara climbed into the back-seat with Kim. Barbara stroked Kim's shoulder, and Stacy said, "A . . .nice . . . deep . . . breath . . . that's right . . . nice . . . and . . . deep . . . nice . . . and . . ." There was a van parked directly opposite them on the west side of the avenue; the words "GUM BUSTERS" were painted across the doors, and underneath that, "CHEWING GUM REMOVAL SPECIALISTS." Even with Kim about to suffer a meltdown here in the car with them, Stacy had to smile; she imagined a piece of turquoise bubble gum stuck to the toe of her favorite shoes, and picking up the phone, in a panic, to call the gum busters. What a way to earn a living! She could just see a couple of guys suited up in coveralls rushing into a Fifth Avenue apartment and scraping Juicy Fruit from an antique Louis XV gilt settee, while the client looked on, wringing her hands and praying for a good outcome.

*Doctor, dentist, lawyer, teacher, social worker, chewing gum removal specialist. Hey, what did* she *care, everyone's got to make a living and pay the rent, right?*

"I'm having an anxiety attack," Kim reported somberly, but then, a few moments later, she turned frantic. "Oh my god! Oh my god! Oh my god!" Clutching her head with both hands, she moaned, "I'm having an anxiety attack. Oh, God. Fuck fuck fuck."

It was getting steamy in the car; Stacy unrolled the window next to her, and looked outside, where she saw a pair of smiling blonde women in red peacoats walking abreast with what she could guess were their adopted daughters, two little Chinese girls around six or seven with lovely, perfectly straight, obsidian-black hair that skimmed their shoulders. Thinking of Clare, she imagined the adoptive mothers' protracted struggles with infertility, with pregnancies gone wrong, with teenage mothers who promised them everything but then withdrew those very promises, saying, not-quite-apologetically, *I thought I could but now I see that I just can't.* And the terrible disappointment, one thing after another. Yet here the four of them were now, happy with themselves, happy with each other, two mothers and two daughters, chatting away, swanning along Second Avenue on a cold sunny afternoon in December, turning now into the entryway of a Mexican restaurant, maybe the four of them stopping in for an after-school margarita; how bad could a little tequila and Triple Sec be, even for a six-year-old?

*What? Now she'd gone too far, envisioning those little six-year-old cuties sipping at their margaritas, maybe the glasses rimmed with granulated sugar instead of salt, while their classmates were safely home drinking hot chocolate at the kitchen table.*

"Fuck fuck fuck," she heard Kim say, and, for the first time, Stacy just couldn't listen to it anymore, didn't want to hear it, didn't even want to entertain the thought of ushering a reluctant Kim into Goodwill and pulling together some outfits for her—nice, clean, gently worn clothing that Kim's mother in Greenwich would probably be humiliated to see her daughter wearing. The mother who knew that Kim was out on the street but was tired of footing the exorbitantly expensive bill for her daughter's treatment and rehab at the Sunrise Center, a facility not far from their home where at least she'd been cured of her heroin addiction. If only Kim could be counted on to take her antipsychotic meds, but the dry mouth and drowsiness that came with them were just too annoying, Kim had told Stacy and Barbara, and was that so hard for them to understand? No, it wasn't, and yes, of course they understood, they'd told her patiently, but without the meds, well, just look at her holding her head with both tiny hands, just listen to her moaning *fuck fuck fuck* here in the backseat of the Chevy. Turning her gaze away from Kim and out the windows of the car again, Stacy saw a Latino child with Down syndrome walking hand in hand with his young mother. The woman had a cell phone held against her ear, and, slung over her shoulder, a shiny backpack of purple vinyl decorated with the same Furby that Nathaniel had brought to the engagement brunch a few weeks ago. Stacy smiled at the boy and his backpack, and thought of her plans to spend the weekend shopping for a wedding gown with Clare. She was reminded that, unlike Kim, and the woman with the Furby backpack, she herself inhabited a life that some might actually consider enviable; after all, the man she loved reciprocated that love and wanted to marry her. And, as far as she knew, everyone in her family and his was healthy in every important way.

So, yes—entirely enviable.

A life to be grateful for.

"I'll stay here with Kim, and you go in and find her some stuff," Barbara was saying.

"Are you sure?" Stacy was happy to make her escape, even for just a few minutes. But she didn't want to abandon Barbara, who probably wouldn't make much progress with Kim while Stacy went scavenging for a new wardrobe for her.

"Go on, get outta here!" Barbara encouraged her affably.

The Goodwill store gave off a damp, dusty smell, as if everything in it had, until recently, been stored away in cartons in someone's dank basement or attic. At the front door was a crudely constructed bookcase crowded with hardbacks missing their dust jackets, and thick paperbacks, their dented covers embellished with illustrations of women in Grecian gowns showing off the extravagant bosoms God had so generously bestowed upon them. Seated in a folding chair next to the bookcase was a beautiful child with a dirty face who was reading a book called *Stories from the Bible*, all the while picking her nose enthusiastically and wiping her fingertip on the pages of the book, her parents nowhere in evidence.

*STOP that!* Stacy wanted to say, and headed off to the racks and racks of women's sportswear, where she hit on a couple of pairs of brand-new jeans, their original price tags still attached, and some colorful sweaters that looked perfectly clean. Everything was priced between five and seven dollars; feeling buoyant, Stacy went straight to the cash register with the agency credit card, her arms full. She thought of Kim's mother in Greenwich, a woman she'd never met, but whose pursed mouth and disapproving stare she could so easily imagine.

When she got back to the car, Kim was beating those extra-small fists of hers against the window and crying, *Oh Lord Oh Lord Oh Lord*; even through the closed windows, Stacy didn't have to strain to hear her.

Sliding behind the wheel, with Barbara's help in the backseat, she drove Kim downtown to Bellevue. They got her admitted, an endless four hours later, to the psych ward, her newly purchased wardrobe safely tucked away under the seat of the car.

The next day, when she and Barbara returned to the Chevy, this time escorting a middle-aged, alcoholic client to a nursing home in the Bronx, it saddened Stacy to see the flimsy supermarket shopping bags full of Kim's new clothes, and she wondered how Kim was managing in Bellevue, forced to swallow down her 300 milligrams of Seroquel a day and to confide in the shrinks who were assigned to her. Days or weeks from now, when Kim was ready to be discharged from Bellevue, it wasn't her mother who would be waiting for her in the lobby, but Stacy and Barbara, who were willing to take charge where Kim's own family wasn't. Stacy would never understand how families could turn their backs on their damaged children or parents or siblings. What kind of parents did Kim have who would throw up their hands in disgust at this poor imperfect daughter of theirs? What was wrong with people? If only, Stacy thought, as she had so often, there were official written tests, both short answer and essay, that wanna-be parents were required to pass before being allowed to proceed with a pregnancy—tests that would definitively prove that the applicants could be counted upon to act, at all times, with compassion and generosity during the course of raising their children.

"So, any plans for Christmas?" Barbara asked, as they were driving back to the city from Staten Island. "Do you mind if I smoke?" she added, and lit up a Winston Ultra Light. Barbara had problems of her own—a crappy ex-husband who had once been a successful TV writer, but didn't believe in paying alimony, and a twenty-eight year-old son who needed a lot of help with his rent—but she was endlessly generous. She routinely brought plastic bins of homemade biscotti to the office, handed out inexpensive but beautifully wrapped birthday gifts, and hosted a Thanksgiving dinner every year, in her cozy studio apartment in Hell's Kitchen, for any of her colleagues who had nowhere else to go. That included Stacy, who, the Thanksgiving after her mother was killed, got sucked into a ridiculous argument with Lauren about what time they would be sitting down to dinner, and ended up at Barbara's instead of with her family.

There had always been something pleasingly maternal about Barbara, and Stacy had, from time to time, confided in her; once, the night of that Thanksgiving dinner, after all the other guests had gone, she'd rested her head on Barbara's broad, middle-aged shoulder following a weepy meltdown of her own. Where Stacy's mother had been slimly built and without much padding, Barbara was soft and rounded, better suited, perhaps, at least physically, for the comfort a daughter might need.

Stacy took one hand off the steering wheel and touched Barbara's shoulder now, hidden beneath the puffy down coat she wore. "You asked me about Christmas?" she said, going on to tell Barbara about the five-day trip to Antigua she and Roger had planned.

Barbara smiled. "Antigua? You're a lucky duck," she said, and how could you possibly argue with that?

༄

*It's a long way past midnight, closer to two A.M., and while her family sleeps, Stacy sits alone on the spacious terrace that overlooks the Intracoastal Waterway. She's thinking of a most surprising thing Roger had hidden but Clare had confided to her, and that was the breakdown he'd suffered during his first semester of college—a complete emotional collapse that required a two-month stay at Emerald Hills, a residential facility in northern Westchester. Stacy had learned this small but vital piece of Roger's history during one of the numerous visits she'd made to Clare's bedside in the final months before her sister-in-law died. The two of them had fallen into a conversation about high school and college when Clare, assuming that of course Stacy was familiar with the details, happened to refer to Roger's time at Emerald Hills. Which Stacy at first mistakenly thought was a summer camp. Or country club. Those painful adolescent struggles of Roger's had to do with a first love, a smart seventeen-year-old named Lucy Eisenstein, whom he dated all through his senior year in high school, only to find himself kicked to the curb the day before she went off to the University of Chicago.*

*According to Clare—who was clearly a little embarrassed to share this part of the story with Stacy—the teenaged Roger had believed Lucy was his one true soul mate and that they were meant to spend their lives together. But Lucy didn't want to hear about it, she'd just wanted to get away from Long Island and out to Chicago and the beginning of the rest of her life.*

*According to Clare, Roger had been devastated. ("Totally crushed," were the words Stacy remembered.) And he'd started thinking of Lucy obsessively. He couldn't get her out of his head, couldn't concentrate for more than a few minutes at a time on his school work that first semester of college at the University of Michigan, could barely haul himself out of bed in the morning to get dressed and go to classes. Mostly he could only lie there and think of Lucy and how she was gone from his life. Then one night he went over to student health and confessed that he'd been contemplating killing himself.*

*That kind of thinking got you a bed in Emerald Hills, and it hurts Stacy even now to imagine how Roger had suffered over this Lucy Eisenstein so long ago. (It hurts, too, to think of the worrisome possibility that Olivia or Will may have inherited whatever tendency Roger had once had toward this sort of crippling depression.)*

*"How dare he not tell me!" she'd cried to Clare, who apologized for raising a subject that apparently was, for Roger, just too excruciating to share with his own wife.*

*But Stacy didn't want Clare to be sorry about anything. "You're in a hospital bed trying to get well," she reminded her sister-in-law, "and you shouldn't spend even an instant apologizing to me, sweetie."*

*Hours after she heard the story from Clare, Stacy worked hard to get the kids into bed earlier than usual, and then approached Roger at his laptop in the den. "How could you keep this from me? Why would you ever keep anything from me? Don't you know that you can tell me everything? That you could always tell me everything?"*

*"Listen, it was a lifetime ago," Roger said after a long silence, and finally turned from his desk to look in her direction. His turquoise eyes appeared ordinary; she was no longer impressed with them, and it felt like a loss to her, one that hit her surprisingly hard. "It was a bad*

scene," Roger admitted, "but I got over it, went back to school, and that was that."

Stacy was shaking her head. She'd been rattled ever since talking with Clare in her hospital room; how could she put this breakdown of Roger's out of her mind? She thought of him in Emerald Hills, shuffling in slippers to the dining hall, swallowing down meds from a pleated white paper cup. "You completely fell apart," she said, and tried to keep her voice low and calm. "Seriously, you don't think that was something I needed to hear about?" She waited for him to get up from his seat and come and sit next to her on the couch, but he stayed where he was.

"Look," he said, pointing to the small TV that was set into their crowded bookcase. It was tuned to CNN, and a little boy, perhaps a year or two older than Olivia, was talking into a microphone about the pig who lived with his family in the suburbs of New Jersey. "My pig, Mr. Dilly, is like a brother to me," the boy said earnestly. His voice trembled. "You can't take him away from me and my sister, even if the landlord says you can."

Roger was laughing. "Man, what a fucked-up family," he said. "I mean, come on, where's the pig sleeping at night? In his pajamas in bunk beds with the kids? No wonder the landlord wants to evict them."

He went on, highly amused, about the little boy and his pig, and got up out of his chair and used the remote to replay the clip on the screen. He'd had enough talk of Emerald Hills and the unhappy circumstances that had landed his teenage self there; Stacy saw that whatever he'd given her was all she was going to get from him on the subject. It was pointless to try and steer him back to where she wanted him, willingly discussing something that he'd made clear was ancient history, and, frankly, none of her business.

She locked herself in the bathroom—shutting the door quietly so she wouldn't wake the kids—and could feel *herself grinding her teeth. It was hard to avoid her face in the mirror, and what she saw was a youngish-looking woman, pale and frightened. Of what? A husband who, after his high school girlfriend left him, had ended up on the psych ward?*

*The truth is, she tells herself now, she hates to think of him as someone who'd once been emotionally fragile, and who, these past few weeks, seems to have returned to that worrisome place again. In the days when she was working with her homeless clients, her professional life overflowed with fragile souls, and most of the time she knew just how to soothe them and their fears, just how to quiet their demons. But she isn't even entirely sure what Roger's particular demons are. And isn't able to dig deep into his psyche to uncover them, because he just isn't talking. At least not to her . . . Ah, to have been the smallest insect nesting in a corner of the ceiling in Dr. Avalon's office, the one place where, she bets, Roger was willing to share every last thing.*

*She's always respected the notion of privacy, of a person's right to keep things close to the vest if that's what he chooses. But hey, she thinks, this is different—this is her husband! Doesn't she deserve to know every last thing about him?*

*She realizes just how much she misses talking to Clare, whose cell number is still stored in her phone; once, maybe six weeks or so ago, before Marshall had shut down the account, Stacy accidentally hit the number with her fingertip. Connected to Clare's voice mail, she was startled, and then stricken, to hear her sister-in-law's lovely clear voice, brimming with energy and good will.*

*The very sound of it would have killed Roger, she's sure of it.*

*Sitting on a slightly damp, upholstered chaise longue out here on her mother-in-law's muggy terrace, she draws her legs up under her chin, clasps her arms tight around her knees. A speedboat churns noisily through the water-way; after it's gone, she can hear the sound of drunken voices eight stories below rising from the swimming pool.*

*She hears Olivia cry out in her sleep now, and opens the terrace's sliding glass door all the way, paying close attention, prepared to make a run for it if necessary, to ease her daughter's nightmare. But the apartment is silent, except for the dishwasher, making a bit of a racket in the kitchen where everything is that laughably unfashionable avocado-green, and her children's small sandy feet have left grit on the worn linoleum.*

*She gets into bed beside Roger, slides her hand under his T-shirt, then rests her ear lightly against his heart, listening for all the secrets he's withheld.*

*Maybe she's imagining it, but her husband's heart seems to be fluttering so wildly, it's a miracle he can actually sleep.*

# ~ 13 ~

Stacy wasn't much of a shopper; she'd never been the sort of person who would set her alarm for seven A.M. just to get to Bloomingdale's before the doors opened the day after Christmas. She lost patience as other shoppers—in their eagerness to snap up whatever skirt or pair of leggings they absolutely had to have—unintentionally stepped on her heels as they shoved past her, women gone wild, but for *what*? For another *shmatta,* as her grandmother would say, to hang up in their closet or stuff into their already overstuffed dressers. After an hour or two, Stacy had always had enough, and couldn't wait to get back home to Park Slope and chill.

But, as a bride-to-be, she had to find a dress, and soon, because the wedding had been booked for April 20th, a mere three months from now. The same April 20th that marked Roger's birthday, along with her own. It fell on a Tuesday that year, but Roger insisted they stick to the date even so. (She could already imagine the speech she would make at the wedding, thanking friends and family for staying out late on an inconvenient Tuesday night to celebrate with them.) Even though she would have preferred a more festive Saturday night, Stacy wasn't going to quarrel with him; Roger already had agreed to the Botanical Garden for the venue, though if he'd known the idea came to her from her client Kim, who'd learned everything she knew from Satan, Stacy doubted he would have agreed so easily. They'd agreed, too, on a two-week trip to Italy and Germany for their honeymoon, and Roger was busy after work every night poring over the dozen books he'd bought and carefully checking Internet travel sites. Stacy had been to the outdoor wedding of a colleague of hers at work whose two golden retrievers had trotted obediently down the aisle dressed in tuxedos and carrying lavender, peach, and lemon-yellow calla lilies in their slobbery mouths. She fantasized about having her cats in the wedding party, Shelley in a pink vest and Keats in black, but knew, of course, that they weren't up to the task and never would be. Her twin nieces would serve as flower girls, and already had their dresses and round-toed, pink patent leather Mary Janes. Stacy herself had a humiliating history as a flower girl, a lamentable experience her mother and father had teased her about for years. She'd been asked, as a five-year-old, to walk down the aisle with a beribboned wicker basket of rose petals at her uncle's wedding, though she'd been, in those days, as shy as could be. Promised a Talking Baby Tender Love doll by her parents, Stacy had allowed herself to be persuaded that she could do what everyone claimed was the simple thing that had been asked of her. The doll, which she'd seen advertised on television again and again, could say a handful of phrases like "Uh-oh, all dirty!" and "Mommy's so pretty!" if you pulled the plastic ring attached to the back of its head, and it was so alluring to Stacy's five-year-old self that even the thought of a crowd of people staring at her as she made her way down the aisle of the synagogue was bearable. But as she proceeded bravely to put one very small foot in front of the other, she was thrown off course by all the whispering rising from the rows and rows of seated guests, so many of whom were waving at her frantically and urging her to smile. Unnerved by too many people asking too much of her, she'd pitched the white wicker basket into the crowd, and, weeping, flown back to her mother and father, who were waiting at the entrance to the sanctuary for their own walk down the aisle. She'd understood, even then, that her parents had loved her greatly, because Talking Baby Tender Love in her red-and-white pinafore and white plastic shoes was presented to her nonetheless that night, despite her unsatisfactory performance, her failure to make it even halfway down the aisle.

She and Clare and Jefrie were meeting downtown at a famous bridal salon near the meatpacking district just before noon today. As Stacy waited outside in front of the store, she saw Jefrie, emerging from the subway exit down the street on Seventh Avenue. She was, Stacy was dismayed to see, lugging a collapsed stroller under one arm, and holding onto Tyler, her three-year-old, with the other. *Just what a three-year-old boy would dream of during naptime: spending the day in bridal salons with a trio of adults, two of whom meant absolutely nothing to him.*

Stacy waved to them, watching from a distance as Jefrie struggled to open the stroller and settle Tyler inside it. But what was Tyler doing here? He was supposed to be with Jefrie's partner, Honey, a pediatric plastic surgeon who'd cheered Jefrie on as she'd given birth to Tyler in their bed at home in Brooklyn Heights, under the watchful eye of a midwife.

"I know you're thinking"—Jefrie said when she caught up with Stacy—"*why the fuck is Tyler here*, but I swear there was nothing I could do. Honey had to take care of an emergency at work, some cleft-palate surgery gone wrong, and our regular babysitter's away for the weekend."

"No worries," Stacy told her. Bending down to chat with Tyler, she admired his woolen earmuffs, which were knitted to resemble pockets of fast-food french fries, one sitting against each ear. "Nice earmuffs, kiddo," she said. "Where'd ya get 'em? Burger King?"

"Nah."

"McDonald's?"

"Nah."

"Well, where?"

"Grandma Suzi."

This was Jefrie's mother, who had enthusiastically embraced Honey and her role in Jefrie's life. On the other hand, Honey's parents, deeply conservative people from Ponca City, Oklahoma, were no longer in touch with her and had yet to meet Tyler. According to Jefrie, Honey's mother and father had lost that privilege the day Tyler was born and they'd refused to come to the phone.

"Grandma Suzi, huh," Stacy said, "and who's this?" She pointed to the GI Joe-related action figure in Tyler's sweet baby hand: it was a grim-faced, muscle-bound hunk of plastic sporting a sleeveless green-and-black vest, a military helmet, and combat boots.

"Sergeant Savage," Tyler said reverently. When Stacy tried to touch the sculpted muscles of his chest, Tyler yanked the figure away, and said, "That's *mine.*"

"Oh, I'll bet Sergeant Savage here is going to have a super-fun time shopping for a wedding dress with us," Stacy said, winking at Jefrie.

When Roger's sister arrived, a few minutes later, she greeted Sergeant Savage by name, and bemoaned, with Jefrie, the generally crappy toys their sons were so fond of. Stacy had worried that there might have been some awkwardness between Clare and Jefrie, who'd never met before. She found herself fascinated by the immediate bond between them, a bond that was there merely because they were each the mother of a little boy. It was the sort of bond Stacy would never have noticed before but which struck her as something of interest, perhaps because now that she could imagine herself as a wife, she was beginning to envision, though a bit fuzzily, the enormous step beyond that. She could hear Lauren insisting, a month or so after the twins were born, *You CAN'T IMAGINE what it's like—you think you can, but I'm telling you that you CAN'T!* She'd told Stacy that on any given day there wasn't even time for her to brush her teeth, to take a shower, or get a good look at herself in the mirror. *Your children have to come first*, she said with the weariest sort of sigh, *at least until they're eighteen and finally out of the damn house.*

Well, maybe so, but come on, not enough time to brush your teeth? Stacy had thought then, and continued to think, that it was all hyperbole, that her poor sister, frazzled and disorganized and sleep-deprived, must have been exaggerating wildly.

Tyler was clamoring to get out of his stroller, but when the four of them entered the bridal salon, the saleswoman who greeted them evidently didn't think much of the idea. She was a bosomy woman in her forties dressed in a no-nonsense business suit, high heels, and a number of noisy charm bracelets on each wrist, and she stared with displeasure at Tyler, and then at Jefrie, who, under her soft, nearly translucent white T-shirt, was wearing a crimson bra.

*You should know better than to bring your three-year-old into this sacred space, you idiot, and furthermore, who in her right mind wears a red bra under a white shirt?* the saleswoman telegraphed with her frown.

Stacy wanted to slap her.

The woman introduced herself as Dawn, "your dress consultant," and pointing at Stacy, said, "You're the bride?"

"Guilty," Stacy said. "I mean I'm the one who called to make an appointment for today."

Tyler gnawed thoughtfully on Sergeant Savage's helmet. "We hafta go home," he said. "I wanna watch my *Tiny Toon Adventures* tape."

"I have two questions for you," Dawn said. "One, do you have any ideas about the style you're looking for; and two, how much do you want to spend?" She studied her watch. "Oh, and by the way, I ought to remind you that you have ninety minutes before I'll have to move on to the next customer."

She'd been in the store for ninety *seconds*, Stacy thought, and already Dawn was making her nervous. "I'm not sure I know precisely what you mean by 'style,'" Stacy confessed, and hung her head. She wished Roger were here with her, even though, of course, he knew absolutely nothing about wedding dresses. He was, however, a successful businessman, who knew how to deal with people out there and compel them to do whatever it was he wanted them to. Stacy, on the other hand, knew perfectly well that she allowed people to persuade her to bend to their will simply because she wanted things—everything, really—to go smoothly. Always. More than anything, she hated the notion of anyone at all thinking ill of her. Which she was sure Dawn already did.

"Let's start with style," Dawn said. "Sheath? A-line? Cocktail length? Princess?"

Stacy shrugged one shoulder.

"Any thoughts about the neckline?"

Shrugging both shoulders, Stacy said, "Not really."

"High neck, scoop, jewel neck, sweetheart neck," Dawn said. She kept her eye on Tyler, who was adamant about going home to his VCR and his beloved *Tiny Toon Adventures*.

"How about a pretzel, buddy?" Jefrie said, and dug into the bag attached to the back of the stroller.

Tyler held up two fingers: he wanted one pretzel for each hand, he said.

"So, no thoughts on the neckline? I'm assuming you have no thoughts on the waist either?" The condescension in Dawn's voice was unmistakable, and Stacy considered making a run for the front door without explanation, and taking her entourage with her. "There's dropped, natural, *om-peer* . . ." Dawn continued. Behind them, a bride-to-be, her mother, and a quartet of bridesmaids were waiting for a saleswoman, and Stacy allowed herself to eavesdrop as Dawn talked solemnly about the distinct virtues of capped sleeves and spaghetti straps. What Stacy overheard was so bizarre, she had to inch backward in the wedding party's direction to make sure she hadn't misunderstood what they were talking about.

"Is she out of her mind?" the mother of the bride was saying. "Cheese made out of breast milk? That is truly, unbelievably, disgusting!"

Moving over toward Jefrie to whisper what she'd just heard, Stacy felt herself relaxing. She loved her old friend's high-pitched squeal, and the way Jefrie hid her face against Stacy's shoulder as she shook with laughter.

"What?" Clare said. "What's so funny?"

It was Jefrie who whispered now into Clare's ear, and soon all three of them were laughing, along with Tyler, who attempted to stand up in his stroller, clearly serious about being sprung.

"Let . . . me . . . out," he said, no longer laughing.

"Whenever you're ready, ladies," Dawn said. "I can see we're going to have to start from scratch. But first we need to talk about your budget."

Well, there was the $4,000 gift from Stacy's grandmother, but how could she possibly spend all that money on a single dress? The thought was utterly distasteful to Stacy; if she divided up the money among her various homeless clients, she fantasized, her grandmother wouldn't be happy but her clients would certainly be better off. (Whether they wanted to be, or not, and sometimes they didn't—rejecting free dental care and HIV testing, substance abuse treatment, and vocational counseling; like her client Kim, who wanted none of it, not even the free cell phone she was offered.)

"I just don't know," Stacy told Dawn.

"Ballpark figure? Between one thousand and two thousand? Two thousand and thirty-five hundred? You've got to give me something to work with here, Stacy."

But she couldn't; embarrassed, Stacy kept silent. Why couldn't they all cram themselves into a cab, and pay a visit to a thrift shop, a high-end place on Madison Avenue where she'd be likely to find something lovely but wouldn't have to spend the kind of money that would turn her stomach and make her feel wealthy and entitled, which she had never been and, God knows, had never aspired to be. She would go ahead with this thrift shop idea, she decided now, even though Roger was apparently doing very, very well and probably would be unhappy knowing that her instincts were leading her to a second-hand wedding dress.

"Stacy?" Clare said. "Are you all right?"

"I want to go NOW!" Tyler said, and, just so they knew he wasn't fooling around, tossed Sergeant Savage out of the stroller, where he landed at Dawn's feet.

"We do have to go," Stacy told Dawn. "And I do apologize." She signaled to Clare and Jefrie to head toward the front of the showroom and out the door, while doing her best to ignore Dawn, who was trying to tempt her with talk of the salon's seamstresses and fitters and beading experts, and even their custom-made, miniature replicas of whatever gown Stacy happened to choose for herself—she could have a *gorgeous teeny-weeny* eighteen-inch replica of her own, if only she would take the time to see what Dawn could do for her.

*Sorry, lady, thanks but no thanks.*

*Stacy explains to him that there are only so many nights in a single week when they can serve their children store-brand chicken tenders, lackluster mozzarella sticks, and penne with some sort of undistinguished red sauce, before it's time to give in and take everyone out for Chinese food. And this is how they end up at Jade Pagoda, where there are starched white tablecloths and perky red carnations in bud vases on every table. Never mind the can of 7 Up that Will accidentally tips over with multiple sets of chopsticks clenched in his fist at one time; never mind the wontons that have to be completely divested of their pork filling before Olivia will even taste them; never mind having to escort Will to an exasperatingly dark and narrow men's room three times in a single hour because he "thinks" he has to pee but then realizes that he may as well hold it in until he gets back to Grandma's apartment where the bathrooms smell like vanilla wafers, he says.*

*Trying hard to enjoy—to the extent that he can enjoy anything these days—a stingy forkful of Tangerine Chicken* and Honey Walnut Shrimp, Roger makes the mistake of idly looking past his family to a round table near the front door. Seated there, with a noisy group of friends, is a woman sporting a silver-and-royal-blue silk scarf wrapped tightly around her head. Once he sees that she is missing her eyebrows, it doesn't take him more than an instant to realize that she is bald under that scarf. And that her life is on the line. Reminded, inevitably, of his poor, star-crossed sister, his appetite—diminished as it is—vanishes completely, just like that, and he uses his chopsticks to capture single chunks of walnut, one after another, and deposit them in all four corners of his square white plate.

Then suddenly he hears "Happy Birthday" being sung, accompanied, improbably, by a guitar, and sees that the birthday girl, whose name is Cynthia, is the cancer patient herself.

Except for Will—and the half-dozen gray-haired, fifty-ish friends, including the guitarist, at Cynthia's table—no one else joins in the singing or the applause that follows. The guitarist, apparently thinking it's time for the seventh-inning stretch, segues into "Take Me Out to the Ball Game."

The restaurant is a relatively pricey one, and its patrons are doing their best to ignore the music. The folksy guitarist, who has a decent, if unexceptional, voice, has begun to sing even louder now; she has everyone at Cynthia's table swaying, their arms flung across each other's shoulders.

Elbows on the table, his head in his hands, Roger doesn't understand why no one has put a stop to this little birthday party that's rudely gone so public, and that has, as it happens, given him a hell of a headache.

He thinks of his sister in her hospital bed, savoring what turned out to be her last supper, a small handful of cherry tomatoes and half a bottle of Orangina, Clare eating and at the same time talking to Stacy on the phone, then complaining, all of a sudden, of "the-e worst headache.

~ 111 ~

*Ever.*" She had to hang up then, but would call Stacy back later, she said.

A promise she would not be able to keep.

It's been two months, and Roger hasn't gotten over it.

He is a brother, not a bereaved husband or child, but, even so, it doesn't seem possible that he will ever get over it. He is a bereaved brother, sick with grief, the taste of it in his mouth, on the tip of his tongue, coating the back of his throat, spoiling everything.

His childhood memories of Clare seem to have been temporarily wiped out; the only images that come to him now are those of the most recent past; his bald-headed sister, her delicate face adorned with bronze-colored lipstick and carefully applied eye shadow and liner, sitting in her hospital bed watching DVDs of the first two seasons of Mad Men on her laptop, Stacy seated in an armchair beside her, the two of them so involved in the show, they barely looked up when Roger arrived with a bakery box full of cupcakes—and not just ordinary cupcakes, but red velvet, espresso ganache, and pistachio with almond buttercream frosting. Clare and Stacy shushed him when he tried to engage them in conversation, and so he sat there awkwardly with the bakery box in his lap, listening to Dylan on his iPod while these two women he loved so madly ignored him . . . But now he is conjuring one small thing from his childhood—the way he and Clare and their mother and father were dressed in gray shorts, turquoise-and-white checkered shirts, turquoise bandanas tied around their necks, one summer when they took a two-day trip to Colonial Williamsburg. Roger was eleven and had no thoughts about all of them being dressed identically, but Clare, at thirteen, was already part of a clique of girls at school, already old enough to be embarrassed by the sight of the four of them marching around in their matching outfits. "We look like idiots!" she told their mother, who had reached over, right there in the blacksmith shop in Colonial Williamsburg, and slapped Clare's pretty face. Remembering this now, Roger wants to grab his sweet demented eighty-two-year-old mother and say, "And you never even apologized." He doesn't understand why it should matter after all these years, only that it does. To him, anyway, the only one on earth who remembers what his mother did, doubling his sister's humiliation that morning, causing her to say, like some thirteen-year-old drama queen, "I wish I were dead!"

He gets up from his seat now and approaches Cynthia's table, where they've begun yet another fucking verse of "Take Me Out to the Ball Game." First he wishes Cynthia a happy birthday, then asks, very politely, if they could please keep it down. He doesn't want to hear "Take Me Out to the Ball Game," he explains, at least not when he's eating first-rate Chinese food in this lovely restaurant. Quite frankly, he guesses that everyone else in the room feels the same way. "After all," he points out, "this isn't your private dining room, guys."

The guitarist stops playing, and cradles the guitar in her arms. "You're an asshole, and a cruel, cruel man," she says, nice and loud, stentorian, really, so that everyone in the restaurant can hear, including the maître d', who's already headed their way. "Just because you said 'Happy Birthday' to Cynthia doesn't excuse you. Go back and sit down, asshole, and finish your dinner," the guitarist says. She plays a few chords, and sings, ". . . it's one, two, three strikes you're out . . ."

Furious at his mother for slapping Clare all those years ago, furious at the oncologists who failed so miserably to save his sister's life, furious at the guitarist for her incivility and her simple-minded repertoire . . . and now what? The maître d', a small guy wearing large, tortoise-shell-framed glasses, says, "Please, sir," and ushers Roger back to his seat.

"Please, sir" what? he wonders.

"No trouble, please, sir. And we have a nice dessert for you, tiramisu, and also almond tofu. And green tea ice cream, all for you."

Very nice desserts, on the house, the maître d' says. He's a gracious guy, eager to please, to smooth things over, but the music is going to drive Roger out of his fucking mind. Cynthia's table is singing "Happy Birthday" in French now, but no one seems peeved; everywhere in the restaurant people are eating their dinner, some with ivory-colored plastic chopsticks, some with plain old forks, treating themselves to Grand Marnier Prawns, Dry Sautéed Beef, Crispy Smoked Duck. Not a one of them distressed, as Roger is, by the sight of a woman who's lost her eyebrows to chemo and her guitar-strumming pal who can't stop singing "Happy Birthday" to her, fearing, perhaps, that it might be Cynthia's last.

"Let's get out of here," Roger says, gesturing that he'd like his check, please, to a nearby waiter who is busy assembling someone's Peking Duck.

"Why do we have to leave?" Stacy asks. Because she and the kids are still eating, and what about the tiramisu and almond tofu they've been promised?

"They'll pack it up to go," Roger says, but declines to explain why, of all the people here in Jade Pagoda, he alone just has to get the fuck out.

He leaves his MasterCard on the table, and says that he and his headache will be out in the car. When he gets there, he goes straight to the glove compartment to massage the solid heft of that 9 mm Glock and it feels so good between his trembly hands, better than anything has felt to him in a very long while. Better even than the soft skin at the bend of his wife's surprisingly dainty wrist.

## 14

It was New Year's Day, and as Roger kept his eye on the Rose Bowl, now in its final quarter, Stacy explained to him that although her wedding dress was second-hand, there was nothing to be concerned about; it was merely "delicately used" or "gently worn," whichever sounded better to him. She told him that, as she'd tried on the dress—with Clare's help—in a curtained-off partition at the thrift shop, she imagined the bride before her who'd worn it and then left it on consignment, hung prettily, a couple of weeks after her wedding, among the Badgley Mischkas and Yumi Katsuras. A bride much younger than herself, a care-free twenty-something who—and this Stacy kept quiet about—had left behind the faintest fragrance, which she immediately recognized as Lady Speed Stick "powder fresh" scent. Even after Stacy had it dry-cleaned a whiff of it remained, but so what? Who was going to notice?

"Mischka and *who*? Those names don't mean anything to me," Roger said. He seemed insulted that Stacy had spent so little money on the dress when she knew perfectly well that they could afford something new and expensive.

"Well, guess what, the Wisconsin Badgers and UCLA Bruins? Those names don't mean a thing to *me*." Sitting down beside him on the couch in the den, winding her arms around Roger's neck, Stacy joked, "Come on, babe, why can't you be like all those guys who'd be thrilled to have a fiancée who saved them some money?"

But the Bruins were only minutes away from losing to Wisconsin, and Roger was no longer paying attention to her.

She went back into their bedroom and took another look at her dress; she now knew what a sweetheart neckline was, and all about Alençon lace, which dated back to seventeenth-century France, and would, years from now, be added to Unesco's Representative List of the Intangible Cultural Heritage of Humanity.

༄

It had drizzled on and off earlier in the day, but then had finally cleared around four o'clock; luckily for the wedding guests at the Botanical Garden, it was an unseasonably warm April night. The pain Stacy felt at her parents' absence hit her hard as, just before sunset, she made her way down the six broad stone steps that led from the Garden Terrace Room and then, still on Marshall's arm, strolled along the well-lit flagstone aisle, nodding and smiling at the guests. There were seventy-five of them seated, on either side of the aisle, in immaculate white-painted wooden folding chairs on the large patio overlooking the Bronx River. Stacy's eyes were wet, and her nose actually began to run, and by the time she reached Roger in his tux—waiting for her so sweetly, so hopefully, halfway down the aisle—she was desperate for a tissue or handkerchief, neither of which was on hand when she reached the wedding canopy under which the ceremony would be performed by the baby-faced rabbi of Beverly's synagogue. So Stacy had to use the clean white linen napkin that was meant to cover the wine glass Roger would soon, as was the custom, smash to bits with the heel of his glossy black patent leather wingtip.

"Happy Birthday!" he said as he took her arm, then lifted her veil to kiss her.

"And to you, monsieur," Stacy said, but just couldn't stop herself from thinking of Adolf Hitler an instant later. It wasn't the first time she'd found herself wishing that Roger hadn't shared that small piece of trivia with her the day they'd met.

༄

She heard both during and after the wedding that the hors d'oeuvres were spectacular—what she remembered were the carmelized shallots with gruyère, pan-seared crab cake sliders, seafood fortune cookies, and miniature BLTs—but, as both her grandmother and Clare had predicted, Stacy barely had a taste of anything at all. She was too busy chatting up the guests—old friends; friends of Roger's from New Orleans, San Francisco, and Chicago whom she'd never met before; Barbara Armstrong and several other people from her office; some far-flung cousins of Roger's from Argentina; and people he'd worked with before going out on his own, most of whom seemed to be big tall guys like Roger himself, but with petite wives dressed all in black. These were the same guys who volunteered to hoist Stacy and Roger high in their chairs, as the band switched to some festive Hebrew music and the guests danced wildly around them and applauded, Jefrie and Clare most vigorously of all. It was, Stacy discovered, a little unnerving up there over the shoulders of Roger's friends, and she was surprised at how uneasy she felt, afraid that she would bounce off her chair and land unceremoniously on the dance floor, her white dress and its twelve-foot velvet sash creased and torn and darkened with dust. But of course no such thing happened; she was, after all, completely safe, Roger (now her husband!) not six inches away from her high up in an identical chair, a brilliant, joyous smile displaying those lovely, perfectly straight teeth of his. She reached across the space between her and her husband and grabbed the tips of his fingers with her own.

‌⁓⁓

*The first item on the local cable news this morning is about a thirteen-year-old middle schooler here in Florida who savagely kicked a fifteen-year-old girl in the head half a dozen times with his steel-toed boots, merely because he was angry about a text message the girl had sent him. Now* the fifteen-year-old victim is in a medically induced coma and her thirteen-year-old assailant is in custody, charged with first-degree attempted murder.

"All this over a text message, for God's sake!" Stacy says. "What the hell is wrong with this world? I mean, who raised this murderous thirteen-year-old?"

"Good morning to you, too," Roger says, standing at the bathroom sink, foaming at the mouth, toothbrush in hand. After he finishes, he gets down onto the carpeted floor of the bedroom, where, with a pillow behind his head, he does two sets of fifty sit-ups, grunting and quietly counting aloud as Stacy describes the Flamingo Gardens to him. And explains why, exactly, Will and Olivia, still asleep in their beds at the moment, should have the opportunity to get a load of all that endangered wildlife—alligators, bobcats, river otters, and seventy species of birds, including falcons, hawks, and bald eagles. "Whatever," Roger says. "Whatever you'd like to do is fine with me."

He seems, Stacy thinks, a little more energetic today, a little sunnier, brightened by something, but who knows what? All she knows is that she's grateful and relieved, and looking forward, with genuine excitement, to flying home to New York the day after tomorrow.

"I'm thinking we should buy a couple of souvenirs for Magnolia. We're only paying her ten dollars a day, you know," she says, referring to the elderly, divorced neighbor who has been looking after their cats this week, feeding them, freshening their water, and getting down on her plump, arthritic, seventy-six-year-old knees to clean out the litter box—the very thought of which makes Stacy feel guilty.

"Whatever," Roger says agreeably. He's running in place now in nothing but his boxers, directly in front of the modest-sized TV, its screen, Stacy notes, coated with the thinnest film of dust.

"You keep saying 'whatever,'" she points out. "Please stop saying that, okay?"

"Whatever," Roger says, and, still jogging, rotates a half turn so that she can see, by the expression on his face, that he's teasing her. She sees, too, the graying hair on his chest and it feels like a blow of some kind, a kick in the gut that reminds her that he is nearly a decade older than she is, that his youth is a great distance behind him, and that most people would probably consider him surprisingly old to be the father of such young children. Not that he hasn't taken exceptionally well to fatherhood; save for the past couple of months—since Clare's death and the reversals his business has suffered—he's always been closely attentive to the kids, never dismissive, listening to them patiently when they go on and on about their favorite shows on the Disney Channel or which classmate spilled what all over himself at snack time; sitting on the floor with Will for as long as it takes to build a small village out of Legos; keeping watch over Olivia as she stands on a chair at the kitchen sink and insists on helping to wash the dishes. And he does love to read to them: one of Stacy's favorite photographs captured him lounging in Olivia's crib, his long, long legs hanging out over the top of the wooden bars, reading Goodnight Moon to his baby daughter.

Stacy approaches him now, standing behind him and casting her arms around his waist as he jogs; she kisses one bare shoulder, then the other. "You're such a good father," she says, and he just keeps running in place, breathing heavily, giving away nothing but the scent of toothpaste and deodorant.

## 15

Other than the excellent pizza, thin-crusted and loaded with baby arugula that had been lightly dressed with extra-virgin olive oil, and served by a Japanese waitress in the small Italian town of Praiano, what Stacy would remember most vividly about their honeymoon was the terrifyingly narrow, serpentine roads tracing the Amalfi coast. How she and Roger, walking back to the hotel after dinner that night—Roger five yards ahead of her—had been forced to flatten themselves against the mountainside as a large, noisy truck came hurtling along in the surrounding darkness, its headlights offering the only illumination except the moon, Stacy's heart thumping in terror as, for an instant, she contemplated the possibility that she and Roger would die together on this honeymoon, their bodies crushed beyond recognition, their friends and family back in New York sick with grief and not knowing whom to blame. Then, moments later, when the danger had passed and the truck was gone, and Roger reversed direction and walked back toward her, she could sense, even in the dark, that he was laughing, that this was his idea of an adventure, and that, unlike Stacy herself, not for an instant had he imagined them to be in any real danger.

After dinner, returning to their room in the small, family-owned hotel where they were staying, the two of them stripped off most of their clothes and got onto the bed together, where they played a heated game of Scrabble on their travel-size board. Roger was an intensely competitive player, *insanely* competitive, Stacy sometimes thought. That night he hit his personal record-breaking score of 161 points for the word "injury"—there was a triple letter "J" ultimately worth a remarkable 120 points; and if that weren't enough, Roger ruthlessly wiped the floor with her with words like "zygomatic" and "amelioratory" and "callithumpian"—a word Stacy had never heard of, but which he assured her was in the dictionary, and that it meant, oddly, "a participant in a boisterous parade." *Fine, if you say so,* she said. He'd jumped off the bed and done a momentary but joyous victory dance dressed only in his boxers after totaling up that 161 points, shouting "Yesss!" so loudly and with such brio that Stacy had to laugh. But it was kind of juvenile, really, the silly dance and all that effort focused on racking up points. Why, she wondered, was it so essential to win? Why did he need so badly, so desperately, really, to beat his previous high score, and, of course, to triumph over *her*, his friendly, rather half-hearted opponent? It was a game they were playing—for relatively smart people, sure—but still, in the end, only a game, made of plastic and paper. It was useless to try and point this out to Roger, she knew. And she knew, as well, how much he hated to lose. He'd lost to her just last night, though not by much, not long after she arranged the word "blitzkrieg" on the board. He sulked afterward and had to be coaxed into making love; tonight, though, in the wake of his victory, there was no coaxing necessary.

Later, when Roger fell asleep, Stacy went into the tiny shower, which had a folding plastic door and beautifully tiled walls. She enjoyed relaxing in the stream of steamy water after a long day in the passenger seat of that BMW convertible that Roger took such pleasure in driving—those sinuous roads that scared the hell out of her were, for him, a great thrill to navigate. He'd promised her that they would arrive safely at the hotel by the end of the day, and they had. Even so, the thrill of getting there was his alone. But that was fine, she thought; surely there were other pleasures awaiting them.

Shutting off the water in the shower now, she reached for the handle of the door that was meant to fold inward, and pulled. And pulled. Again and again. But it simply would not budge.

She soon understood that the door, which had fallen off its tracks, was not going to open, not tonight, anyway, and that Roger was dead-to-the-world sound asleep and could not be awakened, no matter how loudly and insistently she shouted his name, or how fiercely she pounded on the cheap plastic door. She could see her bath towel where she'd left it, draped across the sink, out of reach; her halter top and drawstring pajama bottoms imprinted with cupcakes, and the books and magazines she'd brought along, were all in the other room. She sat with her back against the pretty, pastel-colored tiles and cried in frustration, feeling sorry for herself and pissed off at Roger, nice and comfy in their double bed, failing to hear her as he snored rudely into his pillow.

To add to her discomfort, she was goosebumpy-cold now that the steam had dissipated. Hugging herself miserably, she thought of her clients so stubbornly living out on the freezing streets of the city, huddling in concrete corners, hoping to shield themselves from an icy January wind. She remembered the day, this winter, when she and Barbara Armstrong had escorted a client—a freckled, alcoholic Vietnam vet named James Blackerby—out to the Bronx, where they were going to get him settled into a room at a nursing home, the only one of the several dozen Stacy had phoned that agreed to take him. After returning from Vietnam in the seventies, James had gone back to school and become a successful landscape architect, but the drinking eventually took over his life. His wife had kicked him out of their house in the suburbs just after his fiftieth birthday, a half-dozen years ago, and his grown children had given up on him as well. On the way to the nursing home, he peed in his pants, and earnestly told Stacy and Barbara that getting drunk and staying drunk were his only goals in life. At least there was a trace of embarrassment in his husky voice when he'd confessed to wetting his pants. Without that, Stacy would have thought him utterly hopeless.

They had to open all four windows in the car, but the stench of urine was overwhelming, and Stacy carefully pulled the Chevy over on the Major Deegan Expressway. She went to the trunk, and found, as she knew she would, a spare pair of men's work pants for James, who requested a cigarette and a change of underwear when Stacy returned to the car with the pants for him.

"I'm sorry," she said about the underwear. It was chilly outside, and chilly in the car because they still had all the windows open even though the temperature was barely forty degrees. She was afraid to turn on the heat, worried that the scent of James's piss would linger even longer if she did.

"Just put the pants on," she told him. "You'll be fine."

"Not even one cigarette? Just give me three minutes and I'll smoke it outside and won't ask you for another one, I promise." James hung over the front seat, begging.

Stacy and Barbara, a longtime smoker, exchanged a look: the agency they worked for had a no-smoking policy, and it was supposed to be strictly enforced. But what the hell, if the guy wanted a cigarette, at least it wasn't alcohol he was pleading for, Barbara and Stacy quietly agreed.

"Put your pants on," Stacy said, "then you'll get your cigarette, okay?" She handed James a plastic bag and told him to deposit his wet things into it. She and Barbara got out of the car to give him his privacy.

Cars whizzed past them at sixty miles an hour as they shivered in the cold waiting for James to get himself out of his pissed-upon pants, then the door behind the driver's seat suddenly opened. As James stepped out of the car, lusting after his cigarette, Stacy knew, he passed along the plastic bag containing his sopping clothes to her, as daintily as if he were an heiress handing off a small shopping bag from Tiffany to the chauffeur—not a homeless drunk whose family no longer had any use for him.

Stacy took the knotted bag from him gingerly, unable to avoid the smell through the thin plastic. In the distance she could see a pair of gas stations, and beyond them, Yankee Stadium. No one had to tell her that she needed to toss the bag into the trunk, lock it up, and return to the car; no one ever had to tell her to do the right thing. This time, however, she just couldn't bring herself to do it, and, instead, pitched the bag into some frost-covered foliage nearby as James lit up his longed-for cigarette and Barbara pretended to look the other way. Stacy, who was so accustomed to doing the right thing, had just done the wrong thing, and all she wanted was to hurry back into the car and drive away from the scene of the crime. But first she had to wait for her client to finish his cigarette. So she had waited, as she waited now, only tonight it was hours and not minutes, and instead of waiting in her down coat and soft woolen scarf, she sat here on the floor of the shower naked and shivering and unable to do a thing to help herself.

At first light, Roger got up to use the bathroom, and it was the sound of the toilet being flushed that awakened her. She burst into tears at the sight of him, then came his cry of astonishment at the sight of *her* behind the clear plastic. He fiddled with the shower door, cursing, and finally had to wrench it off its tracks to rescue her, stepping into the shower that was scarcely wide enough for the two of them, embracing her with such contrition, with so many apologies on his lips, that she saw, for the very first time, she was the one who had to comfort *him*.

After they'd returned from their honeymoon and would tell this story to their friends, they recast it as something hilarious—Roger, the big dummy, snoring away in bed while poor Stacy, the other dummy, couldn't manage to figure out how to get herself out of the shower. *Oh, they were a real pair, weren't they, they said laughingly to their friends.*

～

# FIRST DRAFT

*To my dear family and friends—*

*I am a tortured soul. My love for my family is everything to me, and I do not want them to suffer. I have thought things through again and again, and each time the result is the same: there is no way out. I am deeply ashamed of my failures, both as a businessman and as a human being, but you must believe me when I tell you that there is no way out . . .*

*Please forgive me for starting so many sentences with the word "I."*

In addition to all his other failings, his handwriting is an abomination. His third grade teacher, Mrs. Weber—the old bag who taught him what used to be called "cursive writing"—would be disgusted.

✑

Roger's barely eaten all day, but he hasn't offered up a single word of explanation. He had no breakfast at all, Stacy knows, not even a tentative sip of coffee or a single, half-hearted bite of toast; lunch was half a navel orange, which she peeled and sectioned and handed him in a purple plastic bowl, as if he were a child; dinner is a mere handful of the thick, dark pretzels he likes so much, he'd brought a bag of them along from New York.

"Why does Daddy get to eat pretzels for dinner?" Olivia wants to know, and when Roger snaps, "Because I'm a grown-up, that's why," Stacy doesn't argue with him, though normally the two of them try never to fall back on lazy, reflexive answers like that, those that do nothing to enlighten their children and only reinforce the idea that adults can do anything they damn please.

Roger's elbow is upright on the dinner table, the side of his face cupped forlornly in his open palm. Sit up straight! Stacy wants to say, like some cranky teacher close to retirement age in a classroom full of exasperating twelve-year-olds. Sit up straight and eat your damn dinner!

"Soooo . . . when I'm a grown-up, I can have pretzels for dinner if I want?" Olivia continues.

"Absolutely," Stacy promises her. "When you're a grown-up, you can eat, let's see, a bowl of whipped cream for dinner, and you don't even have to use a spoon if you don't want to," she adds, as Olivia shrieks happily at the news.

"When I'm a grown-up," Will says, "I'm going to eat Goldfish for dinner. 'The snack that smiles back,'" he says, and shows off his mouthful of baby teeth outlined in the melted, orangey cheddar of his mac 'n' cheese dinner.

"Yuck, you're an idiot," Olivia says amiably. Then, reconsidering, she says, "Actually, you're not an idiot, you're just stupid."

"We don't talk to each other like that!" Roger scolds her. "Not in this family—do you understand me!" He's gone from the table an instant later; even though Stacy's afraid to go after him, she forces herself up and out of her chair and into the master bedroom, where she finds Roger at the window, staring out at the Intracoastal Waterway and a distant figure parasailing in the sunset, flying off into the ether.

Even though he's facing away from her, she can tell, as Roger rocks back and forth silently at the window, that he is weeping.

"Please don't," she says. "Don't cry like that, baby." She's at his side now, leaning her head against his shoulder, whispering, "Baby, don't," into his ear. He doesn't shake her off, but he can't seem to stop crying, and Stacy's more worried about him now than she's ever been, and *guiltily considers, though only for a moment or two, what it might be like to scoop up her kids from the dinner table and tear out of there, leaving Roger behind standing at the window of his parents' condo, sobbing like a child who has lost his way.*

*The suddenly audible sound of his weeping makes her stomach hurt, but she stays at his side, listening to him talk about the taste of grief on his tongue and for the very first time she wonders if he's crazy. Nuts. About to go off the deep end, as he once had long ago. She's thrown off balance by the thought and imagines the lovesick guy he'd been thirty-five years ago, a gaunt figure sitting around in the day room at Emerald Hills during arts and crafts class, meticulously folding a flock of origami cranes or a rabble of butterflies, a melancholy teenager sitting in silence among his fellow patients, none of them ready to reclaim their lives.*

*She lifts her head and watches out the window now as the parasailer, someone in a brightly colored bathing suit, miraculously returns to earth.*

## 16

He was dying to start a family, but Stacy wasn't entirely sure she was ready. "What's the big hurry?" she would say to him, though she knew perfectly well the nine years between them made a difference, and that Roger had every reason to want to get things going. The September after they were married, she gave in and tossed her birth control pills into the kitchen trash, along with a plastic container of cream cheese that had some mossy-looking stuff sprouting around the edges.

The miscarriage, in the eighth week of her pregnancy, was a sorrowful disappointment to both of them. They were still living on the West Side and on their way in a cab to Clare and Marshall's early one spring night when, without any warning at all, Stacy felt some painful cramping; on a scale of one to ten, she gave it about a seven and a half. And soaked through her jeans right there in the cab, more blood than she'd ever seen. Roger called Clare on his cell phone, and she came running out with bath towels; one for Stacy to wrap around her waist, the others for Roger to clean up the blood that had pooled in the backseat of the cab. The driver, a Sikh in a pumpkin-colored turban, seemed both horrified and disgusted; he took the fifty-dollar tip and tore off down East End just moments after Roger helped Stacy out of the cab.

The cramping continued in a way that would have to be called *relentless*, Stacy thought, and it was Clare who took charge of everything while Roger and Marshall stood around looking grim. She ushered Stacy into one of the bedrooms, wiped the blood from her thighs with warm washcloths, helped her into a nightgown, and covered her with a quilt. But a few minutes later, Stacy flew toward the nearest bathroom just in time to feel something slide swiftly out of her and into the sleek, sand-colored toilet; though she could barely bring herself to glance beneath her, she saw what she could have sworn was a large, particularly nasty-looking hunk of calf's liver. And thought she might faint.

She held on to the edge of the marble countertop, and counted very slowly to ten, and then to twenty. In the mirror, she could see that her face was drained of its natural color and tinted an ashy gray. She looked ghastly, as her mother would have said.

She was thirty-five years old; would she ever stop missing her mother?

Standing in the doorway now, she called for Clare, who bravely took a look.

"That's the placenta, sweetie," Clare explained, then dialed the obstetrician for her and held the phone to Stacy's ear.

What Stacy heard was Dr. Burnes calmly telling her that yes, that was the placenta she'd seen floating in the water, and that she needed to come in for a D and C tomorrow. "These things, you know, happen from time to time," Dr. Burnes added. The doctor herself had once been "Miss Indiana" in a beauty pageant and had two daughters and an infant son. She always managed to sound dispassionate, which never failed to disappoint Stacy just the slightest bit. She waited now for Dr. Burnes to say she was sorry about the miscarriage, but quickly understood that the silence at the other end meant the conversation was over.

"That bitch should have been more sympathetic," Clare—who never cursed—told Stacy. The two of them were the closest of friends these days, even though Clare was eleven years older. "Did she at least tell you to rest?" she asked Stacy.

"I can't remember," Stacy said. Clare escorted her back to bed and covered her with the quilt again, and it hit Stacy, who'd been thinking only of herself, that Clare had been through this a number of times, that she'd had several miscarriages of her own, and that this thing that had happened to *her* tonight must have evoked distressing memories for Clare. Even though, of course, Nathaniel was a big boy of ten now, and that struggle of Clare's to carry a baby to term had ended years ago. "I'm so sorry," Stacy said. "I mean, sorry you had to see this."

Still looking grave, Roger knocked politely at the open door.

"She'll be fine," Clare told him. "And please, no apologies," she said to Stacy. "Don't be nutty!"

Roger sat down on the edge of the bed and put his hand on her belly.

"Gone," Stacy said. She thought again of Clare's attempts to have a baby on her own, and wondered if she and Roger would also be faced with the prospect of having to travel to Colombia—or China or Vietnam—if they wanted a child. Was this a journey she was prepared to make? She wasn't sure, and kept the thought to herself.

The cramping had subsided, and she was able to smile at Roger, whose disappointment was apparently so great, he couldn't bring himself to smile back at her.

## SECOND DRAFT

*To my dear family and friends—*

*I am a tortured soul. My love for my family is everything to me, and I do not want them to suffer.*

IT'S BEST FOR ALL OF US THIS WAY.

I am drowning in debt and have thought things through again and again, and each time the conclusion is the same: there is no way out.

Listen to me, please: There. Is. No. Way. Out.

None.

Hard as it may be, please find it in yourselves to forgive me.

## 17

"Hate to say it, but these Lamaze classes are kind of a joke, actually," Jefrie confided. It was a little more than two years after Stacy's miscarriage, and Jefrie rode along next to her in a hospital elevator packed with pregnant women and their husbands, most of them carrying pillows from home tucked under their arms so that they could do their exercises on the floor. Roger had apologized for missing the class, but he'd been delayed at work and couldn't get here in time, and Jefrie had instantly agreed to take his place when Stacy called her. "I mean, who are they kidding?" Jefrie continued. "Pain-free childbirth is a fucking oxymoron if I ever heard one," she whispered. "Not that I'm trying to frighten you, sugar, but you don't know the meaning of the word 'pain' until you're eight centimeters dilated and stuck there, contemplating death and how much you'd welcome it if only your labor coach would just let you die right then and there."

"Hmm, let's see, you were in labor six long years ago," Stacy pointed out. "How come your memories are so . . . um . . . horribly vivid?"

"Are you kidding? Who could forget a nightmare like that?"

Filing out of the elevator, the group found its way to a big drafty classroom—with all the desks and chairs pushed against the walls—where they were met by a thirty-something nurse in a lavender uniform, new white rubber clogs, and what looked like an optimistic smile.

"Get comfortable on the floor, people," the nurse said. She insisted that everyone introduce themselves in a "loud, clear voice" and encouraged the mumblers to speak up.

"We wanna know who you are," she told a woman in a saffron-colored sari, who, faint-voiced, said she was named Raihana.

"I don't wanna know, do you?" Jefrie whispered to Stacy.

The nurse Gabriella stood alongside a blackboard wiped clean of everything except a diagram of a uterus and a set of ovaries and fallopian tubes. "Do you have something you'd like to share with us?" she asked Jefrie.

Flashing an insincere smile, Jefrie said, "Oh, I was just remembering what a fabulously rewarding experience giving birth was for me. Without all those unbelievably helpful Lamaze classes, it might have been a disaster, though."

A woman seated between her husband's legs heaved herself up from the floor. Her earrings—a black enamel question mark in one ear, an exclamation point in the other—swung as she yelled, "You're SUCH a liar! You think I didn't hear you in the elevator saying Lamaze was a joke? And if I were you, Gabriella, I'd throw this . . .this . . . *person* right out of here. We don't need any negative karma in the room, that's for sure."

Gabriella wrung her hands. "All right, you guys," she said, "let's all take a deep cleansing breath and start over. Labor coaches, that means you, too."

"Excuse me, what exactly did you mean by 'start over'?" Jefrie called out, not the least bit embarrassed, Stacy was glad to see.

"I meant that we're going to pretend we just walked into the room this minute and that our minds are empty of everything negative, especially fear."

"I'm terrified," Stacy murmured, as the sound of deep breathing pervaded the room and a feeling of dread filled her chest. There was Jefrie beside her as Stacy stretched out on the floor, a pillow reeking of fabric softener beneath her head.

Rubbing Stacy's belly, her palm moving in endless concentric circles, Jefrie took Stacy's hand and said, "Now *you*."

Together their hands swept along the hard mound of her belly, performing a dance so slow and intimate that Stacy nearly wept.

∽

## *THIRD DRAFT*

*To my dear family and friends—*

*I am a tortured soul.*

*I am drowning in debt.*

*I am trying as hard as I can to get this exactly right, but I'm at a loss here. Please forgive me.*

*And please know that my love for my family is EVERYTHING to me, and that I do NOT want them to suffer.*

*IT'S BEST FOR ALL OF US THIS WAY.*

## 18

Stacy and Roger officially became parents in the middle of a heat wave during the summer of 2002. Because of the varicose veins she'd developed during her pregnancy, Stacy, who normally went around bare legged all summer, had been forced to wear support hose, every damn day, that were twice as thick as regular pantyhose, and that kept her miserably uncomfortable over the course of one of the city's hottest summers. She'd never been a complainer, but for the last month of her pregnancy, she couldn't seem to stop squawking about the substandard air-conditioning in her office, the thirty-two pounds she'd gained, and her puffy feet which, by the end of her ninth month, fit into nothing except flip-flops, which went beautifully with her support hose. She also cursed a lot, referring to "the fucking hot weather," her "fucking varicose veins," and even, once or twice, "this fucking pregnancy," as in, "When will this fucking pregnancy ever be over?" (Roger hated to hear this, but out of deference to Stacy's suddenly high-strung temperament, all he did was roll his eyes.)

Fortunately for both of them, Roger thought, he kept his equanimity all summer long. He replaced the four air conditioners in their apartment with the most powerful ones their co-op would allow, made it home from work early almost every night—by seven thirty or so—and cooked dinner and washed the dishes afterward so that Stacy could relax until bedtime. He sympathized with her when she complained she couldn't sleep at night, and when she worried about the direction she had allowed her life to take. Though he knew he had no idea what he was talking about, he promised that the deepest sort of love and contentment would make their way into her life—into *their* life—once the baby arrived. And reminded her that Clare had assured them there was nothing like the lovely weight of a baby in your arms.

"Yeah, yeah, yeah," Stacy said, sounding like some impatient, unappealing seventeen-year-old, albeit one he treasured.

*꙰*

Stacy lay in bed in a labor room listening to the music flowing from her iPod. She listened to the same three-minute movement from Handel's *Water Music* over and over again, a serene, delicate piece simply entitled "Air." When Roger asked if she was finally ready to move on to the *andante* movement, she happened to be breathing through a particularly fierce contraction, and yelped, "Stop talking to me, dumbass!" And then, as the contraction ebbed, "Sorry! Sorry, sorry, sorry, okay?"

"Listen, you're entitled to be as mean and bitchy as you want. Tomorrow it'll all be forgotten. By me, anyway," Roger said.

"How is it possible," Stacy asked in between contractions, "that every child who ever came into this world caused this much pain?"

Roger shrugged; what, after all, could he possibly say? Still, she wanted him to say *something*.

"Honestly, I can't take too much more of this," she announced, hating the sound of her own lament. Another contraction built, sweeping her along all the way from discomfort to agony. It hit her that for the first time in her life she actually wanted to die, and that she didn't have the faith or strength to see past this unbearable moment. "You did this to me!" she yelled. "You, you idiot!"

"Guilty!" Roger said, and she heard a jaunty note in his voice that infuriated her.

But then *she* felt guilty. "Sorry, did I just call you an idiot?"

"I certainly hope not," said the labor nurse who'd come to check on Stacy's progress. "So how are we doing?"

"We," Stacy said, panting, "want an epidural."

"Too late for that now," the nurse informed her briskly. "Sorry, but you should have spoken up earlier."

"You're not sorry," Stacy heard herself say. "Why are you saying you're sorry when you're not?" She listened to Roger drawing in his breath.

"Hey!" Dr. Burnes said, appearing at Stacy's side in surgical scrubs. "They told you I had to do an emergency C-section on another patient, right? I wish I could have been here sooner."

"They told me a lot of things," Stacy said. "They told me this Lamaze crap would work like a charm, which, under the circumstances, I find pretty hilarious."

Rubbing her shoulder, Roger said, "Well, it's been a long seven hours." And then, "Hey, look, the sun's coming up."

"Like I give a flying fuck," Stacy said.

"Don't mind *me*," Roger said as he walked toward the window for a better look, "I'm just making polite conversation."

"Go away, please," Stacy begged. "All of you go away and leave me alone to die, which is actually my goal right now."

"*I'm* not going anywhere. I'm your knight in shining armor," Dr. Burnes said. She drew a plaid curtain around the two of them and after examining Stacy, said, "Yup, this patient's on her way to the delivery room even as we speak."

"She is?" Stacy said.

There were, she noticed immediately, remarkably bright lights overhead in the delivery room. *Too* bright: she had to close her eyes against them.

Now she could hear Dr. Burnes's voice commanding, "Bear down! Push!"

Stacy gave it everything she had as Roger's hands pressed down on her shoulders.

She leaned back, drained. "Eulogy or elegy, what's the difference between them?" she asked Roger, her voice so small and tired even *she* could barely hear it.

"You're not concentrating," Dr. Burnes said crossly. "You've got to help me out here."

But Stacy was no slacker; she was pushing as powerfully as she could. Again and again until hours might have passed. She was trapped in this hellish place where there was only appalling pain and loud voices cruelly ordering her to work harder when, honestly, she was more exhausted than she'd ever been in her life; she was half dead, really. And, too, she was certain that if she pushed any harder, she'd explode, and they would be gathering bloody pieces of her from all four corners of this dazzlingly bright room.

"Again!" Dr. Burnes insisted. "Push against my finger!"

"Come on, Stacy! Come on, come on, come on!" the nurse said, and Stacy envisioned this hefty middle-aged woman in a cheerleader uniform, pale dimply thighs revealed, the white Air Jordans on her feet even whiter than her thighs.

"Put down your damn megaphone!" Stacy yelled at her.

Dr. Burnes was muttering angrily now. "It's been forty-five minutes, it's enough."

"Don't be angry at *me*," Stacy said.

"No one's angry at you, babe," said Roger. He had no right to look so tired and spent, Stacy thought, not when she was the one who'd been doing all the work.

"And don't call me 'babe,'" she told him.

"Stacy!" Dr. Burnes said sharply. Shining in the fluorescent light was a tool that resembled a pair of tongs, with extra-large spoons at the ends.

"What the fuck is *that*?" said Stacy.

"We're going to get this baby out with forceps. And no worries, I'm going to be very careful."

"Okay." How meek and innocent she herself sounded, Stacy thought; hers was the voice of a woman you could walk right over. A woman so innocent, you could feed lies to her without her even noticing. But *she* was not such a woman. "Come over here," she told Roger. "Where I can see you."

"I'm right here," he said. "We're going to watch for the baby now."

The baby, whom Stacy had forgotten all about. Already she'd proven herself a bad mother, and wanted to weep.

Something was sliding out from between her legs. Something wet and slippery, grayish-pink and greasy-looking; in truth, it was kind of hideous.

*That's a baby?*

Well, apparently it was.

"There's your daughter!" the doctor announced, all smiles for the very first time, as she held Olivia up for Stacy and Roger's approval. "Good work, Stacy."

*Good work!* A high school teacher's enthusiastic scrawl across the top of your AP English essay, calculus quiz, world history exam.

Olivia let out a small cry of outrage as she was placed on Stacy's stomach. "You want to go back where you came from, little girl?" Stacy said, and dropped a first kiss on Olivia's greasy, matted hair. "Oh, and by the way, that's your old man over there," she said as Roger lowered his head to kiss them both.

Hearing this, Olivia whimpered, and closed one blue eye.

❦

She was a lightweight: five pounds, thirteen ounces, with heartbreakingly spindly arms and legs, the pale hair on her head soft as down.

"Don't you just love her?" Roger said.

Had she already fallen in love with Olivia on this very first day of the baby's life? It was an unfair question, really, Stacy reflected. Because Olivia was a stranger, wasn't she, someone Stacy had been introduced to barely twelve hours ago. But she loved the sweet, velvety feel of the baby in her arms, just as Clare had predicted.

Clare and Marshall were Olivia's first visitors; as soon as she walked into Stacy's hospital room, Clare let out a cry at the sight of the baby asleep in her arms.

"She's a beauty," Marshall said kindly.

Well, to be honest, *not exactly*, Stacy thought; Olivia's nose was a little squashed, and there was some bruising on one side between her eyebrow and hairline, thanks to the forceps. Bending her face now, Stacy touched her lips to one of the bruises.

Isabel, the patient in the other bed, a first-time mother in her forties, was watching *Jeopardy!* on her TV with her husband. "What is . . . the Spanish Inquisition?" she said.

"It's amazing, this fatherhood thing," Roger told everyone, and deposited Olivia back into her Lucite bassinet next to Stacy's bed. "There's nothing like it."

"Who is . . . Albert Speer?" Isabel called out excitedly.

Marshall sighed. "Did I mention my BlackBerry has a cracked screen?" he said.

"What happened?" Stacy asked him.

"Oh, the usual—your sister-in-law flung it onto the floor of the terrace in a moment of unchecked rage," Marshall said.

"Ha ha," said Clare.

"Who is . . . Benito Mussolini?" said Isabel. She and her husband high-fived each other.

"Seriously," Marshall said. "I dropped the BlackBerry on the bathroom floor. And that's marble we're talking about."

"I just heard on the news that 67 percent of all people surveyed admitted to texting while in the bathroom," Roger said.

"Yeah, but how big was the survey?"

Stacy's eyes were closing and she was about to doze off. When she awoke, twenty minutes later, she heard Clare say, "You want perfect happiness for them, perfect contentment, but trust me, even when they're babies it's not always a possibility."

∽

Waiting for Roger and Clare to swing by the hospital and pick her up for the crosstown trip home, Stacy sat at the edge of her bed eyeing the baby, and had to acknowledge that beyond holding Olivia and feeding her those four-ounce bottles of formula every few hours, she'd done very little for her daughter. She had yet to change a diaper, to get Olivia in and out of the plain white hospital-issue Onesies the nurses had dressed her in. Several of the nurses had offered Stacy the opportunity to do these things on her own, but she'd decided to pass, claiming exhaustion, and a soreness everywhere that made her dread the mere act of getting up and moving around the room.

So what was it, exactly, that she was so afraid of? Snapping Olivia's fragile arms as she tried to slip them into the sleeves of her shirt. Taping her diaper too loosely or too tightly or backward or upside down. Handling her too roughly, or even too gently. Roger shared her fears; the two of them were kind of pathetic, she thought, a couple of bewildered amateurs who had about three minutes to get their act together before taking the baby home with them.

When Clare finally showed up, half an hour late, she explained that the traffic coming from the West Side had been terrible, and that Roger was downstairs in an illegal parking spot. "But why isn't this baby dressed and ready to go?" she asked, laughing when she heard Stacy's excuses. "Oh, honestly, don't be such a coward!" she said, and went into the bathroom to wash her hands before she touched the baby.

Stacy stood by helplessly as Clare took over, dressing Olivia in a pink terrycloth Onesies, punctuating her movements with silly, singsongy murmurs of "this little arm in this little sleeve, *this* little arm in *this* little sleeve."

Riding in the wheelchair the hospital insisted she use for transportation to the lobby, Stacy felt self-conscious and foolish, as if everyone who passed her in the hallways knew that she was fully capable of walking out on her own. She kept her head down to avoid their gazes.

Outside in the hospital's circular driveway, Clare arranged herself next to Roger in the front seat of the BMW; Stacy sat in back, watching over the baby in her rear-facing infant safety seat. As they drove through the park, heading back to the West Side, Olivia began to cry. "She's probably hungry," Stacy said, though without much confidence. "Or maybe she's wet. What do *I* know?"

"You'll figure it out," Clare told her, "trust me."

Stacy slipped the tip of her pinky into the baby's mouth and watched as Olivia sucked on it greedily. No longer crying, she stared at Stacy with her unblinking, slate-blue eyes. For her the world hadn't yet come into focus, and everything she saw was in basic black and white. If only it were that simple for *her*, Stacy thought; if only she could see black and white everywhere she looked.

At home, walking past the doorman, Olivia in her arms, she tried her best to look like someone who knew what the hell she was doing.

The front door of their apartment was decorated with a glossy pink bow stapled to a piece of copy paper that said "WELCOME HOME, GIRLS!" in Roger's cramped, sloppy script, and Stacy found herself choked up at the sight of it.

Embarrassed by her own sentimentality, she felt a need to apologize. "Dumb, stupid hormones!" she said, shaking her head.

Instead of going directly to the baby's room, she carried Olivia into the master bedroom, and lowered her onto the vast, king-size bed. As Roger and his sister looked on, she held her breath and eased one marble-smooth leg, then the other, out from the Onesies.

She put Olivia's sweet-smelling foot in her palm, and silently marveled at its perfect, doll-like beauty.

∽

*He remembers, from his childhood, a cartoon he'd seen on television only once, though for years he'd kept hoping to discover it again. Its tone was surprisingly dark and melancholy, as were its colors, the darkest browns and grays and greens. In the cartoon's narrative, a little boy was desperate to find the beloved pocketknife he'd carelessly lost near the creek behind his home. Observing the child's misery, his pet goldfish, large and friendly and eager to help, sprang from its bowl, and suddenly blessed with the power of speech, announced that they would travel together on the ocean to someplace the boy needed to see. They sailed along in a glass-bottomed boat until the fish said, "Right here—look!" Through the floor of the boat the boy could see his pocketknife at the bottom of the ocean. Not only his knife, but dolls and toy soldiers, rings of keys, quarters and dimes—everything that had ever been lost by a child. It was the place where all lost things came to rest, and the boy was supposed to take comfort in the very notion of it. Instead he wept, wanting to rescue the knife he could see so vividly through the water, an ugly dark swirl of colors that was somehow perfectly transparent. But, as the fish patiently explained, once something was sent down there, it had to stay forever.*

*Why not, Roger thinks now, why not just empty himself of everything he wants to lose, every bleak, oppressive thought, and let it all rest where it can't possibly be retrieved, at the bottom of an imaginary ocean.*

## 19

When Stacy and Roger moved to their new apartment on the Upper East Side, Will was barely a month old and Olivia had just turned two. It meant nothing to a two-year-old, of course, but Stacy couldn't resist pointing out to her daughter—in the cab ride to Park Avenue the day of the move—the hospital where Stacy herself and Roger were born, and whose rooftop Olivia would see from the window of her new bedroom. Their apartment on the West Side had been more than comfortable and Stacy would have happily raised her children there, but Roger had other ideas: their new home, in a Park Avenue high-rise, was house-sized at well over three thousand square feet—a three-bedroom condo with an eat-in kitchen, a quartet of marble bathrooms, and generous views of Central Park and the Manhattan skyline from nearly every room. And, too, it had central air-conditioning, and its own washer and dryer, a necessity for Stacy, since she had, by choice, no housekeeper to help her, and, with an infant and a toddler, more laundry to take care of than she could ever have imagined. The apartment was considerably larger than the house she had grown up in, and considerably more luxurious. She hadn't worked with the homeless in the two years since Olivia was born, and Stacy was, from time to time, plagued by feelings of guilt about both her departure from that world and also her good fortune, and she instinctively reached into her wallet in search of a twenty-dollar bill for any homeless person she happened to encounter loitering outside in front of her neighborhood subway station on Lexington Avenue.

Whenever her sister came to visit with the twins, who were now ten years old (and, shockingly, already interested in makeup and fashion), Stacy tried to downplay the views of the Empire State Building from her twenty-seventh floor windows, the custom-made cabinetry in the kitchen, the heated bathroom floors. The first time Lauren saw the apartment, she came without Chuck, and murmured to Stacy, "Whoa, Roger must really be raking in the big bucks from those shopping malls!"

"I guess," Stacy had said with a shrug, because this kind of talk would always make her uncomfortable. And, too, in the five years since her wedding, she'd kept her distance from the financial aspects of their marriage; there was always more than enough in their checking and savings accounts, and that, for her, was pretty much all the information she needed. Though she knew, too, that this willful ignorance might come back to haunt her someday, for the moment, she thought, it was all fine.

Her sister looked at her sharply. "Don't take this the wrong way, Stace, and it's not a criticism, just an observation, but honestly, I don't think you realize how lucky you are."

"No, no, *of course* I do," Stacy said, and could feel herself blushing. In the few months they'd been living here in the new apartment, she had never felt entirely at ease and worried that she never would—worried that, instead, she would continue to feel out of place. Who, after all, really needed four bathrooms? And doormen who would deliver your mail directly to your door. And carry even the skimpiest bag of groceries to your apartment for you, even if you tried to explain that it simply wasn't necessary—tried to explain that the truth was, these services rendered made you feel foolish and spoiled. She just didn't feel entitled to any of it and only wished there were a way of explaining this to Roger that wouldn't make her sound ungrateful.

"*Of course* I realize how fortunate I am," she repeated to her sister. She thought, at that moment, of going back to work for a nonprofit, of getting out there again in the world of the disenfranchised and putting both her heart and soul into the sort of work that, according to Roger, most people wouldn't dream of embracing. (The sort of work, he'd told her when they first met, that he couldn't help but admire her for doing.) As if the baby heard what she was contemplating—if only momentarily—Will began to shriek from his bassinet, and it was that urgent newborn wail that went right through you, yanking you from your deepest thoughts, the deepest sleep. It was an alarm that could not be ignored, and it went off many times, both day and night. There was also Olivia, still a baby herself, even though she could identify all the letters of the alphabet and could type her name on Stacy's laptop. And had recently taken to cheerfully asking, "What's your password?" to strangers in the supermarket.

It was so retro, Stacy knew, but she had willingly allowed her beloved children to transform her into someone whose universe did not extend much beyond the borders of motherhood. If her friends had told her, when she was an undergraduate studying literature and feminist theory, that she would, a decade and a half later, be a stay-at-home mother, she would have said, "Yeah, hysterical. You guys really crack me up!"

But it wasn't funny. Being a mother, she'd discovered, was serious business. You were on call twenty-four/seven and had to protect those kids of yours from myriad dangers—the full bathtub they might tumble into, the open bottle of wild cherry-flavored milk of magnesia they might find all too alluring, the playmate at the park who might just feel a sudden urge to rip out a small fistful of your daughter's hair.

You would do anything to protect those kids of yours; you couldn't, and wouldn't, take your eyes off them even for a moment.

❧

*Olivia approaches Roger poolside now, wanting to play Scrabble Junior while Stacy and Will are fooling around in the shallow end, splashing each other and shrieking happily.*

*Roger doesn't want to play Scrabble Junior, Scrabble Senior, Scrabble Deluxe Edition, doesn't want to do anything at all, but he agrees to play nevertheless, keeping his sunglasses on as Olivia, in her tie-dyed bikini, arranges the Scrabble board on the chaise longue. She already knows how to spell "candy" and "sun," "tiger" and "water," but just wait, she says, until she's in first grade next year and will be able to spell hard words like "arithmetic" and "science" and "apartment."*

*Just wait until next year! his beautiful daughter says excitedly.*

*It occurs to Stacy that maybe a few sessions of couple's counseling might be helpful. She knows that Jefrie and Honey began seeing a therapist when Tyler was three or four months old and Jefrie was suffering from some sort of low-level postpartum depression that made her nearly impossible to live with, according to Honey. Not that Roger is impossible to live with; it's just, Stacy's thinking now as she washes her already perfectly clean hair in the shower, that here in Fort Lauderdale being around him pretty much all day, every day, has sharpened her awareness of what feels like his perpetually bleak moods, his face creased with desolation and worry and something else—maybe it's an uneasiness about the future, a fear that nothing will ever get better, only worse. What's wrong, sweetie? she's heard herself ask him again and again. But he's not much of a talker when he's like this, not when his mood darkens and he can't stop thinking about his sister and his mother and the downward spiral of his business, the tailspin that's so*

*rudely cast their family two blocks east onto what Roger considers the déclassé shores of Third Avenue. Where, honestly, Stacy sees no reason why they can't be happy. But she senses that Roger just can't envision that happiness, that he can only see that their finances have taken a nosedive, can only believe that the shame he feels won't ever go away, but will, in fact, only deepen . . . Maybe Dr. Avalon can recommend someone when they return to New York, a marriage counselor who will get Roger to look Stacy straight in the eye as he unburdens himself of all the crap that, she finally acknowledges, is threatening their happiness, their marriage, their life together.*

*In the shower, she turns off the faucet, uses the rubber blade of the squeegee to clear the water from the glass door. But she hasn't done a very good job of it; there are streaks left behind on the translucent glass and she can't figure out how to make it right. Maybe it's the squeegee blade that needs to be replaced; maybe it's just that she doesn't know what the hell she's doing anymore. It hits her that now and then over the past few months she's been all-too-willfully and stubbornly detached from Roger's worries, which makes her either a selfish idiot or a coward, she tells herself. Or maybe a selfish, cowardly idiot who sometimes refuses to look head-on into the pitch-black darkness of her husband's despair. Just thinking about that darkness is dizzying, and she has to reach for the edge of the bathroom sink to steady herself.*

∽

*On another one of those nights when sleep is impossible, he tortures himself imagining Stacy rummaging around for something or other in the front seat of the Toyota and finding the paper bag with the Glock stuffed inside it.*

"What the hell is THIS doing here?" he hears her say. Stacy lays the gun in the palm of one hand, and grasps the paper bag with the other, as they sit up front in the car waiting, as usual—before they go upstairs to his mother's condo—for their dozing kids seat-belted in the back to awaken.

"Oh, sorry, I—" he begins.

"Sorry? Are you kidding me, you're keeping a gun in the car? Seriously? What's wrong with you? Seriously, what's WRONG with you, huh?"

"Of course I'm not keeping a gun in the car, what would I be doing with a gun?" he says, and knows, with all certainty, that she will believe—as she always has—whatever he tells her. "It's a rented car, babe, the person who had it before us obviously left the gun in here by accident when he turned the car in," he explains, carefully taking first the Glock and then the paper bag from her.

The relief on her face is plainly visible, and she slaps her right hand over her heart as she says, "I KNEW it couldn't have been yours, I mean, that would make no sense at all, right? I mean, come on, what would someone like you be doing with a gun?"

"Don't look at me," he says, smiling now. He slides the Glock into the paper bag and returns it to the glove compartment. "I'll bring it back to Hertz tomorrow morning and let them deal with it, okay?"

"Promise?"

He pictures the gun safely out of sight again, pictures himself leaning across the seat of the Toyota and stroking a long silky strand of Stacy's dark hair.

In the darkness of the bedroom now, his sleeping wife folded beside him, he mouths the words, "I promise."

## 20

Stacy's fortieth birthday had come and gone uneventfully six months ago, and as a gift, she'd treated herself to a writing class at the New School; with all the time she spent with her children, she'd recently begun to feel an urgent need to jump ship once a week and do something slightly more intellectually stimulating than reading *The Runaway Bunny* over and over and over again. (An undeniably beautiful book, she thought, but reading it aloud to Will three and four times a day was just too much.) Or else she'd have to shoot herself, she teased Roger.

She was, by far, the oldest of the dozen people in the class; even her teacher, Professor Sarno—a thirty-two-year-old guy who wore the same pair of worn-out khakis and silly long-sleeved black T-shirt imprinted with the words "Hyperbole is the **BEST!**" to nearly every class—was years younger than she was. He was the author of a single published book of what he called, mysteriously, "speculative fiction," a book that hadn't, he confessed on the very first day of class, gotten much attention in the literary world—the ruefulness of his voice as he spoke of this disappointment instantly calling up Stacy's sympathy. The rest of the class, mostly people in their midtwenties, it seemed, regarded Stacy with a kind of respectful curiosity, especially the girls, who wanted to know what it was like to have been pregnant and given birth, and to be responsible for two young children, all of which seemed unimaginable to them. The class met within walking distance of Union Square from six to eight on Tuesday nights, and Stacy looked forward to it perhaps more than she should have, she realized. She had a bit of a crush on Professor

Sarno, who, though pale and unshaven and dressed in that dopey T-shirt, was a good-looking guy in that heroin-chic way she normally didn't go for. He played in a band in Brooklyn, and had recently invited the class to come to their show in a club in Williamsburg.

Stacy arrived tonight with a Tupperware container of cookies she'd made for the class (not from scratch, she admitted, just the ones you sliced from refrigerated dough and baked for nine minutes at 350 degrees), and tried, as usual, not to monopolize the workshop discussion. Though tonight, as so often happened, it seemed as if it were only Stacy and Professor Sarno lobbing comments back and forth across the beat-up plastic seminar table while the rest of the class sneaked looks at their cell phones—which of course were supposed to be turned off but which sometimes rang jarringly, their owners muttering "Fuck!" and pretending embarrassment as they fumbled to silence them. For a few months now Stacy had been working on what she thought might be a novel; its protagonist was a young homeless woman from a WASPy family, and she had revised the first couple of chapters again and again. In truth she had nearly given up hope of ever getting them right, but Professor Sarno and some of her fellow students strongly encouraged her to keep at it, a few of them going so far as to promise to read her newest revisions even after the course had ended.

It was almost eight o'clock now, and Professor Sarno was reminding them about the show his band would be playing on Friday night. He described their music as off-kilter post-punk, and laughingly warned Stacy—the oldest person in the room—that earplugs were a must. Stacy, who was a big fan of James Taylor, John Lennon's solo albums, and the Lemonheads, knew that Professor Sarno's band would not, in all likelihood, appeal to her, but, even so, she had the urge to hear them play. As the other members of the class made their way out the door, most of them already talking on their cell phones or checking their text messages, she approached

~ 151 ~

Professor Sarno and asked him to repeat the address of the club where his band would be playing.

He was standing at one end of the seminar table, the sole of one sneakered foot raised onto the seat of a rather flimsy plastic chair. He took her by the wrist, gently swiveled her hand around, and wrote the address on her palm in blue ballpoint ink.

"Okay, thanks," Stacy said, and feeling that first flush of embarrassment that she knew would, in the next moment, heat her everywhere, she withdrew her hand. Though why was *she* embarrassed? She had, after all, done nothing but ask a simple question.

"You know, it blows my mind that you've got two kids," Professor Sarno said. His first name was David, and even though he'd told the students on the opening day of class that they should feel free to call him "Dave," surprisingly, no one ever did. (Surprisingly, too, his doctorate was in sociology, which he taught at the New School as well—a fact Stacy had discovered when she Googled him.)

"Really? Why?" Stacy said. Her phone, jammed in the back pocket of her jeans, was vibrating now. "Excuse me, Professor," she said, and saw that there was a text from Roger, asking her to please pick up a sesame bagel for him on her way home. "*2nd choice cinn raisin xox.*"

"I dunno," Professor Sarno said. "Maybe it's that you're way too cool to be anyone's mother."

Stacy laughed. "I'm not so cool," she said. "Actually, I think you're confusing me with someone else."

Leaning toward her, he fingered the tip of one of her long peacock feather earrings, which, these days, she never wore anywhere except to class.

"I'm not confused at all," he said. "And what the fuck do I have to do to get you to call me 'Dave'?"

∽

She tried to convince Roger to come with her to hear Dave's band, but he let her know that he had no interest whatsoever in standing around a noisy, crowded club filled with stoned and drunken kids grooving to set after set of deafening music.

"Okay," Stacy told him, "you made your point." *Jesus*, she said under her breath. A simple "no" would have sufficed, she thought. But later she was grateful to him for staying home and babysitting so she and Jefrie could go to the show together.

Olivia had a meltdown just as Stacy was walking out the door to meet Jefrie, and she had to go back inside the apartment to soothe her, promising her three-year-old that she would be right there when Olivia woke up the next morning. But that wasn't enough for Olivia; what she wanted was for Stacy to stay with her *now,* until she fell asleep. Or else to take Olivia with her to the show. Those were Stacy's choices, Olivia explained, her arms folded against her Strawberry Short-cake pajama top, her pale lashes already darkened with tears as she kicked the heels of her bare feet against the glossy living room floor. Stacy imagined a time when, years from now, Olivia would be laughing her head off, saying, "I wouldn't let you leave the apartment without me? How funny is *that*?"

Roger, who was always reliable in situations like this, whisked Olivia from the floor, and carried her off, tickling her under the ruffles of her pajama top, and gesturing to Stacy that she should bolt.

He really was an uncommonly good father, she told Jefrie later as they had the inside of their forearms stamped in dark ink at the entrance to the club, so that they could come and go as they pleased without having to pay again. Jefrie had been complaining about her partner, Honey, who, she claimed, was never around when you needed her.

"Seriously," Jefrie continued, "I could count on one hand the number of hours she's spent with me and Tyler this week. She's a surgeon, for Christ's sake, not the president of the

United States! I mean, come *on*, why bother to have a family if you're not going to be there at all the right times? I can't tell you how many meals Tyler and I have eaten alone, how shitty it was to go to back-to-school night all alone, or even to take him to the pediatrician by myself when he fell off the kitchen counter and got that huge bump on his head."

"Oh, I'm sorry," Stacy told her, feeling her gratitude to Roger intensifying as Jefrie griped about Honey. "Maybe you need to talk to her about all this."

"Been there, done that," said Jefrie. "We've talked the subject to *death*."

As they made their way through the bar into the back room where the band was already playing, they crossed paths with someone dressed as a fuzzy white bowling pin in a costume that, Stacy estimated, was close to nine feet tall.

"So tell me, are you animal, vegetable, or mineral?" Jefrie asked, laughing, as the bowling pin bowed to them.

Stacy had forgotten to bring earplugs with her, but the music wasn't as loud as she'd been warned. She and Jefrie were all the way in the rear of the crowded, overheated, dimly lit room, and it was hard to see Dave, who played lead guitar and was backed by a drummer and two other guitarists. Leaving Jefrie behind, Stacy managed to get closer to the small stage, and immediately saw that Dave wasn't wearing his "Hyperbole" T-shirt; in fact, he had no shirt at all, and the chest that he'd bared was pretty damn scrawny. But she also noted the nipple ring glinting in the spotlight, and it was a turn-on, though she had no idea why, only that it was.

As she and Jefrie danced side by side now, rockin' to the rhythm of the raucous music whose lyrics she struggled to make out, it came to her that without Roger here, she was free to savor—just for the evening in that dark, sultry room— the sight of a silver ring suspended from Dave's endearingly scrawny chest.

∽

# FOURTH DRAFT

To my dear family and friends—

I don't want to take up too much of your time,
but I'm begging you, please PLEASE believe me:
There. Is. No. Way. Out.

IT'S BEST FOR ALL OF US THIS WAY.

Another busy year had passed; it was late summer now, and Roger was on a business trip in Boston, driving in congested traffic along Mass Ave near the Prudential Center, when Clare called him on his hands-free cell.

"I need to talk to you," she said, and Roger could hear Marshall's voice in the background saying, "Not if he's driving, for God's sake!"

Roger's stomach was already churning, and his hands tightened around the beautiful mahogany steering wheel he'd installed himself in his Porsche.

"What's wrong?" he asked Clare. He had a lunch meeting with a contractor he owed money to, and had taken a Xanax just before he left the hotel a little while ago. It was an old prescription, and he'd forgotten to check the expiration date; for all he knew, the pill he'd swallowed was totally worthless.

"Roger?" Clare said. "I think Marshall's probably right, that I shouldn't have called while you're in the car. Maybe you should just call me later, when you're back at the hotel."

He assumed this was all about his mother, whom they'd moved into assisted-living several months ago, and whose Alzheimer's diagnosis had been no big surprise.

"What's wrong with Mom?" he said.

Clare paused. "It's not her . . . it's *me*."

Roger hated the wireless Bluetooth that amplified his sister's voice so that it filled the car. He heard her say she and Marshall were going to fly up to Boston next week to the Dana-Farber Cancer Institute for a second opinion, and that they'd been lucky enough to score an appointment with an oncologist there who specialized in solid tumors, the type of tumor that was coiled around the base of Clare's spine. Her lower back had been bothering her for months, Roger knew, but not one of the half-dozen doctors she'd seen had been able to determine why.

But now they knew, Clare was saying, her voice oddly clinical, and not at all tremulous; perhaps, Roger thought, she was still in a state of disbelief. As he was.

Reflecting on the words "oncologist" "tumor" and "Cancer Institute," he fell victim to an attack of hiccups. He needed water, he thought, and also to pull the car over somewhere so that he wouldn't jump the curb and mow down some poor pedestrian in downtown Boston, someone out on his lunch hour innocently looking for a decent place to pick up a tuna wrap and fries to go.

He wasn't one of those people who, upon hearing bad news about someone else's life, would nod his head and say, *Whoa, that's a shame, dude,* and go back to eating his dinner. Even if the news was about a friend of a friend of a friend, a person he'd never met, he wouldn't have an easy time letting go of it—he would ask questions, always wanting to know more, and sometimes even pressing too hard for information he wasn't entitled to. Like Stacy, he secretly thought, he was a wellspring of empathy. And of course *this* was his beloved sister, his only sibling, and this news of hers had taken his breath away; the hiccups were coming faster and faster now.

He pulled the Porsche over to a fire hydrant on this busy street, and put the car into "park" but kept the engine running. Nearly overcome with anxiety now, his legs began to tremble and he thought of his breakdown in the middle of his first semester at Michigan. And he remembered how, after his high school girlfriend Lucy Eisenstein had dumped him at the end of that summer, he couldn't get out of bed and would have stayed there twenty-four/seven if not for his mother and sister. Both of whom had worked so hard to pull him from his bed and back into the world, so that he could leave home and go to Michigan and start his freshman year. Clare or his mother would sit with him patiently as he struggled to eat a few mouthfuls of dinner at the kitchen table, and on his worst days, when she just couldn't get him up and out, his mother would bring food on a plastic tray for him so he could dine in bed, even though his father vehemently disapproved and shouted at his mother to stop treating Roger so tenderly. This had continued for a week or so, but then he went off to college right on schedule. But he ended up in Emerald Hills a few months later anyway, and it turned out to be a place where he spent far too many hours at the pool table in the patient lounge, playing eight-ball and one-pocket with a couple of his fellow nutjobs, as he thought of them.

His hiccups had finally subsided, he realized now, and he put his hands over first one knee and then the other to stop his legs from shaking. Maybe he should cancel his lunch meeting—not a smart move—but how would he be able to concentrate on business knowing what he'd just learned about his sister? When was her meeting at Dana-Farber? Could he join them and hear what the doctors there would have to say?

What he heard was the dead silence as Clare and Marshall considered his request, and then his sister saying, "No, no, thanks, but not necessary. It's just going to be Marshall and me . . . Oh, and Stacy's already offered to have Nathaniel stay with you guys while we're away overnight next week. And I bet you can guess how well *that* went over with a sixteen-year-old," Clare said, laughing slightly. "He was totally insulted that we didn't trust him to stay home alone, but of course he's got to stay with you anyway."

Wait, Clare had called Stacy before she called *him*? Roger knew it was petty and maybe even juvenile, but he was offended that he hadn't been Clare's first choice. She and Stacy had become close friends over the years, but, even so, *he* was Clare's brother, not an in-law, and deserved to be at the top of her list, didn't he?

"I understand," he said, but, in truth, he didn't. He looked out the window of his Porsche, and saw a dwarf in khaki shorts and a red T-shirt light up a cigarette as he stepped out of a convertible that hadn't bothered to pull over but merely stopped in the middle of the street. The little guy had a sleeve of tattoos on each arm, and had slammed the door with real force; maybe, Roger thought, he was pissed off about something. As the convertible drove past, he saw that its license plate said "NICEHUH" and that it was a new $90,000 Mercedes SL.

Nice, huh.

His sister had a malignant tumor the size of a grapefruit wrapped around her spine.

He put his head down on the steering wheel and shut his burning eyes.

&#x221E;

He was back from Boston, and the next day it seemed imperative that the whole family go to see his mother. Will, who had officially entered the Terrible Twos though his birthday wasn't for another month, turned around and went straight for the front door almost as soon as they arrived at Renaissance Living Center to visit Beverly. The doors parted automatically, and Will was out on Second Avenue moments later, beguiling the handful of elderly residents who were seated on plastic lawn chairs in front of the building, enjoying their cigarettes.

"I'll get him!" Stacy yelled over her shoulder as she headed for the door. "You take Olivia and go upstairs to your mother, and I'll be there in a couple of minutes."

Holding hands, Roger and Olivia boarded the elevator, which was nearly filled to capacity—with a pair of elderly women and their metal walkers, a single man in a wheelchair, and three caregivers from the West Indies and south Asia dressed in pink uniforms. A thread of saliva hung from the old guy's lower lip, reminding Roger of his father, who'd suffered from Parkinson's for too many years before his death.

Just before the elevator door closed, a man with white hair in a shoulder-length ponytail got on, along with his companion, an attractive woman in her seventies who was wearing too much dark eye shadow. "In your own sick way, I have to say you're perfectly normal," she said loudly to the ponytailed guy.

Roger tightened his grip on Olivia's small warm hand.

They got off on the Alzheimer's floor, and Olivia, who was four now, dropped Roger's hand and ran toward Beverly's room. The walls of the hallway were painted a soothing lavender and adorned here and there with framed artwork that had been done by residents of the floor. They resembled the drawings and paintings Olivia brought home from preschool, Roger noted, and sighed. His mother's work was not among the things that were displayed, for which he found himself grateful.

Halfway down the hallway a door opened, and a woman and her caregiver emerged from the apartment. The caregiver held a cell phone to her ear with her right hand, and put her left arm around the woman's back. "Come, Jewel," she said, "we're going to take a nice long walk up and down and up and down, okay?"

The woman with Alzheimer's had a wide, expressionless face and stooped shoulders. She was wearing a pleated plaid skirt, and like a teenager in the fifties, saddle shoes and bobby socks.

"You're Beverly's son." The caregiver smiled at Roger. "Jewel and Beverly are best friends."

Roger smiled back at her, though he had no idea what she could possibly have meant by "best friends." His mother could hardly hold a thought in her head and rarely engaged in conversation for more than a few minutes at a time. "That's nice to hear," he said lamely. "Thank you."

Starquasia, his mother's caregiver, stood at the door to Beverly's apartment, and ushered him in. "Your mom had a little accident, but she's all cleaned up," she reported, and gestured toward the palm-sized darkened area on the pale gray carpeting. "Just watch where you step."

"Look what Starquasia gave me!" Olivia said, and ran to Roger with a lollipop in her mouth. "My lips are such a pretty green!"

He wanted to tell Starquasia not to give his kids teeth-rotting candy, but he knew that she was wonderful with his mother and it seemed best not to say anything.

Walking farther into the living room, which smelled faintly of pee, he smiled at his mother, who was seated in a reclining leather La-Z-Boy and dressed in black sweatpants and a long-sleeved black shirt even though it was summer. He hugged her, and prepared himself for what he knew would come next.

"Such a lovely young man, do I know you?" his mother said.

Olivia, arranging herself at a snack table now with a set of colorful markers and some blank computer paper, didn't look up; she'd heard it all before and seemed to understand that Beverly had lost her way and could not be led back again.

"That's your son," Starquasia said helpfully. "That's Roger, he comes here all the time, Beverly."

Beverly looked skeptical. "He does? No, I don't think so. Honestly, I'm quite sure I don't know you, young man, but it's a pleasure to meet you." She put out her left hand for Roger to shake. Her nails were painted a cheerful crimson, and her hand, which he held in his own, was soft and a little puffy. He'd been warned by both Beverly's neurologist and geriatrician that Alzheimer's patients often turned angry and mean-spirited, but, if anything, his mother had lost her edge; she'd become the proverbial sweet little old lady, and, in a way, he found it disconcerting.

"It's me, Mom," Roger said, because Starquasia had told him that there were moments now and again when his mother was lucid—what the hell, who knew, she might actually recognize him, if only for an instant. He no longer called her on the phone since the conversation generally went nowhere and for some reason it pained him less to talk with her in person. But it was all so fucking depressing, and there was no getting around it.

"It's my pleasure to meet you," his mother said delightedly. "But tell me why you look so sad."

"Clare is very, very sick," he was surprised to hear himself say. "If I seem sad, that's the reason."

Olivia looked over at him now, and Roger regretted not having kept his big mouth shut. "What's wrong with her?" Olivia said.

His mother's face filled with compassion. "That's terrible," she said. "Is Clare a friend of yours? Whoever she is, please tell her how sorry I am to hear that she's ill."

"Clare's your daughter," Starquasia called from the other side of the room, where she was washing a couple of dishes in the tiny aluminum sink near the door.

"You never told me I had a daughter," Beverly said. "Are you sure?"

"*I'm* sure," said Roger, who was standing awkwardly beside her chair, still holding on to her hand. He contemplated dropping it and backing away, but it seemed cruel, and so he continued to stand there, like a sentry on duty, though one with less than exemplary posture.

"You know," said Beverly, "it occurred to me that I haven't seen my mother and father in ages. Do you have any idea where they are?"

"They're gone, Mom."

"Gone?"

"Dead," Roger whispered. "Since 1951 and 1968, respectively," he mumbled.

His mother seemed even more bewildered than usual. "But that can't be. I saw them in Neiman Marcus in the Bal Harbour shopping center the last time we were down in Florida."

"Daddy?" Olivia said. "Don't IGNORE me. You said Aunt Clare was very sick." She had a thick orange marker in hand, and a slash of purple ink at one corner of her mouth; her formerly white baby teeth were stained a startling chartreuse, thanks to the lollipop Starquasia had given her.

Now Stacy appeared at the door with Will at her hip. She greeted Starquasia, and went to Beverly and kissed her.

"Please come back soon!" Beverly told her. She ran her finger across Will's bare knee. "What a sweet little boy," she said. "Who do you belong to, darling?"

"Hmm, that reminds me," Stacy said. "Knock knock."

"Who's there?" Roger said obligingly.

"Two," Stacy said, holding up a couple of fingers.

"Two who?"

"To *whom*!" said Stacy. "You like that?"

"Love it," Roger said, deadpan.

"Me me me!" Olivia said. "Knock knock."

"Who's there?" Beverly said, and Roger patted her shoulder.

"Water," said Olivia. She looked at Beverly, who was staring into her lap now.

"Water who?" Roger and Stacy said in unison.

"Water you doing in my damn house!" Olivia said, laughing so hard she slipped off the folding chair she was seated on, and landed on the floor.

Beverly was smiling now with what appeared to be the greatest pleasure. "You're such lovely people," she said. "It was so nice to meet you, and I hope you'll all come back soon."

Roger and Stacy gave each other a look; he wished he could turn his mother's pathetic routine into something funny, wished he could see the humor in the way her severely diminished brain insisted on seeing the world, but, instead, he found every visit here unnerving and disheartening . . . And now there was his sister, whose life, he suspected, had been permanently altered by the MRI that revealed the monstrous mass of unruly cells that were trying to kill her. Something poisonous and sinister and, her oncologist said, as large as a grapefruit—why couldn't it have been the size of a lemon or an orange instead? And why the citrus fruit analogy? Why not large as a runty cantaloupe or an enormous tomato? Why malignant and not benign? Why *his* sister and not someone else's? Why had this good, *menschy* human being been dealt pain and suffering and not pleasure and comfort instead?

He worried that the odds were not in Clare's favor and that optimism would not, in the end, prove helpful. But perhaps he—along with the MRI and the radiologist who reviewed it, and the oncologist who reported it—was wrong. Perhaps (and here was where he gave his most recent brand of atheism the heave-ho and mentally fell to his knees and prayed) Clare would live a good long life and be lucky enough to trade knock-knock jokes with her grandchildren someday.

*"Knock knock," Roger tells his wife.*
*"Who's there?"*
*"Dwayne."*
*"Dwayne who?" She looks at him expectantly.*
*"Dwayne the bathtub, I'm dwowning. And twust me, it's no joke," Roger says.*

*He wakes her up to inform her that he's feeling sick. Sick with grief, he tells her tearfully, and she doesn't know what to say. He tells her that the taste of that grief coats the length of his tongue and the roof of his mouth, and that he doesn't think it will ever go away. She understands*

that he is speaking metaphorically, but, even so, he sounds like someone in urgent need of help from a mental health professional, and so Stacy suggests that a call to Dr. Avalon right this minute, in fact, might be a very good idea.

"Let me dial the number for you," she says.

"It's five in the morning," Roger points out. "And anyway, I'm done with the guy. Finished. Finito."

She hands him a honey-colored Kleenex, but he lets it drift from his fingers onto the bedroom carpet. She takes another from the box on the night table and wipes his eyes for him, as gently as she does for their children. She thinks of her recent phone call back in New York to her old colleague Barbara Armstrong, who'd listened with the greatest sympathy as Stacy allowed herself to confide in her. They'd talked about Roger and the remote possibility of a short, soothing stay in Emerald Hills—still in business after all these years, but way too expensive these days. And Stacy knew Roger would never agree to it anyway, no matter how hard she might plead with him. There was an uneasy pause in the conversation, and then she'd heard Barbara use the words "New York State psychiatric facility" and "involuntary admission," phrases which Stacy had routinely employed in the old days when she'd worked with her homeless clients, but which she now found intolerable. She knew, without Barbara reminding her, that with certification from a couple of doctors and an application for admission made by her—as next of kin—and based on a claim that Roger had a mental illness likely to result in harm to himself or to her and her children, she could have him admitted for treatment. Against his will.

Serious harm to himself or to her and Will and Olivia? Of course not, she told Barbara. He's really depressed, but he's hardly what anyone would call a psychopath.

I'm sure he's not, Barbara assured her, but got Stacy to promise to keep a close eye on him. Call me anytime, she said. Text me. E-mail me. Whatever you need.

*I will,* Stacy promised her.

*"I'm pretty sure it won't be the first time Dr. Avalon's been awakened by a patient,"* she says now, picking up the landline next to the bed.

*"NO!"* Roger says, and he means business: his fingers are around her wrist, squeezing it so fiercely, she actually cries out in pain before dropping the phone.

*"You're hurting me!"* she says. *Never, in all the hours and days and years they've been together, has he ever hurt her.* *"Let go!"* she says.

*But he keeps on squeezing until finally, with her free hand, she makes a fist and smacks him in the chest with it, though not hard enough to bruise him.*

*She contemplates saying,* If you won't let me call Dr. Avalon for you, I'm leaving you.

Leaving. You.

And taking Olivia and Will with me.

*But how can you threaten a broken-down man with tears in his eyes? You can't, and though it kills her not to speak up, she keeps her mouth shut and her threats to herself.*

Between his mother and his sister, Stacy thought, Roger had too much on his plate these days, sorrowful burdens that weighed him down so heavily, you could actually see it in his posture—those slumped shoulders of his that she gently reminded him to straighten whenever she happened to notice. There were some business problems as well, she understood, watching as he examined his BlackBerry at the dinner table every night, studying text messages and e-mails so intently, you would think his life depended on what he found there. His answers to her questions about the projects his real estate company was developing were never greatly detailed; rather, he responded in the most noncommittal way possible, then followed up with a shrug, a vague shake of his head, and, occasionally, a roll of his eyes. The truth was, Stacy wasn't as interested as she might have been. It was the business world, a world she'd ignored her whole life and probably would, she thought, continue to ignore. It was, perhaps, a failing of hers and she knew it, but this was who she was, who she had always been.

Now that Olivia was in kindergarten and Will in preschool (*finally* in preschool, she thought, as if it were an accomplishment she'd been aiming for since the day he was born), she had, at long last, a few good solid hours a day to devote to the umpteenth draft of the novel she was still working on for Professor Sarno's class. This was the novel about the homeless, WASPy twenty-something, partly modeled on her former client Kim Sutherland. Stacy had taken one course after another with Professor Sarno (whom she'd finally been able to call "Dave") over the past couple of years, and when he left the New School and moved over to Columbia's School of General Studies, she went with him. She still had a minor crush on him, though she'd admitted it to no one except Jefrie, who thought it was "cute" and assured her that crushes were perfectly healthy.

The students in the class at Columbia were an interesting mix; the current bunch included an elderly Christian Scientist who'd shed his religion and gone to medical school, a former dancer on Broadway, and a pretty—if androgynous-looking— guy originally from Bangladesh. Dave seemed fascinated by them, and Stacy found herself having to work harder to get his attention from her seat at the seminar table. One night after class, seven of them went out to an espresso bar for coffee with Dave. Stacy texted Roger to let him know where she was, and he wrote back immediately: "*Enjoy. XOX.*" She felt bad nonetheless, even though she knew the kids were asleep and that Roger was free to relax in front of the enormous high-def, flat-screen TV in their den, where he loved to watch his favorite cooking shows like *Iron Chef America* and *Hell's Kitchen*. But his worries about Clare and his mother tainted just about everything, Stacy thought, and she felt a burning twinge of remorse, there in the restaurant, seated between Dave and Kumar, the mysterious guy from Bangladesh.

She wasn't even a coffee drinker, and felt like a jerk ordering a Diet Coke in the espresso bar. Dave had smoked a cigarette on the way over, and she could smell it in his short, unkempt hair, and on his ratty maroon sweater with the ripped, misshapen V-neck. His head was turned away from her now as he spoke to the white-haired, retired MD who'd been writing a memoir about his days as a Christian Scientist; Stacy was close enough, if she wanted, to rub the flat of her hand against the stubble that traced Dave's sharp jaw. He seemed a thousand years younger than Roger, and was, she couldn't help but recognize yet again, attractive in that slacker way of his—torn sweater, bristly face, sneakers that had seen better days. The bristly face was marked by dimples and what you would have to acknowledge were outstanding cheekbones. Whenever he happened to smile at her in class, Stacy was reminded of her inexperienced, vulnerable high school self, and what it was like to be set afire by some boy you knew would never be yours.

"I have to go," she told Dave quietly, and as she rose from her seat in the espresso bar, handed him some folded singles for the Diet Coke and her share of the tip. Her classmates, who filled up the four tables for two that they'd pushed together for themselves, turned in her direction to call out their good-byes.

She was pleased that Dave accompanied her to the door, and flattered when he grabbed his jacket and went out with her and then stayed at her side while she waited for a cab to come by. It was October and no longer warm, the streets of Morningside Heights quiet and wet with drizzle. They stood in the middle of Broadway, neither of them saying a word. When Dave flagged down a cab for her several minutes later, she put her hand casually on the sleeve of his jacket and started to thank him. His mouth found its way to hers, resting against it very lightly and only for a few moments, but long enough for her pulse to pick up speed.

It was surprising how guilty she felt. And, too, how gratified, how filled up with pleasure.

~∽~

When she got home, Roger looked so distraught, she almost could have been persuaded that someone had snapped a picture of her and Dave together and posted it on Facebook for all the world to view and pass judgment upon.

"*What?*" she said. "What is it?"

He was at their front door, in what their real estate broker had grandly referred to as "the entrance gallery" (but which Stacy called "the foyer"), waiting for her in sweatpants and an old, old Harvard B-School reunion T-shirt, and that glossy sheen she saw in his eyes must have been tears, she recognized. And was astonished by them.

What she didn't fully understand was the failure of his current and most important development project and how, as a result of that failure, they were going to have to move from this beautiful apartment of theirs. Which, by the way, *was no longer theirs,* he told her.

Or would no longer be theirs in the very near future.

"*What?* What are you *talking* about?" Stacy said. She rested one hand on the small antique desk in the foyer to steady herself.

The new mall, the one they'd been building in Seattle for the past two years? The $100 million deal he'd needed $5 million in cash for? Well, he'd gone to his pool of investors, who'd put in a million and a quarter each, and then to the bank to borrow $5 million more and to secure a construction loan. The lender had approved the loan, but insisted that Roger pledge the other mall, the still-profitable one in Atlanta, as collateral. (Roger had agreed to it, though in retrospect, God knows, he shouldn't have, and God knows, as well, that Roger would continue to beat himself up over this for the rest of his life.) And he'd gone ahead and closed on the project and hired the contractor. But now, nearly two years later, now that the mall in Seattle was almost completed, his anchor tenant—a huge national chain of home-improvement stores that had been having problems of their own—had pulled out of their lease. Learning this, the rest of the tenants pulled out as well. Even worse, because of all the construction overruns, there just wasn't enough cash to finish the project. And now the bank, envisioning this empty mall with not a single tenant in sight—no Victoria's Secret, no Foot Locker or Ann Taylor or Banana Republic—well, they weren't interested in throwing good money after bad, and so they'd foreclosed on the mall.

"We're in trouble," Roger said, as if, after all that, he still needed to underscore his point. "We're in the deepest shit, and I'm so sorry." He looked down at the floor after his apology. "We owe the contractor big bucks. I had a meeting with him last week and he gave me two choices—either put our apartment on the market and pay him off with whatever we get for it, or just give the apartment to him outright in lieu of the money we owe. But then tonight, while you were out, I got another call from him, and he—" Roger took a deep, noisy breath—"he said he wasn't going to wait for us to sell, he just wanted us to turn the apartment over to—"

"Wait!" Stacy said. "Wait wait wait wait WAIT! What kind of contractor is this? Who *is* this person? He tells you to turn over the apartment to him and you agree? That's insane, Roger."

"And here's kind of the worst part," Roger said. His eyes were squeezed shut now. "The guy is someone . . . well, let's just say he's comfortable hanging out with the bad guys in Brighton Beach, if you get my point."

"The Russian mob? Is this your idea of a joke?"

"There's no fooling around when it comes to this guy, Stace, no asking for favors or extra time. He wants what we owe him, and that's that." Roger was staring at the floor again, and Stacy waited for him to raise his head. When he did, he blinked two tears from his eyes. "The lawyers are going to take care of all the paperwork, and then we'll have extinguished our debt to this guy."

"I don't understand how this could have happened," Stacy said slowly. "I just don't get how—"

"STOP LOOKING AT ME AS IF I'VE LOST MY FUCKING MIND!" Roger howled, and his voice sounded hoarse, as if he'd been ranting all night.

It hit Stacy then, that until a moment ago—when he'd shouted at her—she hadn't even been particularly angry, hadn't even thought much about blaming him for this disastrous failure. (But dealing with a mobbed-up contractor—what was he *thinking?*) She and Roger had never yelled at each other like that, or at the children. Neither of them came from families who were ruled by parents wielding bad tempers. Shouting was unacceptable and she had to remind him of that.

"First," Stacy said, "keep your voice down, or I'm going back out that door. And second, you're telling me that we have nothing left, that's implicit, right?"

"I'm telling you," Roger said, "that essentially we no longer own this apartment and will have to move as soon as we can find a reasonably priced rental somewhere. Oh, and you can forget about the kids' private school. We'll have to take them both out. I mean, they might give us emergency financial aid for one kid, but for two, never gonna happen. And I'm telling you right now there's no way we're having one kid in public school and the other in private." He put his face into his hands, and how could her anger not be tempered with sympathy? That was the way it went in the business world—you took risks and sometimes you were rewarded. Greatly rewarded. But sometimes you got screwed. Big time. So no, she wasn't as angry as she might have been. Certainly she was grief-stricken, and certainly more than a little frightened. But they were two smart people, and they would manage.

After all, in whose bible was it written that the only happy families were those who lived on Park or Fifth or Central Park West in enviable apartments worth a hefty seven figures and then some?

Her husband staggered toward her now, and she caught him by the shoulders, telling him, over and over again, in her softest voice, what she had just told herself—that they were two smart people and that they would manage somehow.

It was the sweet soft voice she employed to comfort her children when they were unhappy, and it had never failed to do the trick.

If only she didn't believe in karma, didn't believe that somehow that pulse-quickening kiss from Dave was connected to all of this.

# ~ 23 ~

His appetite wasn't what it used to be; used to be at dinner Roger would routinely finish up two large chicken breasts, several servings of basmati rice, a couple of helpings of a mixed green salad ornamented with red pepper, mushrooms, and olives, and then, an hour or so later, return to the kitchen for an apple or an orange or a handful of extra-dark pretzels. And an hour after that, help himself to a good-sized bowl of caramel-truffle-flavor ice cream, and not the low-fat kind, either. He was a pretty big guy, six three, a hundred and eighty-five pounds, and all his life he'd enjoyed food. He did one hundred sit-ups on his exercise mat every morning, and ran on his NordicTrack for half an hour before breakfast. His stomach was still fairly well-muscled, he thought, and he'd never worried about his weight even as he settled into middle age and watched some of his friends develop what they sheepishly referred to simply as "a belly."

These days, he woke up every morning, exercised—though his heart wasn't really in it—and bypassed breakfast altogether. The thought of putting food into his mouth so early in the day had begun to nauseate him. He had a banana for lunch at his office, and washed it down with several bottles of water. When he came home at night, he wasn't hungry for dinner, though he knew he should have been and that it was a worrisome sign that he wasn't. Stacy, who had worked, over the years of their marriage, to turn herself into a confident—and excellent—cook, couldn't help but take it personally when, night after night, he sat down at the dinner table, took a quick look at what she was offering, and turned away.

Tonight he had more important things to be concerned about than the made-from-scratch tacos Stacy insisted on filling his plate with and the offended look on her face when he couldn't even make the effort to swallow down more than a baby-sized portion while *she* took her time eating every last bite of her dinner.

"What's wrong with you?" she asked him, and reached across the table to lay her hand on top of his. "You really need to start talking to me, baby."

His BlackBerry was next to him on the glass tabletop, as if he were seated in a restaurant; he couldn't keep his eyes off it. He thought of the two young guys in suits he saw smoking out in front of the Citicorp building today in Long Island City. As Roger walked past them, he heard one say to the other, "So, how many $100 million dollar investors you got?" Though he'd wanted to continue past them, he brought himself to a dead stop in order to hear the other guy's disappointed response: "Just two."

*Just two.*

"What's wrong with you?" Stacy asked him again.

*What was wrong with him?* Well, let's see, his business was going down in flames, his mother had been assigned to the Alzheimer's floor in the assisted-living residence whose monthly charges he could no longer afford to kick in his share of, his sister was seriously ill with cancer, his precious children were about to be yanked out of the private school where they'd been treated to the best possible kindergarten and pre-K education money could buy, and, lastly, they were about to lose their spacious home and panoramic views on one of the choicest streets in this choicest of cities.

He apologized now for not being himself, but maybe this was simply his *new* self; the one who had little interest in food or sex, or anything other than keeping his family and his business afloat. And, too, just getting by from one day to the next without sustaining any more losses didn't seem like much to ask for.

"No apologies," Stacy said. "You know we're going to be fine," she added, but she couldn't possibly have meant it, could she?

⌒

She and her sister haven't spoken since the night before she left for Florida, she realizes, and decides to give Lauren a call while Roger is grilling turkey burgers and ears of corn outside on the terrace overlooking the Intracoastal Waterway. In the master bedroom, Olivia and Will are lounging around, watching Dumbo on the portable DVD player.

Tomorrow afternoon they're all flying back to New York, and no one's complaining. Fortunately both of her kids seem happy at their new schools; why wouldn't they want to get back?

"Hey, just thought I'd check in," she tells Lauren's voice mail, and seats herself at the foot of the bed with the kids, who are flat on their stomachs, chins sunk into their raised palms, as they watch their DVD.

Stacy is surprised to learn that Dumbo's real name is "Jumbo Jr." and that "Dumbo" is, in fact, just a mean-spirited nickname.

Then she gets a call from her grandmother, whom she's been speaking to every other day since they've been here.

"I need you to hold on just a sec," Juliette says. "I have to put my coffee cup down someplace safe." She is ninety-two years old and still of impressively sound mind and body—except for her eyes, which are suffering from the earliest stages of macular degeneration. She's still in her tiny apartment in Brooklyn, in a neighborhood that's still none too cool and not especially safe, though certainly more so than a decade ago.

Juliette's just finished reading fifty pages of This Side of Paradise, she reports to Stacy. In one of her few concessions to old age, she's enjoying Fitzgerald on her e-reader—a gift from Stacy and Roger—where she can adjust the light and the size of the print to suit her. (The other concession is Mary-Magdalene, the caregiver who looks in on her once a day and prepares dinner for her every night.)

"Did you know that the poet Rupert Brooke died of sepsis caused by nothing more than a mosquito bite? The poor thing was only twenty-eight years old when that mosquito got him!" Juliette says, sounding outraged.

"Wait, I thought you were reading This Side of Paradise," Stacy says.

"Well, where do you think the title comes from? It's from a Rupert Brooke poem," her grandmother tells her. And Stacy thinks how lucky she herself will be if, at ninety-something, she'll be interested in having a conversation about poor, tragic Rupert Brooke.

She hears the call-waiting beeping now, and sees that it's her sister.

"Hang on, Gram."

"Hey, gimme your flight info," Lauren says.

"I'll be right back," Stacy says, and clicks back to Juliette, promising to call her later.

"I don't think you will," her grandmother says. "But I'm busy here with my F. Scott Fitzgerald, and in a little while what's her name, Mary-Magdalene, will be here to make me my pasta. So I'll see you soon, babydoll, when you get back from your trip."

"See you soon, Gram."

"Got anyone to pick you guys up at the airport?" Lauren asks when Stacy switches back to her. "Because I can drive in from Connecticut if you need me to, it's not like it's a weekday and I need to be at work or anything."

Stacy is both surprised and pleased by her sister's offer, but says, "Oh, we'll just catch a cab, no problem." She's already imagining, with some excitement, the taxi ride back from Kennedy—she and the kids packed into the rear of the cab, Roger up front with the driver—the familiar, uninspiring landscape of the parkways, the Van Wyck and the Grand Central, both of them probably clogged with cars as usual. And she realizes now just how much she's been longing to get home.

Pretty much since the moment they got here, if you really want to know the truth.

## 24

Roger was sleep-deprived, but this time around, there was no baby to blame, no hungry infant shrieking in the middle of the night and forcing him or Stacy to haul themselves out of bed at two or three or four A.M. for a diaper change and a soothing bottle of Enfamil. This time around, he just couldn't sleep through a single night without getting up and out of bed at least once, and sometimes twice, for lengthy periods. He usually went to bed with Stacy at midnight or so, and envied the way she fell asleep, within a few minutes, it seemed, her head resting against her bent arm, her knees tucked together, her breathing even and nearly silent. He arranged himself around her, hoping the warmth and weight of her body, that perfect calm and stillness she gave off, like a delicate scent, would somehow lull him to sleep.

No dice.

For weeks now, it had been the same thing every fucking night; it would take him a miserable hour or so to fall asleep, his mind racing from worry to worry, his stomach all worked up as he thought of his business debts, the dwindling money in his checking and savings accounts, all his investments in the stock market he'd been forced to sell at a loss. He'd awaken a couple of hours later, the back of his neck moist with sweat even though it was already December and they never slept with the heat on.

He would go into the den and onto the Internet, send e-mails to his accountant asking questions he already knew the answers to. And then he would torture himself by visiting the websites of the top-ranked cancer hospitals throughout the country to see if there was something better out there for his sister than what she was already getting.

There wasn't.

He found himself wishing he drank, or did the kind of drugs that made you high, high enough to lift him from the pitch-dark place he currently inhabited and could not—no matter how strenuously he tried—figure out a way to abandon.

Some nights he collapsed on the rust-colored leather couch in the den watching bad news on MSNBC, and once he fell asleep at his desk, his head on the keyboard of his open laptop, foul-smelling saliva trickling from the corner of his mouth into the crook of his bare arm. That time, Stacy discovered him there at six A.M. and led him back to bed, whispering gently into his ear all the ways in which she loved him.

Often it seemed she knew just the right thing to say, and it was good to be able to count on that. And also on the Xanax that he now took multiples of multiple times a day, never mind what Dr. Avalon would have thought.

Lying to his shrink was a new low, no doubt about it.

## 25

Happily, through a friend of Jefrie's, they had been able to find a two-bedroom rental on the Upper East Side that they could actually afford. They would be relocating only a couple of blocks east of the Park Avenue apartment they were being forced to leave behind, and yet, in certain painful ways, it would feel as if they were worlds away. In the meantime, in the few weeks remaining before the first of the month when they were scheduled to move, Stacy would have to endure numerous visits from the Varushkins—the wife and grown daughter of the contractor who would be taking over their condo. The first time they arrived—both of them in mink on a mild December day—Oksana, the chunky, sixty-something wife, swept through the front door of Stacy's apartment with a very small dog tucked under the sleeve of her coat. It was, Stacy learned, a teacup Yorkshire terrier, and it was wearing a sparkly silver bowtie around its undersized neck. Oksana introduced herself and Albina, the thirtyish, bejeweled and heavily made-up daughter whose face reflected her own. She lowered the dog, who was named Totoshka, onto the parquet floor in the foyer, where he immediately peed.

Vague apologies were offered, and while Stacy ran off to the kitchen to get some paper towels and the odor-and-stain remover she used on the floor on the very rare occasions when her cats might have strayed from the litter box, the Varushkins helped themselves to a tour of the apartment. Stacy caught up with them in the master bedroom, after she'd cleaned up Totoshka's mess. The two women were poking around inside her walk-in closet, and Totoshka was curled up on her bed, relaxing against a silk-covered decorative pillow that Roger's mother had once given her.

"I think I saw a dust bunny or two in there," Oksana noted as she stepped out of the closet. "You really should tell your housekeeper it could use a good cleaning before we move in."

"We don't *have* a housekeeper," Stacy said, and carefully removed Totoshka from her bed. Her two cats, she knew, were cowering in terror behind the shower curtain in the kids' bathroom.

Oksana frowned. "I don't get it," she said. "I mean, who does your cleaning for you?" Although she was closer to seventy than she was to sixty (which Stacy had discovered on the Internet with a couple of clicks of her mouse) and boasted a pair of hefty legs, she was dressed like her daughter, in a foolishly short black skirt, and a dangerously low-cut scarlet satin blouse that displayed more of her breasts than anyone might have wanted to see. Both Varushkins wobbled uncertainly in what Stacy and her friends would have referred to in college as "fuck-me pumps," the sort which she herself had abandoned at about the time she became a mother.

"I don't understand what you mean when you say you don't have a housekeeper," Oksana insisted, and she and her daughter stared at Stacy, both of them looking baffled.

The thought of this woman and her family setting up shop here and taking over *her* home—and Roger's and their children's—made Stacy want to weep. But would it have been any more palatable if Oksana were a different sort of person, someone smarter and better dressed and just a little more gracious? Well, probably not. Still Stacy would have gotten at least *some* satisfaction out of saying, *Honestly? Just the thought of you moving in here makes me want to kill myself.*

"You look upset, everything okay? You all right?" said Albina, who, like her mother, had necklace upon necklace draped around her—Stacy counted a half-dozen long gold chains adorned with good-sized diamonds, some reaching almost to her waist, and also a couple of strands of pearls, and she remembered the armfuls of silver bracelets she herself had worn long ago. But thin silver bracelets were one thing, she thought, thick gold chains another.

She shrugged off Albina's question, and ushered the Varushkins into the master bathroom.

"You know, I wanted to ask you," Oksana said, "how come it's almost Christmas but there's no tree in the living room?"

"Yeah, how come?" Albina said. "And is this marble? Because we only like granite. And why didn't you put in a Jacuzzi?"

"We're Jewish," Stacy murmured. She looked around for Totoshka, who was nowhere in sight. Maybe, she thought, he was contemplating leaving the Varushkins behind and getting home to Brighton Beach on his own.

"Jews don't have Jacuzzis?" Oksana said.

"Jews don't have *Christmas trees*," Stacy said.

"Says who? That's ridiculous—everyone has a Christmas tree."

"I don't think so, Mom," said Albina. "There are a hell of a lot of Muslims in this country now." She flipped the light switch on and off several times. "That's kind of an ugly light fixture you've got up there, no offense."

"I agree," Oksana said. "Thank God Daddy's a contractor and can whip this place into shape for us."

What Stacy imagined was a whip-wielding guy in work boots and carpenter's overalls ferociously ripping out all the carefully chosen tiles and faucets and showerheads and his and hers double sinks that she and Roger had taken some pleasure in during the three years they'd lived here. (Not that she couldn't have lived without all those expensive things—it was just stuff, after all, though stuff she liked to think reflected her good taste.) Three years that had whizzed by as Will learned to walk, both kids outgrew their diapers, made friends beyond the walls of the apartment, and learned to read.

She'd never, not once that she could remember, allowed anger to get the best of her, and so she pretended now that Roger was entirely innocent, that he could not, in any way at all, be held responsible for their downward tumble.

There was good luck in this life, and there was bad, and no family—no matter how smart and deserving they might have been—ever got through life without bumping up against the darkness that was out there. It would be wrong, wouldn't it, to regard her family as special, as if they deserved better than any other in this world. This was what she tried to accept, and she thought she was doing a pretty good job of it.

She heard Oksana say that she wanted to take another look at the kitchen, and as the three of them walked out into the hallway, Totoshka strutted toward them, one of Stacy's bright pink disposable razors clenched between his lips. He dropped it at Oksana's feet and wagged his tail.

"He just loves to go through people's things," Oksana said. "Hope you don't mind." She swept him off the floor and brought him along with them into the kitchen, where she and Albina nodded approvingly at the Sub-Zero refrigerator and all the other stainless steel appliances Stacy had burnished with a special spray cleaner just before the Varushkins arrived, wiping off the kids' fingerprints wherever she found them. As if she'd wanted to impress Oksana, wanted to say, *Look at the beautiful things in this beautiful home I'm handing over, against my will, to you and your possibly mobbed-up husband.*

And then there were the washer and dryer in the small utility room off the kitchen—more stainless steel that gleamed impressively. Oksana opened their doors and slammed them shut carelessly.

*Take it easy!* Stacy wanted to say, but what did it matter, she realized a moment later; what did *she* care how Oksana handled her things? Let her slam the doors as hard as she wanted. Who cared if they broke off their hinges, or if the $2,000 dishwasher (which Stacy would have loved to take with her but which was too big for the new apartment and would have to stay put) overflowed because Oksana added too much Cascade, or the edge of the granite counter chipped after she dropped a dinner plate on it? Who cared *what* Oksana did?

They trooped into the living room now, where the roller-coaster Marshall and Clare had given Will for his third birthday stood in all its green-and-yellow plastic glory, a big monster of a thing that seemed to swallow up a good portion of the room and would not be moving along with them to Third Avenue—no matter how hard Will and Olivia begged—when they decamped to the new apartment.

"Seriously?" Albina said. "A roller coaster?"

The kids were on separate playdates this afternoon with pals in the building, but Stacy could still hear their delighted squeals as they rode tandem down the single slope of the roller coaster, Will seated between Olivia's legs in the car, her arms around him protectively, the two of them just thrilled to death.

*He watches his beautiful, tired children struggling, at the end of the afternoon, with their slightly overcooked turkey burgers around his mother's oval dining table, and thinks, Don't you want to see them grow up? Don't you want to see how lovely Olivia will turn out to be when she hits fourteen or fifteen (her eyes that arresting color close to his own, her hair light as his in childhood), and, someday, what profession she will choose for herself? Her IQ has tested at 148—doesn't Roger want to see her make something of herself? And what about Will, who, at three and a half, already knows how to read? Didn't his pre-K teacher at his new school already tell Stacy that Will is*

*exceptionally bright? Not to mention one of the most pop-
ular (how funny is it that a three-and-a-half-year-old could
be described as popular?) kids in his class, sought after by
everyone, even the girls, for playdates after school. Though
maybe a little overly exuberant at times, he's a charmer,
and always has been, pretty much since the day he turned
five months old and laughed joyously for the very first
time, his face reflecting what Roger and Stacy immediately
recognized as the baby version of joie de vivre.*

*Will's given up on his turkey burger now and is crunch-
ing a little too quickly on the handful of potato chips he
scooped out of a glazed orange serving dish shaped exactly
like a catcher's mitt.*

*Roger puts his hand on Will's wrist and says, "Slow
down, boy, slow down, okay?" because he's worried that
his son might choke.*

*He's a born worrier, absolutely.*

Even before they'd settled as comfortably as they could into their new apartment, Roger and Stacy found themselves in Memorial Sloan Kettering, sitting in a small waiting room, biding their time before they donated blood. Clare, whose tumor had returned, would be undergoing what had been predicted to be a marathon surgery next week, and she would likely be in need of several transfusions during the operation. Though Roger's B negative blood was not a match and he would be donating to a stranger, Stacy's was O negative, the universal donor, and her blood would, they hoped, go straight to Clare.

The only other people in the waiting room with them on this Monday afternoon just hours before New Year's Eve, were a trio of nuns in traditional black-and-white habit. Instead of counting their rosaries, two of the nuns were texting or e-mailing on their BlackBerries, and the third was plugged into her iPod, listening to God knows what—maybe it was Beethoven's "Pathétique," Roger speculated, but then again, maybe it was Chuck Berry singing "Johnny B. Goode." He hated being here, hated thinking of his sister in such terrible jeopardy, but had to smile at the thought of a nun, especially one dressed in her wimple and scapular, silver cross hanging from a black cord around her neck, grooving to Chuck Berry, pretty much the inventor of rock 'n' roll. He leaned over in his seat and whispered into Stacy's ear, and both of them stared at the nun for a moment, hoping she would give something away, just a hint of what she was listening to. But her eyes were closed now, and classical music was a good bet,

Roger decided. Or better yet, some otherworldly thirteenth-century Gregorian chant about the End of Days.

He and Stacy had already filled out a lengthy questionnaire about their medical history, and now he was being summoned by an RN into a small private office, where she took his temperature by sticking a thermometer into his ear, and told him to relax.

"Ever given blood before?" she asked him. Though a plastic badge on her uniform indicated her name was M. Crookendale, she was a small, dark-skinned woman with a whiff of an accent.

Roger could hear a child's voice whining out in the waiting room. "I wanna see the 3-D version, NOT the regular one!" the kid insisted.

"My sister is very sick," Roger murmured.

"Oh, so sorry," the nurse said. "Have you been tattooed in the past twelve months?"

"What?"

"If you have, you won't be able to give blood today."

He thought of the tiny heart, just an outline, actually, that Stacy had tattooed on her wrist. (She and Jefrie and another friend had gotten matching ones together when they were in college, but years later Jefrie had paid to have it removed with a laser because her partner, Honey, found it trailer-trashy.) . . . Roger thought of how disappointed in him Stacy had to be, though she would never have said so. When the moving van came for their things last week, and Thomas, his favorite doorman, had asked if they were leaving the city, Roger had hung his head, embarrassed to admit that their new home was on Third Avenue—where the sullen-faced doormen wore ill-fitting uniforms and sauntered leisurely from their station to the heavy glass door that led to the inner lobby of the forty-two-story high-rise. The apartments there, with their narrow galley kitchens and plastic-coated cabinets and linoleum counters, and tiny bathrooms with shower floors made of textured concrete, were nothing to write home about. But Stacy kept reminding him how lucky they were to be able to stay in the city, how lucky they were that Jefrie's friend had gotten them in there, and Roger wasn't going to argue with her. Thomas, who wore white gloves and a well-pressed uniform that hung on him perfectly and was ever the professional, always addressing Roger as "Sir," and never failing to open the door for him, shook his hand gravely as he and Stacy and the children had made their way through the elegant marble lobby—with its coffered ceiling graced by a flock of winged putti—and out the door for the last time. Roger had resisted the urge to turn and take one last lingering look over his shoulder at what they were leaving behind.

"In the past twelve months, have you had sexual contact with, or lived with, anyone who has had active viral hepatitis?" the nurse asked.

Roger shook his head.

The nurse continued to read from a sheet of paper in her lap. "Have you ever had a positive test for the AIDS virus? Have you ever used illegal intravenous drugs, *even once*?"

No. And no.

"If you are a woman, have you, since 1977, given or received money for sex, *even once*? Or, if you are a man, have you, since 1977, paid to have sex with another man, *even once*?" the nurse asked matter-of-factly.

Roger had to laugh. "I just want to make it clear that I'm not now, nor have I ever been, a woman."

"Oh, no problem, I didn't mean to suggest that you were. It's just that I'm required to read everything on this questionnaire to you," the nurse explained.

Stacy had apparently been led into a small office next door, and Roger could hear her laughing now.

"Best of luck to your sister," the nurse said. She asked what kind of cancer Clare had. When Roger told her, her face turned grim, but she said nothing.

In a few minutes, when they were finished, he and Stacy met in the hallway between the two offices, and immediately

Stacy said, "Hey, did I ever tell you that I received money for sex, just this one time, back in the late seventies, when I was in middle school?"

"Bad girl," Roger said. He smiled at her. "I hope you at least put the money to good use."

"Damn straight I did!"

It was chilly in the large room where the two of them gave blood, and Roger accepted the cotton blanket that was offered him as he arranged himself in the fake-leather recliner where he would be spending the next half hour. He looked away when the needle, which was more painful than he'd expected, was slipped into his vein. Stacy was in a recliner on the other side of the room, and they waved to each other. They had lost their home—correction, *he* had lost their home—but, inexplicably, Stacy didn't seem to hold it against him, or, if she had, she'd soon forgiven him. Last week when they were unpacking in the new apartment, he overheard her voice rising, with what sounded like genuine enthusiasm, as she told Olivia and Will how lucky they were to be sharing a room with bunk beds. *Bunk beds! How cool is that!* he'd heard her saying. Never mind that in the old apartment the children had each had a room of their own, a room twice as large as the new one they were sharing. They were babies, three and five years old; what, after all, did they know or care about the dimensions of a room? Stacy asked him. But *he* cared, he whose responsibility it was to provide the best of everything for his family.

*Stop it!* Stacy had said to him. *We have a roof over our heads and it's a pretty good one. Get over it!*

But he couldn't get over it—not what he'd done to his family, not what he'd allowed to be taken from them. Waking up in the new apartment for the first time, he couldn't get his bearings, couldn't endure the view directly into the stranger's apartment that faced his bedroom window. He wanted to kick himself for having taken for granted the beautiful glimpse of the Empire State Building from his former bedroom window, the views of the glittering East River from his dining room.

His family, or at least Stacy, had grown well accustomed to those views, and to the life that accompanied them, a life that offered the luxury of always having more than enough money. Substantially more than enough. But now, because of his failures, his shortsightedness, his inability to predict the future with any degree of wisdom or accuracy, there was the worry of never having enough.

Never mind that Stacy had so quickly forgiven him; he hadn't been able to forgive himself and could not imagine that he ever would.

⁂

Every visitor they passed—on the escalators, in the lobby, waiting for the elevators, walking through the hallways on Clare's floor—every last one of them was sick with worry over whatever patient he or she had come here to see, Roger was sure of it. The nurses and doctors went about their business nevertheless, chatting at the nurses' station as if nothing were wrong, as if every patient in this hospital weren't engaged, as Clare was, in the fight of his or her life.

As Roger and Stacy prepared to go into Clare's room now, a young guy dressed in blue scrubs was standing in the hallway talking to a woman whose scrubs were a deep purple. "So you know I'm a vegan, right?" he said.

"Wait, you don't even eat tuna fish?" the woman said.

"I don't eat anything that has a mother," the guy explained, "and that includes tuna."

"Excuse me," Roger said, and, with Stacy, made his way between them into his sister's room. Last year, Clare had lost her hair to several rounds of chemo that started a month or so after her diagnosis; following her most recent round toward the end of the summer, she'd been sporting a microshort haircut and large gold hoop earrings. And today was in her own pajamas, rather than the hospital gown she hated. She was without a roommate (though this was subject to change at any moment), and one wall of the room had a small corkboard embellished with get-well cards and photographs of Marshall and Nathaniel that were attached with pushpins.

Nathaniel, who was eighteen now, a senior in high school, was sitting in an armchair at Clare's bedside.

"Hey, how's it going?" he said, and jumped up to offer Stacy his seat. Like Roger, he was an afficionado of cooking shows on TV; the one playing now on the television set next to Clare's bed was, Roger recognized, *Good Eats*. He felt a pang of sympathy for the kid—all the high-priced tutors Clare and Marshall had hired for him apparently hadn't done Nathaniel much good; his SAT scores had caused them no small degree of anguish, he knew. Nathaniel had recently dyed his spiked black hair white-blond, in homage to Guy Fieri from the Food Channel, whose show, *Guy's Big Bite*, was one of his favorites.

Roger kissed the top of his sister's head. She was fifty-four years old, and every morning when he awoke, he prayed that she would hit fifty-five. And that twenty years from now, Clare and Marshall and he and Stacy would all be sitting around over dinner and complaining good-naturedly about how impossibly old they all were.

"I'm sorry we came empty-handed today," Stacy apologized, taking Nathaniel's seat. Often when they'd visited Clare on the numerous occasions she'd been hospitalized over the past year, they brought with them expensive chocolates from a boutique in Grand Central, beautifully scented hand lotion, or paperbacks of novels and stories Stacy particularly loved.

"Empty-handed? Are you kidding? You brought me blood!" Clare said.

"Or at least Stacy did," Roger said. He didn't much care about the unknown patient who would be receiving his own B positive blood, but of course he would never say so out loud.

Stacy drew her chair closer to her sister-in-law. "You're looking good," she said cheerfully. "And after you get my blood, you'll be looking even better," she teased. "Taller, considerably more beautiful, and, oh yeah, a lot more glamorous!"

"Got anything to eat around here?" Roger went rummaging through the small cubby where Marshall stored all the treats that friends had brought for Clare. Despite the cookies and orange juice he and Stacy had been encouraged to sample in the snack room to which they were escorted after giving blood, Roger felt a little weak, a little drained, he announced.

"No pun intended," Stacy said.

"What?"

"Yeah, maybe I'll feel like a vampire when they transfuse me," Clare said. She smiled at Stacy, and at Nathaniel, who found a bag of gourmet white cheddar popcorn chips for Roger among her stash. "Tell them about your plans, honey," she said to Nathaniel.

"Can't *you* tell them?" he said, and fooled with the snapshots on the corkboard, straightening and flattening their edges as Clare talked about his application to the Culinary Institute of America, where he hoped to get a bachelor's degree in baking and pastry arts. To fulfill their application requirement of a half year of hands-on food prep, he'd been working after school in the kitchen of the Sugar Sweet Sunshine Bakery on the Lower East Side. During the seventeen months since Clare's diagnosis, Roger knew, Nathaniel had prepared dinner for the family nearly every night; after each round of chemo, Clare told them, he'd brought her homemade miso soup with tofu and deep-fried bean curd on a tray, with Jell-O in fluted parfait glasses for dessert. He'd been sweetly solicitous of her, soothing her with the news that miso was a favorite of samurai warriors because it was so rich in protein, vitamins, and minerals, stuff Nathaniel knew to be just what Clare needed for her recovery.

"Samurai worriers," Roger said absently. "Who knew they had a thing for miso soup?"

He didn't understand why Stacy and Clare were laughing at him now, the two of them screaming with laughter, their heads thrown back, tears leaking from their eyes in his sister's hospital room as they shrieked "samurai worriers!" He didn't like being laughed at, but what a pleasure it was just to see the two of them enjoying themselves like that, in Sloan Kettering of all places, a place you'd never, ever want to find yourself.

∽

*As she's cleaning up the mess in the kitchen after Roger's little barbecue on the terrace—she should have been smart enough to stock up on paper plates, Stacy realizes, annoyed at herself—her sister calls back.*

*"I've been thinking about it, and look, just let me pick you up at the airport tomorrow," Lauren says. "Just let me do this for you, all right? The plane gets in around five? After the twins' gymnastics practice, the three of us will drive to Kennedy in the SUV, pick you up and bring you into the city, and we can all go out for an early dinner. Nothing fancy, maybe that coffee shop sort of place in your neighborhood, okay?"*

*Bemused by Lauren's persistence, but touched, too, Stacy realizes they haven't seen each other in a couple of months; hey, why turn down the opportunity to spend some time with her sister? And her nieces, fourteen years old and probably none too keen on being in the company of relatives . . . Lauren doesn't know much of anything about their financial crisis, though she must have assumed something was up when Stacy told her she and Roger were moving to a smaller apartment, one that was several blocks east of Park. She has never offered Lauren any details; their relationship just isn't the sort where either of them shares with the other the particulars of their bad news. (Only Jefrie knows; when Stacy told her, the night after they went to hear Dave/Professor Sarno's band, Jefrie said, "Wait, Roger put up the Atlanta mall as collateral? But why would he do something so risky and, well, so just plain stupid?" Then she'd apologized to Stacy, who had no answer to her question. Or no intelligent answer anyway.)*

*She remembers something her grandmother is fond of saying:* What was, was, what is, is.

*And what was the point, Stacy asked Roger, of torturing himself with the heavy weight of blame and guilt that he insisted on shouldering and which served no purpose except to grind him down, little by little, day after day.*

*"Well, if you're absolutely, 1,000 percent sure it's not too much trouble," she says now to Lauren, and shakes some Ajax vigorously into her mother-in-law's scratched and stained sink.*

*"See ya tomorrow," her sister says.*

~ **27** ~

In the laundry room of her new building, Stacy soon discovered, the housekeepers who worked for her neighbors were from all over the world—Russia, Poland, the Philippines, Korea, but mostly the Caribbean. They had plenty to say, most of it uncomplimentary, about their employers. As she transferred armloads of wet clothing from the washing machine to the dryer in this big brightly lit room that opened onto a brick patio and smelled mostly of the too-sweet scent of a variety of fabric softeners, she heard a litany of complaints: about dogs who did their business on Wee-Wee pads in kitchens, foyers, and hallways; spoiled children who, disgracefully, threw tantrums in the neighborhood branch of the New York Public Library; and employers with crumbling marriages who used the F word right there in front of their children.

Stacy listened now, over the continuous whirring of spinning washers and dryers, as one of the housekeepers, who was named Louise, stood with her hand on her hip and announced that the woman she worked for had been arrested for trying to run someone down in the building's underground parking garage.

"Whoa!" a woman named Josie said, pulling a long stream of plaid boxer shorts from a washing machine. "What the fuck wrong with her?"

"She got a whacked-out problem, that girl!" someone else added. She was a middle-aged housekeeper in jeans, and a pink-and-white T-shirt that said "100% KOSHER— ALYSSA'S BAT MITZVAH SEPT 8, 2007."

"Well I hope she end up in Rikers where she belong!"

"Nah, the husband posted bail and she's back home. And here's her brassieres, right here," Louise said. She pointed to the three leopard-print bras she'd draped over the crook of her arm.

It was hard for Stacy to ignore the fact that she herself was the only woman of the dozen or so in the room who wasn't a housekeeper; she observed, as well, that there was merely one male here among them, and, inexplicably, he happened to be wearing a pleated black knee-length skirt that showed off his thick, hairy legs as he bent over into one of the large plastic recycling bins neatly lined up opposite the door. He was fishing for treasure, apparently, and walked off with a pile of magazines, his tennis sneakers squeaking against the shiny linoleum floor. Watching him leave, Stacy tried, and failed, to imagine who he might have been and what possessed him to dress up in a skirt merely to scavenge some recycling bins for his neighbors' abandoned magazines. She listened to the housekeepers as they continued their eager, spirited talk about the woman who'd turned violent behind the wheel of her car—if she didn't belong in the slammer, then certainly she belonged in the loony bin, they decided. Stacy stood among them, ignored, and felt a flicker of something resembling loneliness at one o'clock on a weekday afternoon as her load of towels and child-size socks and pj's spun noisily. At her feet, littering the floor, were needles from discarded Christmas trees, the trees themselves shoved against the wall near the entrance. On a long plastic table where tenants in the building customarily displayed, as if in a thrift shop, things they no longer wanted, there were Christmas ornaments, best-selling paperbacks with shiny gold or silver covers, a computer monitor, its screen cloudy with dust, an array of dolls with uncombed hair and dingy-looking clothing. And one Dora the Explorer doll positioned slightly apart from the rest, a pristine Dance & Sparkle Ballerina Dora, her plastic hand grasping a violet-colored plastic barre, her feet in pink toe shoes. After a moment's hesitation—because despite her *gently worn* wedding dress, she'd never given her children secondhand anything—Stacy scooped up Dora and her barre, and slipped out of the laundry room. Feeling as if she'd gotten away with something illicit.

She would never tell Roger that Olivia's new doll was a gift from the laundry room; despite their failing finances, he would, she knew, be mortified by what she'd done.

∽

The public school where Olivia was now a student was only four blocks from their new home. This was one of those schools for the "gifted and talented"; it had a low acceptance rate, and Stacy knew the principal's long friendship with Clare and her willingness to pull a string or two on Olivia's behalf was another stroke of good luck, something to be grateful for if you were keeping score of these things, which Stacy was. As she stood and waited in the cold for Olivia this afternoon, she couldn't help but take note, as she had every day since Olivia had enrolled here last week, that the mostly middle-class students who were streaming forth from the front doors were sloppily dressed, the laces of their sneakers untied, their backpacks food-stained, their hair not quite as clean as one might have hoped. And then there were the mothers, some of them sneaking cigarettes while they waited for their kids, the mothers looking—in their baggy sweat suits—as if they were part of the bridge-and-tunnel crowd instead of from right here in the city. But one of them, Stacy knew, was the wife of a former star who'd played for the Knicks years ago; another was a frizzy-haired philosophy professor at Columbia. An interesting mix of families, and a far cry from the crew who waited outside the Griffin School, just a few blocks west of where Stacy stood now. This was the school Olivia had transferred from, a school whose tuition was a cool $32,000 per year. In truth, Stacy had never felt the least bit comfortable among the crowd of chicly attired mothers and high-priced housekeepers who assembled at the front of the school every afternoon at dismissal time; she'd developed not a single friendship among the mothers of Olivia's classmates—classmates who came to school dressed in miniature Burberry trench coats and cashmere sweaters, their infant siblings arriving in their strollers wearing black patent leather Gucci baby shoes on their teensy feet. This was a world Stacy had little interest in making her own; it was Roger who'd insisted that this was where their children belonged and where they would get the best education their money could buy. She'd often thought of her former life, of the homeless people she'd lavished such attention on, and reflected ruefully that she probably shouldn't have allowed Roger to have his way when it came to decisions about their children's education. But all that was moot now: she and her family would not be dipping their toes in that world of privilege again, certainly not in the foreseeable future, she imagined.

"Sweetie pie!" she said now, greeting Olivia, as she always did, as if it had been weeks since they'd seen each other rather than hours. Will, who attended preschool in another part of the building, had been dismissed earlier and was off on a playdate with one of his new friends, who happened to be a neighbor and lived several floors beneath them.

Olivia was lugging a castle she'd made in art class with shoeboxes and aluminum foil fashioned into turrets. A doll's head, the size of an adult fingertip, poked through one of the castle's windows forlornly.

"That's *some* gorgeous castle," Stacy said. When it came to her children's artwork, the lies flowed easily, and were always accompanied by what she hoped passed for a genuine smile.

"This is Jazzmin," Olivia said, pointing to the pretty girl standing next to her, who also held a castle in her arms and had a backpack slung over her shoulder. "We're having a playdate today, okay?"

It was okay, but only if Jazzmin's mother agreed, Stacy explained to the girls. "Where's your mom, sweetie?" she asked.

Jazzmin, whose skin was the color of iced tea, pointed to a tall white guy around Stacy's age, dressed in jeans and a thin corduroy jacket that couldn't possibly have kept him warm on this cold day in January. His eyes were remarkably bloodshot, his long hair was in an oily ponytail, and most disconcertingly, his feet were in flip-flops. He would not have been out of place among her homeless clients, Stacy suspected, and when she approached him, the stink of a freshly smoked joint was all over him. *This is how you come to pick up your little girl from kindergarten?* she wanted to say. The guy was completely wasted, and she wondered how he'd managed to get here on time to collect his child.

Introducing herself, Stacy presented the idea of a playdate as something he had no right to refuse.

"Hey, you'll get no argument from *me*," Jazzmin's father said, and laughed. "Keep her as long as you'd like. Just gimme your address and I'll come get her later."

Stacy tore out a piece of paper from the small notebook she always kept in her purse just in case she had an idea she wanted to include in her still-unfinished novel.

"Love you, Daddy," Jazzmin said after he took the paper from Stacy, but he'd already turned his back and started to walk off.

They stopped at a candy store on the way home, where Stacy, who was seething over her brief encounter with the poorest excuse for a father she'd met in a long while, bought the girls Kit Kat bars. It was the social worker in her, and the mother in her, that made her loop her arm around Jazzmin and pull her close. And that was when she noticed the aroma, which wasn't a pleasant one, of a young child's body, one that hadn't been washed in a long while. When they arrived home, just a few minutes later, she told the girls that before they could play, they'd have to take a bath.

"You're silly," Olivia said. "We don't take baths in the afternoon."

"Well, we do today."

Stacy ran the water for the bath, and stood by as the girls undressed and tossed their clothing on the floor. She nearly gagged at the odor, but was relieved to see there were no bruises on Jazzmin's body, something she'd been worried she might find. Just because Jazzmin's father was a stoner and wore flip-flops in the winter didn't necessarily mean he was an abusive parent, she realized. Or at least not physically abusive.

"So . . . where's your mom today?" Stacy said casually.

"In South Carolina with her boyfriend," Jazzmin said. "We don't see her," she added, and said yes, Stacy could wash her hair for her.

"That's silly!" Olivia said. "Moms don't have boyfriends."

"Some do," said Stacy, but went no further than that. She thought, for the first time in a long while, of her ex, Rocco Bassani, who she'd heard—via Jefrie—was recently divorced and the father of a toddler named Dylan, whom his then-wife had given birth to after Rocco had his vasectomy reversed. Some of the best sex of her young life had probably been with Rocco, she recalled now, as she put bubble gum-scented Tame Your Mane Lazy Lion conditioner through Jazzmin's hair and then Olivia's. One summer night, when he was in med school and the two of them were living together, she and Rocco had sex in his parents' pool at their house in East Hampton. She'd worried that his mother or father might wake up and decide to go into the kitchen for something to drink and look out beyond the door that led to the patio and the pool. *Yeah, and then what?* Rocco had said, making fun of her. *Like they can possibly see what's going on out here?* She knew they couldn't, but the fear stayed with her as Rocco pulled off her bikini bottom there in the shallow end of the pool where they could smell the ocean just beyond them. It embarrassed her slightly now to realize that the fear of being discovered had heightened the experience. And also that she still thought of Rocco with affection.

She missed the adventurous sex they'd had together all those years ago, missed being young. She had one small tattoo, and eight holes in her earlobes, but she was forty-two years old and wasn't her youth way, way behind her? And yet one kiss from Professor Sarno was all she'd needed to remind her that she was still very much alive and kicking.

She and Dave had yet to speak of that kiss in the couple of months that had passed since then, but it occurred to her now, that if he were to approach her again, at the end of a class when her fellow students were gone from the room, she might very well be tempted to caress the stubble on that bristly face of his. But of course this was pure fantasy and she knew it.

"I'm cold!" Olivia announced. "Also, I want a snack."

"Me too!" Jazzmin said happily.

Her father, Steve, came to get her hours later, after Stacy had called him twice, fed the children dinner, and put Will to bed.

"Bet you thought I forgot about my little girl, huh?" he said as he stood in the small foyer and waited for Stacy to help Jazzmin into her down jacket.

His eyes were still bloodshot, and he still had his flip-flops on, but at least he was wearing a warmer jacket, Stacy observed. She handed Jazzmin her Sleeping Beauty backpack and her shoebox castle, and it was only later, when she went to give Olivia the ballerina doll she'd helped herself to in the laundry room, that she realized it was gone from the bedroom closet where she'd hidden it. Though she hated to think of Jazzmin ransacking the closet and ripping off the doll—only because of what it might have reflected about the little girl's life and her desperation to improve upon it—the truth was, Stacy was glad it was gone. And relieved that she wouldn't have to argue with Roger over its secondhand provenance.

Roger, who, of late, needed to be handled with what her father used to refer to as *kid gloves*.

One wrong word, one mistaken look, who knew what it would take? How about a little transcendental meditation to restore clarity to his thinking, to calm his thoughts, and maybe even a little yoga to invigorate that surprisingly lean middle-aged body of his. Speaking of which, she'd have to look at a calendar to remember the last time they'd made love or had sex; frankly, at this point, either one would do just fine.

⁂

*Roger and Will are in Stuff-U-Like, a convenience store just a few minutes from his mother's condo, where they've been sent in search of ginger ale and also the kid version of Tums or Mylanta, all for Olivia's upset stomach. Roger sees a young mother walking by with her small son, a first-grader in a Donald Duck bathing suit just like the one Will is wearing.*

*"Are you fucking KIDDING me, Christopher? You don't know how old you are? Ask me again and I'm going to hurt you," the woman says to her child, who shrinks back from her and hangs his head.*

*Roger puts his hands over Will's ears.*

*"I don't want to, but I WILL hurt you," the woman says fiercely, and Roger doesn't doubt it*

*His hands are still covering his son's ears, though Christopher has been yanked along by his mother and they're both out of sight now.*

*What sort of monster would talk to a child—any child— like that, Roger wonders. He sees that the woman's cruelty has actually raised a field of goose bumps across his own arms.*

*Monster, he says in a whisper.*

## ~ 28 ~

Roger was not a religious man, and might, if pressed, have classified himself as a former agnostic and current atheist, but, even so, he found himself today in Cambria Heights, Queens, visiting the grave of the Rebbe Menachem Schneerson, believed by thousands of fervent followers to be the messiah. Someone who was more than willing to answer your prayers, which you simply had to write down on a sheet of paper, then tear into pieces, and toss into the open-air mausoleum where the Rebbe was buried.

Clare was on life-support, and there was nothing left to do but pray.

Telling Stacy that he was taking a subway and a bus to Queens to pray for his sister's unlikely recovery wasn't a conversation Roger felt up to having; he'd told her, instead, simply that he was going out for a walk and might not be back for a few hours. In the old days, he would have gotten into his Porsche Carrera and driven out to Queens, but there was no longer a Porsche (or any car at all, for that matter) in his life—the annual seven grand he'd paid the parking garage to keep the car in the city was no longer even a possibility. So he'd sold his $75,000 Arctic Silver Metallic 911 Carrera back to the dealer for $25,000 less than he'd paid for it only a year ago, and had already used the money to pay off some business debt. He missed the Porsche badly, and would have said that he grieved for it, but given his sister's precarious connection to life, he had no right, he knew, to be grieving for a car, no matter how beautiful, no matter how much color it had added to his existence.

*Clare Clare Clare.* She was supposed to be well enough to leave the hospital a couple of weeks after the surgery, a surgery that had lasted a horrifying fifteen hours and change, and was meant to remove the fucking tumor that, as it turned out, no chemo or surgery could possibly kill off. She had been doing well, or so it seemed that first week post-op, but then, just like that, she'd been hit with a cerebral hemorrhage caused by a metastasis to the brain. It was Stacy who'd been the last person to talk to her, Stacy who'd been so pleased to hear how Clare was enjoying those cherry tomatoes and that bottle of Orangina in its pebbled glass that she loved, both of which Nathaniel, sweet kid, had brought her from home for dinner. Then Nathaniel had left because he had a midterm to study for, and so it was Stacy who kept her company over the phone as Clare ate and drank, waiting for Marshall to finish up with his last patients of the day before he came for his nightly visit. But by the time Marshall arrived, Clare, who'd suddenly been stricken with a horrific headache, had already hung up on Stacy. And then, a short while later, slipped into a coma, from which she had not awakened these eight long, long days.

Staring idly at Stacy's diamond ring—something he couldn't bear to sell though certainly he needed to—glittering in the fluorescent light of their elevator the other day, Roger had remembered the jewelry store on Forty-Seventh Street where he'd bought it, and the photograph of the blue-eyed Rebbe taped to the wall. And the jeweler's promise: *He vill help you even from beyond the grave.*

Fine: why not give it a shot? It couldn't hurt, could it?

The Rebbe's twenty-four-hour visitors' center was a mundane little saltbox of a house just outside the grounds of the cemetery where he was buried. Making his way up the walk that led to it, his prayer for his sister folded into the back pocket of his jeans, Roger saw Orthodox families arriving and departing and hanging around out front, the unsmiling women and little girls in their long skirts, the earnest-looking men and older boys in their black hats and suits, white *tzitzits*, the knotted ritual fringes, drooping from the waistline of their pants. No one looked particularly happy, not even the smallest of the children, some of whom were as young as Roger's. *No texting on Shabbos, not ever*, he heard one teenager say to another. He was astounded to see a pair of tiny, mixed-race boys wearing yarmulkes and speaking Yiddish to their Japanese mother, the father nowhere in sight.

Inside in the small lobby, there were signs posted in English, Hebrew, and Yiddish that said, "Please turn off your cellular phones," and a Sony Panasonic flat-screen TV—its frame inexplicably draped in plastic ivy—that played, in a continuous loop, a DVD of the Rebbe giving a speech in Yiddish. On the wall hung a large photograph of the man, one that appeared to be an official portrait; what you saw was an elderly Jewish guy sporting a long white beard and a black felt hat, but you just couldn't ignore those blue eyes. Roger noticed, as well, the Rebbe's long fingernails, clearly in need of a trim. He picked up a brochure that reported some impressive stats: seven thousand e-mails and four hundred faxes arrived here daily from people all around the world asking for the Rebbe's help. With all that competition, Roger wondered gloomily, what were the chances of the Rebbe answering *his* particular prayer?

Walking farther, he entered a large, open room with long, cafeteria-style tables; dozens of people were seated here, some studying prayer books, others talking quietly, or writing notes to the Rebbe on plain white copy paper. Up front was a young receptionist in an ankle-length plaid skirt who was checking her cell phone messages. And in case the faithful were hungry or thirsty, there was a free snack bar offering cookies—chocolate chip and shortbread—and envelopes of Celestial Seasonings tea along with dispensers of milk, soup, cocoa, and decaf. Roger had done his homework, and he knew leather shoes were forbidden when visiting the mausoleum and that he wasn't permitted to go bareheaded. He'd brought along a Yankees baseball cap and a pair of green flip-flops, the only footwear he had that wasn't leather. He stuffed his socks in the pockets of his down coat, and left his shoes next to a disorderly pile of black oxfords and sneakers and women's high heels. Colorful silk scarves were available for women who'd forgotten to wear a hat today.

He had no idea why, but his hands had suddenly turned sweaty and his heart banged around in his chest as he walked outside and headed toward the mausoleum. There were two entrances, one for women and one for men, and because he hadn't been paying attention, he nearly went in through the women's side, but was stopped at the last moment. A young woman, her head wrapped in a woolen shawl, wagged a finger at him just in time.

The Rebbe's headstone faced a concrete pool filled nearly to the brim, not with water, but with bits of torn-up paper. Orthodox and Hasidic men and women swayed in prayer, along with a guy in a brimmed cap stamped with the words "Brake Masters: An Honest Brake since 1983." Roger arranged himself among the men and slipped his prayer from his pocket. He knew the drill: he was supposed to read the prayer aloud before tearing it up, but he felt too self-conscious to utter the words he'd composed on the subway today.

Dear Rebbe,

Please save my sister, Clare, daughter of Beverly (my apologies, but I don't know her Hebrew name). I cannot bear to think of my sister gone from this earth.
I greatly appreciate your help.

With gratitude,
Roger, son of Beverly (who, by the way, has Alzheimer's, and should be included in this prayer as well, if you find yourself willing and able to cure her dementia)

p.s. Just between you and me, I've never felt so hopeless, so close to giving up on that small flicker of hope I'm still nurturing. And I don't just mean my sister here, I mean all the rest of it, too . . .

He folded the small rectangle of notepaper into quarters, and ripped it to pieces, which he flung into the pool. Leaning over the edge, he saw fragments of children's letters drawn in crayon, adult letters written on graph paper, composition paper, and even tissue paper. He saw notes in English and French, Spanish and Italian, German, Hebrew, and Yiddish, and something that looked like Polish.

*Good luck to all of us poor shmucks*, he thought, then made his way into the visitors' center, retreating backward, one foot behind the other, the customary sign of respect here.

Later after he rode the bus to the subway, which would soon be approaching his stop on the Upper East Side, he pulled out the brochure he'd taken with him from the visitors' center and studied some of the frequently asked questions:

> *May I pray in English rather than Hebrew?*
> *May I pray using an app on my iPhone?*
> *I prayed to lose weight, but why am I still a size 18?*

Well, the Messiah worked in mysterious ways, and, believe it or not, there actually *was* an app for a Hebrew prayer book. Roger would have loved to have shared this with Clare, who, he was sure, would have gotten a kick out of it. But his sister was deep in a coma and unavailable for conversation of even the lightest sort. He understood that there were people who sat by the bedsides of their comatose loved ones and chattered on and on, because, well, you never knew, did you?

As Clare's oncologist said just the other day, when Roger inquired about the infinitesimally small possibility that she would emerge from wherever she'd been hiding, *From your lips to God's ear, sir.*

❧

*Even as she holds Olivia's hair behind her with both hands now while her poor little girl retches over the toilet,*

Stacy can already envision that moment tomorrow when Olivia will, along with the rest of the family, board their JetBlue flight to JFK. A little weakened, perhaps, and still without much of an appetite, but most likely well enough to return to school on Monday or Tuesday.

"Better, sweetie pie?" she asks Olivia, and wipes her daughter's face with a washcloth moistened with warm water. Stacy leads her back to the big bed here in the master bedroom with the en suite bathroom conveniently close. She helps Olivia onto the bed, smoothes the summer blanket around her small shoulders, and says, "You're going to be fine, sweetie pie, trust me. You've just got to get this out of your system." She thinks it might be those turkey burgers Roger grilled just a few hours ago, though Olivia is the only one who's sick. Maybe it's a virus, who knows?

"I hate throw-up. It's disgusting," Olivia says. She closes her eyes. "I mean, it _tastes_ disgusting."

"Daddy will be back soon with some ginger ale and medicine for you, okay?"

"I _hate_ ginger ale," Olivia says.

"Just keep those eyes closed, sweetie, and maybe you'll fall asleep," Stacy says. "Then when you wake up, you'll be much better, how does _that_ sound?"

Olivia doesn't respond and is already drifting off. Stacy strokes her daughter's hand; ornamenting her tiny wrist is an elastic bracelet of pastel-colored wooden beads. Stacy raises the little hand to her mouth and kisses it. She will not leave her daughter's side, though she needs to go back into the bathroom and see what has to be cleaned up in there. She'll put out fresh towels for herself and Roger for one last shower in the morning before they leave tomorrow . . . She thinks with excitement of the prospect of returning to work sometime in the near future, of making some phone calls Monday morning, sending out some feelers, shooting some e-mails in the right direction. Barbara

*Armstrong had been promoted to associate head of the nonprofit where they'd worked together, and she's the first person Stacy will call next week . . . She's surprised Roger hasn't made a point of warning her that in this economy, the likelihood of her quickly finding a job is slim to none, especially after a five-year absence from the field. It's not in her to harbor pessimism, to wallow in it, as she thinks Roger sometimes does. Roger who has been so dreadfully unhappy, so terribly worried about everything and anything. Business, their family's financial well-being, his sister, his mother . . . all of these, she suspects, are on his mind all day, every day, and who can fault him for that, really?*

*When they get back to New York, she hopes, he'll start seeing Dr. Avalon again, even though he says he's finished with the guy.*

*They can't afford it, but he can't afford not to.*

*She hears the front door opening, hears the hushed voices of her husband and little boy as they come toward the bedroom now, bearing necessary things from Stuff-U-Like. Olivia, thankfully, is asleep, and Stacy ushers Roger and Will back toward the living room, where she goes through the bag they've brought home with them.*

*"What's this?" she says, and pulls out a multicolored business card from the bottom of the plastic bag. Imprinted on the card, against a roiling, powder-blue sea, is Noah's ark, inhabited by coyly smiling giraffes, pandas, walruses, and tigers. "The Lord is faithful to all his promises," the card informs her, and when she flips it over, there's a message on the other side that merely says, "Pass it on!"*

*Laughing, Stacy says, "Hey, do you think someone at Stuff-U-Like is trying to tell us something?"*

## 29

Clare had been on life-support for thirteen days now, and after making Stacy promise that she wouldn't tell Roger, Marshall had confided last week that it was time to let Clare go. He, Nathaniel, Stacy, and Roger were seated now in a short row of comfortable faux-leather chairs in the lobby of Sloan Kettering, not far from the gift shop, where the walls were made of glass and you could look inside and take a gander at those upbeat *Get Well Soon!* balloons and also the collection of stuffed animals, large and small—all of which were meant to console those patients who were recuperating nicely and would be heading home shortly, as well as those who, tragically, would never have that chance.

The oncologist who came down to the lobby to speak with them was a young woman named Kelsey Whitacre. She had a mouthful of square white teeth lined up like Chiclets, and long, severely straight hair. As the doctor talked to them about Clare's future, Stacy found herself deliberately ignoring what she could not bear to hear. And thinking, instead, about the oncologist standing before her and whether or not she'd had the Brazilian Blowout to straighten her hair, never mind those carcinogenic formaldehyde fumes that came along with it.

Dr. Whitacre was telling them now to take their time in deciding whether or not to remove Clare from life-support. She understood, she said, that this was a heartrendingly difficult decision for most of the families who had to make it, and she didn't want them to feel rushed.

A man whose face and shaved head were completely covered in tattoos sauntered by with a bouquet of flowers under his arm.

"You have my cell, right?" Dr. Whitacre said, and then—unforgivably, Stacy thought—she yawned. Exhaustion or boredom; whatever the reason for that yawn, Stacy would neither forgive nor forget.

"We appreciate that," Marshall was saying, and after the doctor left them, he draped his arm around Nathaniel and said quietly, "Listen, I don't think there's anything more we—"

"No!" Roger cried, and you could hear all the grief he'd poured into that single word. "If we're voting, I vote NOT to let Clare go."

But what authority did he have? Stacy tried to think of the kindest way to point out to him that, in fact, he had none.

"I'm sorry, Roger," Marshall said gently. He stretched out the fingers of his left hand, examined them, and with the inner edge of his pinky and the tip of his thumb, began to rotate his wedding ring. "Don't be insulted by this, okay, but you need to understand that it's my decision to make, not yours."

Near the reception desk, a woman in her twenties in leggings and dangerously high heels was talking too loudly into her phone. "I was, like, really, really hungry, and I opened Kendra's pocketbook and was totally excited because I thought I saw a candy bar down at the bottom there, but then I realized it was only an address book and I was *so* disappointed."

"Fuck. You."

At first Stacy thought Roger was talking to the woman who'd mistaken the address book for a candy bar. But the instant he tore himself out of his seat and headed for the escalator that would get him to the lower lobby and out the front entrance, she knew the score. But did not run after him.

"Marshall," she said, leaning across Nathaniel to touch her brother-in-law's knee, "you'll forgive him, right?"

Marshall looked bewildered. "We've been married for twenty-eight years," he said, "and you know, this has got to be the worst fucking day of my life."

As if she might have thought otherwise.

"I know," Stacy said. "I know . . . I know . . . I know." She squeezed his knee. "The worst fucking day of your life." She tried very hard not to cry in front of Marshall, but quickly failed, and tears fell from her eyes and rolled past her chin and down the V-neck of her sweater. She remembered the first time she'd met Clare, and the mushroom-and-asparagus ravioli her sister-in-law had made from scratch that night, and the chocolate mousse, chosen because it would be easy for Stacy to eat after the root canal she'd had a couple of days before. With the tip of her tongue, she touched the tooth now, the very last molar up there on the left side. Clare had always been so generously solicitous of her; after her mother was killed, there hadn't been many people like that in her life, Stacy recognized—and oh how lucky she'd been to have Clare. Who'd even wiped the blood from her thighs when Stacy was in the throes of her miscarriage. It was ten years from start to finish that they'd known each other, and it wasn't nearly enough time.

"I'm going to say good-bye to my wife now," Marshall announced. He struggled to stand up; like an old man, he needed help getting out of his chair. Stacy and Nathaniel walked him to the elevator bank, and Stacy left the two of them there as they went upstairs to Clare's bed in the ICU. She didn't want to hear what Marshall would be saying, didn't want to imagine what it would be like for him to walk away knowing that after twenty-eight years he would not get another chance to warm his body all night next to that beloved person whose life had been his.

It was an unutterably sad, harrowing day, and how could she ever forget it?

⁓

She had no idea where Roger was, Stacy realized, and had no expectation, when she called his cell phone out here on York Avenue within spitting distance of Sloan Kettering, that he would answer. (He didn't.)

It was Clare's last day on this earth, but Stacy still had to get home and pay the babysitter fifteen dollars an hour, and feed her children their dinner: chicken nuggets in the microwave two nights in a row. Which was what you got for dinner when you had a distracted mother and father for parents. This reminded her of Olivia's friend Jazzmin, who had not been back for another playdate and whose father continued to show up at dismissal time with those bloodshot eyes of his, stinking of weed. Stacy needed to do something about this, she thought, and thought, too, that she had never been very good at minding her own business. Maybe she would make an anonymous phone call to the Administration for Children's Services and see if they could send someone over to Jazzmin's home to take a look at what was happening behind closed doors.

But not before she got Roger safely through the next few days and weeks.

༄

At the funeral, which was mobbed—a tribute to just how much Clare had been liked and admired by the teachers in the middle school where she'd worked her magic as a shrink for so many troubled, disenfranchised kids—Stacy held hands with Roger as he sat beside her in the very first row of burnished wooden pews. Next to Roger was Marshall, and then Nathaniel, both of them soberly dressed in their black woolen suits, rep-striped ties, and highly polished penny loafers, Marshall looking particularly pale and handsome, Stacy observed. There were shining quarters in the slots of Nathaniel's loafers; Marshall's were empty. Kissing the back of Roger's hand, Stacy thanked God—or Whoever Up There might have been responsible—for her own family's good health. She wondered whether Clare had ever acknowledged out loud that she was probably dying, ever acknowledged that the cancer was apparently immune to round after toxic round of chemo that brought painful sores to the insides of her mouth, banished her appetite and her hair, and, on the very worst days, had her puking her guts out. She and Clare had never, in the sixteen-month trajectory of her illness, talked about the future, except in the vaguest way; not once had she heard Clare worry aloud about whether she would live to see Nathaniel marry or open his own restaurant or, beyond that, bring grandchildren into her life. If Clare had had her suspicions, her fears, that her life would be abridged, she never raised them. At least not to Stacy, or to Roger either, and Stacy was grateful to have been spared the sadness of that. But now was the time for her to reflect on the tragedy of Clare's life, on the undeniable fact that her sister-in-law had been cruelly robbed of decades in which there would surely have been much to savor.

But when she got up there to deliver her eulogy from the lectern in the funeral chapel, it came to her that there was only one thing she wanted to talk about. Several years ago, she explained nervously into the microphone, she herself had fallen off a ladder and badly broken her leg; because of the surgery that had been necessary to pin the bones back together, she'd been bedridden, and unable to shower for two endlessly long weeks. Now she told the room packed with several hundred people how Clare had so sweetly, so thoughtfully, volunteered to wash her hair for her, arriving with fancy bottles of shampoo and conditioner and—get this—a child's inflatable wading pool that she'd bought just for the occasion, so that Stacy could lie on her back across her bed, lean her head over the edge, and all those pitcherfuls of water could flow directly into the wading pool without soaking the carpet beneath it.

"It was purely an act of love, one of the most loving things anyone has ever done for me," said Stacy. "But ultimately there was nothing, not a single thing, that I could do for Clare to save her. And believe me, it killed me. *Kills* me."

She stepped down, and returned to her seat, where Roger—who was too distraught to offer even a single word about his sister, let alone a eulogy—waited for her, stiff and silent, as if he hadn't heard a thing she'd said.

∽

## FINAL DRAFT

To my dear family and friends—

I have been struggling to say the right thing and this, I'm afraid, is about as close as I will ever get.

My life has taken a nosedive, I'm drowning in debt, and the outlook is increasingly grim. I am deeply ashamed of my failures, both as a businessman and as a human being. I can no longer provide for my family in the way that they deserve.

But you have to understand that my love for my family is EVERYTHING to me. And more than anything, I do not want them to suffer.

Please don't judge me too harshly—I've already done that myself. Again and again and again.

If there were any other way out, I would take it. But there is none, trust me.

IT'S BEST FOR ALL OF US THIS WAY.

In the end, this is what it comes down to: I can no longer live with myself.

## 30

Roger went alone to Renaissance Living Center to break the news to his mother. He put it off until three days after the funeral, and even though Stacy had offered to come along with him, he didn't want her to witness what he could already predict would be a kind of pathetic farce. He signed in at the front desk now and tried not to see all the old women cluttering up the lobby with their wheelchairs and metal walkers, the bars of the walkers often adorned with dried food and the sticky residue of spilled beverages, the heads of the old ladies sadly bent from osteoporosis as they pushed themselves along. And there were the old geezers, just a sprinkling of them, gaunt or pot-bellied, their feet in backless leather slippers, walking arm in arm with dark-skinned caregivers who spoke jauntily to them, as if their charges were kindergartners just beginning to make their way in life.

Observing them, it hit Roger, not for the first time, that just like everyone else his age, he did not want to grow old. The truth was, he feared it, and thought perhaps he'd rather die first.

A tiny, short-haired chihuahua dressed in a blue-and-brown striped cotton sweater looked at him eagerly from the lap of a white-haired man in a wheelchair. "Now, in my darkest hour, as I await my pension," the man said, his voice plaintive, "I'm suffering from digestive heart failure; can you help me, please?"

Along with all the other people in the lobby, Roger ignored him, though he did pat the chihuahua on its head as he walked by. It wasn't that he didn't feel for the old man, it was only that he was in a rush to get upstairs and get this sorrowful business with his mother over with. He was on a fool's errand, but it had to be done.

His mother's so-called best friend, Jewel, was out in the hallway when he got upstairs to the Alzheimer's floor, and she was dressed, as always, in her saddle shoes and bobby socks and plaid skirt; perhaps, Roger thought, the fifties had been her hey day, and she still managed to draw some pleasure from even the vaguest memories.

He waved to her caregiver, Bettina, who waved back. "Have a blessed day!" she called out to him.

Starquasia greeted him at the door of his mother's apartment and immediately offered her condolences. Then she hugged him. "Your mother's not having such a good day today and I don't know why. Maybe she already knows what you're here to tell her," she said.

He suppressed the urge to roll his eyes, and thanked Starquasia for the heads-up. His mother was in her La-Z-Boy, catnapping in front of the TV; he hated to wake her. "Hi, Mom," he said, kissing her cheek.

She stirred, opened her eyes, and immediately smiled at him. "Hello there, sir!" she said brightly. "Do we know each other?"

The Xanax he'd taken at home had just kicked in, and he was suddenly aware of feeling almost preternaturally serene. "We do know each other, Mom. For almost fifty-two years, as a matter of fact."

"Huh, imagine that," his mother said. "But I'm very, very thirsty, and need to wet my whistle," she added.

"Got some water for you right here," said Starquasia. She brought it over in a lime-green plastic mug, and didn't seem particularly surprised when Beverly knocked it from her hand a moment later.

Roger jumped back, but the front of his button-down shirt was already soaked.

"That's naughty," Starquasia said. "You got Roger's shirt wet, and that's not nice."

"Who's Roger?" his mother said.

"Mom, it's me," he said uselessly. He took the dish towel Starquasia handed him, but what was the point—his shirt was drenched.

"You're a sad young man, but a nice one," his mother said. "I hope you have a family who's good to you."

"I do," Roger said. "But we need to talk about Clare, okay?"

"I don't know who that is—is she your wife?"

"She's my sister." He was down on his knees now, and he took Beverly's hand. "She was your daughter."

Beverly swatted his hand away and began to cry. "I want my mama," she said. "When is my mama coming back?"

"Oh, Jesus, please don't start that again," said Starquasia.

Even though Roger could tell that the Xanax was shielding him from the worst of it, he didn't have the heart to prolong his visit. Still on his knees, he told his mother not to cry, and that he loved her. Then he left, declining Starquasia's offer to dry his shirt with a hair dryer first. He went out into the cold, his jacket thrown on carelessly and unzipped over his wet shirt. He walked the few blocks home along Third Avenue, thinking not about Clare or his mother, but about his modest apartment where he ate his breakfast leaning against a Formica counter as Stacy packed the kids' lunches, he and Stacy trying to stay out of each other's way in the small, cramped kitchen that made it difficult for her not to bump her hip against his. This recent move had only reinforced his feelings of failure, he reflected day after day, as he awakened in the new home that was less than half the size of his old one and rushed to the subway every morning to get to his office in Long Island City, observing the buses and cabs flying up Third Avenue and down Lex, mindful that on Park, a neighborhood he would never again be able to afford, there were only cabs—buses, that common mode of mass transportation, simply weren't permitted to litter the pricey landscape.

The following morning, he boarded a crowded, litter-strewn subway where of course there were no seats and he was stuck standing in the aisle, until, at Grand Central, he switched lines and found himself seated uncomfortably close to a morbidly obese woman dressed in an enormous yellow sweat suit and breathing wheezily beside him. And across the aisle there was the guy sporting a **REPENT OR PERISH** T-shirt and talking loudly to his companion, saying vehemently, "Why do you keep bringing this up, dude? What's done is done and we're seriously fucked."

This was his new life—Roger got it, he understood with perfect clarity what it was all about. He no longer had a car he could drive to work, a successful business, an enviable bank account or a home on Park Avenue, kids who went to private school, a beloved sister he could summon on his cell phone, a mother with her wits about her, or even an ordinary washer/dryer in his own little conveniently located laundry room right off a gleaming stainless-steel kitchen.

All of this—including his sister and mother, though for those losses, at least, he was blameless—was out of reach and would, he felt certain, remain so. When he told this to Dr. Avalon, told him about this sense he had of himself as an absolute fucking failure, Avalon had suggested, solicitously, that this was "delusional thinking," and asked Roger why he couldn't try and see his way past his pessimism to something akin to optimism.

*Optimism? No way.*

*Sorry, doc, but he was all out of optimism.*

*Permanently.*

He was fucked, man, just like his fellow passenger across the aisle. For a guy with an MBA from Harvard, he had stumbled badly, and could not foresee how he would ever be able to repair things. Ever be able to restore what had been taken from him and his family by his own poor judgment and crappy luck.

*What if he could no longer afford to put food on the table and they starved to death? Then what?* It had been clear to him that Avalon didn't like hearing this, because the doc actually rose from his seat behind the desk and walked to where Roger was slumped on the couch, then bent slightly to touch his elbow.

*Is that what you really think, Roger? That your family is going to starve?*

What he really thought was that this beloved family of his deserved so much more, so much better, than what he was able to offer them, and how could you ever forgive yourself for that?

∽

*Packing for the trip home as Olivia sleeps off her upset stomach and Roger and Will head downstairs for one last dip in the pool while it's still light out, Stacy checks on the damp bathing suits set out to dry on the terrace, empties the dresser drawers in the master bedroom of everything except what she and Roger will be wearing tomorrow on the plane, slips a couple of books into her carry-on bag. She inspects herself in the ornately framed mirror over her mother-in-law's dresser and sees that there's some nice healthy-looking color in her face, enough so that her neighbors will probably ask where she's been and if she'd enjoyed herself.*

*Enjoyed herself? Not . . . so much.*

*Actually, it was very relaxing, she'll say.*

*Because, really, what's so awful about lying to neighbors you barely know, letting them think you've come back well rested after a week of summery days and nights with your family.*

## 31

This was how Stacy requested a conference of sorts with Professor Sarno one night after class: "Hey, got a minute?"

"For you, sure," Dave said. He'd already shouldered his messenger bag, but dumped it back onto the seminar table, and said, "So hey, what can I do for you?"

*Well, let's see, what about that momentary kiss nearly four months ago, which neither of them had seen fit to mention even once in all that time.* Perhaps she'd imagined it, Stacy contemplated saying now.

"I hate to put you on the spot like this," she began, fingering one of her nearly shoulder-length peacock feather earrings, "and please forgive me for asking, but I really do need to know if you actually think of me as someone with . . . you know . . . I guess the word would be 'promise'?" She wanted to say *talent* but couldn't bring herself to pronounce the word out loud.

Dave was looking at her with amusement. " 'Promise'? You mean 'talent,' doncha?"

"It's probably the worst question a student could ever ask you, right?" Stacy said. "I'm aware of that, believe me, it's just that I've been working on this alleged novel of mine for so long now and if you think I should put it aside, or even permanently delete the file from my computer, well, I guess I would probably listen to you." Her phone was buzzing like an annoying insect, but she ignored it. "I want to accomplish something in my life," she said. "But if this is the wrong thing for me to pin my hopes on, I want you to tell me." It wasn't particularly warm in the room, but she felt a little damp behind her neck. And also dry mouthed. "Please just be honest with me," she said, and took a fast swig from her sweating Poland Spring bottle. And even though the classroom door was wide open and there was another class across the hall that was still in session, Dave leaned toward her, putting his hands on her shoulders to balance himself as he kissed her, and this time—without a cab waiting impatiently on Broadway for her to hop in—it seemed that she had all the time in the world to kiss him back.

She recognized that this was Dave's way of deflecting her question, and also—in the deflection itself—of answering it. It wasn't the answer she'd been looking for, not after all those endless hours she'd spent writing and rewriting her manuscript over too many years. But what about the encouraging critiques she'd received from Dave and her fellow classmates? They hadn't been telling her the truth and had only wanted to spare her feelings, was that it? She closed her eyes to all of this and went with what was being offered her, the sexy opportunity that had presented itself here in this empty classroom with its white boards and big, square-faced ticking clock on the scuffed, pale-gray wall.

There was a walk-in closet in a corner at the back of the room; without speaking, Dave led her there, and they went into it and shut the door. Her eyes adjusted to the semidarkness, and she could see that the shelves in the closet were empty, except for a spray bottle of Lysol and a rag. A bare light bulb hung from the ceiling; Dave yanked on the metal chain suspended from the socket. Stacy wanted the light off, but he wanted it on. *To see how beautiful you are*, he said. As they tugged their sweaters over their heads, she remembered the silvery nipple ring that was exposed the night he played with his post-punk band in Williamsburg.

Soon she was licking the metal with the tip of her tongue, surprising herself.

He slipped a condom from his cracked leather wallet, and ripped it open with his teeth.

*All the perfumes of Arabia will not sweeten this little hand*, she thought guiltily as, helping Dave along, she reached down to pull off her underwear. But she was no Lady Macbeth, she told herself; she was only someone who kept waking in the wrong bed in the wrong house, morning after morning, unable to find her old life, the one she would joyfully reclaim in an instant if only she could.

∽

As she and Dave were getting back into their clothes, Stacy mentioned that she was going to have to miss a class when she went to Florida next month, just for a week, just to get away for a while . . .

It was flattering to see how deflated Dave looked, as if he might actually miss her.

"So you're going with your family?" he said.

*Yes, with my family*, she told him as she followed him out of the closet.

Roger seemed so deeply unnerved and unhappy these days, and it pained her to think that learning—not that he ever would—what she had done tonight would only make him unhappier. But she was startled to discover this thought didn't do all that much to diminish the substantial pleasures of the evening.

The piercing spasms of guilt would come later that night as she tried, unsuccessfully, to fall asleep, and she would force herself to deal with them.

Pointing now to the laces of Dave's dusty suede Pumas, she said, "Your spaghettis are untied."

"What?"

It was a favorite line from a favorite book of Olivia's, but how could Stacy tell him that?

∽

Mrs. Feinsilver, the shrunken old lady from two doors down, is apparently standing outside their door begging for change.

"Honey, do you have eight quarters for two singles? Mrs. Silverfein has to do a laundry," Stacy calls out to Roger. Now she's ushering the old lady into the living room.

"Feinsilver," Roger corrects her, and the truth is he doesn't like the sight of her in his apartment; it makes him uneasy to see anyone except his family here. She's an old friend of his parents', originally from Brooklyn, where her wealthy husband owned a couple of nursing homes and was very nearly indicted on various charges having to do with financial shenanigans that attempted to defraud the government of Medicare fees. Her husband is gone now, her son lives in San Diego, and, like a lot of lonely people, she can't help but talk incessantly about herself. Which is why she's someone Roger tries to avoid whenever he's down here in Florida.

He goes through his pockets and the souvenir ashtray from Las Vegas where he's been keeping his change, and comes up with seven quarters, one short of a single load of laundry.

"Here you go," he tells Mrs. Feinsilver, who, it appears, doesn't have the two bucks she would very much like to give him.

Standing in the living room in her flower-print housecoat, pale, bare legs, and satiny scarlet slippers, she says, "Your poor mother. How my heart aches for her!" And goes on to report, in great detail, her own vale of tears, those earthly sorrows which she only wishes her hubby were here to share with her.

Roger and Stacy nod and say they understand how hard things must be. "Please just take the quarters and never mind about the two singles," Roger urges her, but Mrs. Feinsilver wants them to know that she feels bad *about taking their money. Her apology goes on for too long, and Roger can't wait for her to leave.*

*"It's just two dollars," Stacy says. "Honestly, don't give it another thought, Mrs. Silverfein."*

*"Feinsilver," Roger says. He hears Will crying from the bedroom because the TV remote is stuck and Will doesn't want to watch the news, he only wants to watch the Disney Channel, which of course is a premium channel not available in Grandma Beverly's basic cable package. Roger has explained this to Will several times already, but he's three and a half years old and tired and cranky, and seems to have forgotten.*

*"Excuse me, I've got to help my little boy," he tells Mrs. Feinsilver, and, at last, makes his escape.*

## 32

People—like the guy who cut his hair for fifteen bucks at the unisex place on Third Avenue, and Fernando, the one friendly doorman in his new building, and Marshall, his brother-in-law—kept asking Roger what kind of diet he was on. Nutrisystem? Weight Watchers? Slim Fast? They seemed surprised when he said that no, there was no diet, it was only that he had a lot, too much, as a matter of fact, on his mind lately, and sometimes found himself forgetting to eat lunch. Even though Dr. Avalon suggested the problem was in his head, the doc was still worried enough to insist that Roger see his internist for a check-up—to find out why he'd lost so much weight, nearly twenty-five pounds over the past couple of months. Stacy had urged him to go as well, though it had taken a bit for her to notice how much he'd lost, and to finally say, with teary-eyed concern, *God, even your face is too thin.* Once his jeans and khakis began to fall past his hips, he'd been forced to put an extra hole in his belts, using an awl from his toolbox.

But nope, there would be no doctor appointments; who needed a doctor to tell you what you already knew? Which was that it was hard to eat when everything tasted bitter—his favorite cinnamon bagels, Stacy's homemade lasagna, even a teaspoonful of super-premium chocolate raspberry truffle ice cream. Roger had heard Clare complain about this very problem after one of the many rounds of chemo she'd endured; the worst of its side effects had been that her taste buds were altered in a truly fucked-up way, and there wasn't really an antidote. It had hurt to hear about this from her; thinking about it at this moment, only weeks after his sister's death, made him weep. He went into the kids' bathroom now, and sat on the edge of the tub and cried into his cupped hands.

Down the hallway, Stacy was getting the children into their pajamas in their new bedroom where they slept in bunk beds made of shiny, red-painted steel. She called out to Roger; he could hear her even behind the closed door of the bathroom.

She needed his help, but he needed to sit here and cry for his sister, who had known, as he did, what it was like to taste bitterness in everything.

## 33

Stacy was enjoying her own version of coffee (aka a well-chilled can of Diet Coke) with Jefrie in a diner of sorts in Union Square, not far from the site of the very first class she'd taken with Dave. This was the week before she was leaving for Florida, and she and Jefrie were meeting in person because phone calls, e-mails, and texts all seemed to Stacy both inadequate and dangerous, given the nature of what it was she felt so desperate to confide in her best friend. And that was: how, precisely, she and Dave had fallen into . . . well, whatever it was they'd fallen into. Perhaps not a full-fledged affair, exactly, since they'd only revisited the walk-in closet twice since their first time last month. Perhaps it was more of an intimate friendship of sorts, she mused out loud—a friendship that had, more than once, taken a sharp detour from its expected path.

"Professor Sarno? Whoa!" Jefrie said. "And by the way, I believe that in common parlance what you've described is known as 'friends with benefits.'" Along with her decaf, she'd ordered an enormous, ungainly looking black-and-white cookie on a plate that could barely contain it. She kept breaking off pieces and offering them to Stacy, who shook her head "no" each time.

Stacy told her that every so often—when she was poised at the bathroom sink, toothbrush in hand, or standing alone over the stove stirring a steamy pot of capellini—she would suddenly feel sick with guilt. And, too, that she couldn't stop thinking of her sister-in-law and how disappointed in her Clare would be. But Jefrie interrupted and said, "No offense, kiddo, but she's dead, and can't be disappointed, horrified, or anything else. And I don't mean to sound hard-hearted, but we do what we have to do in this world to help us get by . . . *Comprende?*"

It had been painful for Stacy to confess what had gone on in the walk-in closet, and it was mortifying to confide that, after all those classes she'd enrolled in, Dave had admitted he wasn't absolutely certain she had "quite as much talent as it takes . . ."

"Bummer," Jefrie said sympathetically. "You're sure you don't want any of this cookie?"

"Huge bummer, yeah, so discouraging, but he did say that my critiques were, um, truly insightful and a big help to my fellow students."

"All right, okay, that's a nice little something," Jefrie said, snapping off a piece of cookie. "And I take it you have no intention of telling Roger about any of this, right? I mean, some people think that telling your partner—if you still love him, which I'm guessing you do—can actually strengthen the relationship. Like, once the person gets past the hurt of the betrayal, you can focus on whatever else you . . ." Jefrie paused, and waved her hand dismissively. "Oh, I don't know what the fuck I'm talking about, forget it."

"What, are you kidding?" Stacy said. "Of course I love Roger! And let's put it this way: I wouldn't dream of saying a word to him. What he doesn't know won't . . ." It was odd, she reflected, that it wasn't until now that Roger's name had come up, and she only wished there were something sanguine she could offer. "I think," she told Jefrie, "that he's always had a tough time dealing with stress. And failure. He's utterly disheartened about those business losses, and I mean twenty-four/seven, not just these little moments here and there. He's been hitting the Xanax a lot, I think." She was tempted to tell Jefrie about the breakdown Roger had suffered long ago during his freshman year at Michigan, but it seemed disloyal in the extreme, and so she kept quiet.

But then, even though she felt uneasy as soon as she got started—knowing it would only make her husband look bad—she began to enumerate for Jefrie the ridiculous complaints Roger had about the laundry, of all things, which she'd gotten him to help her with only recently. He couldn't even stand the tacky notices on the bulletin board in the laundry room of their building when, occasionally, he went down to take their stuff out of the dryer for her late at night: all those ads for SAT tutors; play groups for stay-at-home dads and their toddlers; Sunday services at Saint Stephen of Hungary Church; $10 off your first electrolysis treatment. Stacy could tell he was humiliated by having to do the laundry in a communal space; it brought him back to those days when he was in grad school, the last time he'd ever had to use a public laundry room.

In his mind, she suspected, it was one more thing that highlighted just how far he'd plummeted.

"*Argh*, I can't stand to listen to this!" Jefrie said. "He sounds like a spoiled baby who needs to grow the fuck up. This minute."

"I guess he always thought of himself as terrifically ambitious. And, until recently anyway, a successful businessman. And then there's his sister . . . It's been dreadful for him," Stacy said, and her voice was soft. "*Too much.*" She didn't tell Jefrie that often during these past couple of weeks, when she spoke to Roger about anything at all—Marshall's bereavement group or Olivia's new teacher or the neighbor down the hall who'd worked for the Secret Service during the Clinton administration—she could see how distracted he was, see in his turquoise eyes that he was beyond distracted. That he was, she feared, *lost.*

Then he would snap to attention, and, greatly relieved, she'd realize that she'd been mistaken.

At the table next to them, a moon-faced woman seated alone was reading *My Diet Starts Tomorrow: A Novel.* Flipping it over, the woman brutally squashed the open paperback down on the table, picked up her cell phone, tapped a few keys, and said, "Hey, I've been thinking a lot about Shawn, and here's the thing I really admire about him; he's not dumb, you know?"

If Stacy had been in better spirits, she would have laughed.

"Look, you need to tell Roger to get his act together," Jefrie said. "If you don't, maybe I will." She grabbed Stacy's wrist. "You and I go way, way back, kiddo, and I can't stand to see you looking so worried."

"Do I look worried?"

"Hell yeah you do!"

"Well, we're going on one of those cheap, child-friendly vacations to Florida next week, so that should be nice and relaxing."

"You *hate* Florida," Jefrie pointed out cheerfully, and Stacy was reminded of what a dear friend she was.

"Hate Florida? Hell yeah I do!" she agreed.

# ~ 34 ~

Sometimes, late at night, when he'd been unable to sleep these past few weeks, Roger sat in the living room of his Third Avenue apartment with a black linen-covered photo album in his lap and stared at one picture after another of his wife and beautiful children. Olivia posed in front of a haunted house in Disneyland, eyes squinting into last summer's sun, her little-girl potbelly protruding beneath her brightly colored psychedelic T-shirt . . . Stacy, with nine-month-old Will held in her arms, Will's small palms pressed against either side of Stacy's mouth, his smiling face turned coquettishly toward the camera . . . Olivia, age two, in a pink-and-white striped summer dress and tiny white leather sandals, sporting an enormous, broad-brimmed straw hat that belonged to Roger's mother.

With his fingertip now, he stroked Olivia's shoulder in a photo preserved behind a veneer of the thinnest plastic. And then covered and uncovered her face with his thumb, as if they were playing peek-a-boo.

It was four thirty in the morning, and he should have been asleep beside his wife. Instead he found himself sobbing over an album full of pictures that so faithfully documented what any fool could see had been their indisputably happy life together.

⁓

*Olivia is feeling better, and might even have some Jell-O, a box of which Stacy was lucky enough to score in the pantry, and which she made with boiling water and ice—a* secret ingredient that will have that Tropical Fusion-flavor Jell-O set to go in no time. Stacy is busy now giving Will his dinner and Roger is sitting here with Olivia on what was once his parents' bed, reading aloud from Horton Hatches the Egg, his daughter's favorite Dr. Seuss.

"I meant what I said, and I said what I meant," the two of them recite together, and Roger gives Olivia a little tickle under her arm, even though she'd tossed her cookies only a couple of hours ago.

"I meant," he told Dr. Avalon not long before Clare died, "exactly what I said."

Dr. Avalon had narrowed his eyes at him in a way Roger didn't like, and said, "You're telling me that you went to the grave of a rabbi thought to be the messiah, and asked him to save your sister?"

Hanging his head slightly, Roger said, "Desperate times call for those proverbial desperate measures, Doc."

"Daddy," Olivia is asking him now, "if I'm still sick tomorrow, will I have to go to school on Monday?"

"No, baby, nobody has to go to school when they're sick."

"That's not true," Olivia says. "Someone in my class had lice in his hair and his mom sent him to school anyway."

"Well, that's a bad mother," Roger tells her.

Stacy arrives with a small Pyrex cup of Jell-O, but Olivia declines to taste it. "That's not strawberry," she correctly points out.

"Of course it is," Roger and Stacy insist, but their daughter, God bless her, is smart enough to distinguish between strawberry and Tropical Fusion, and she's having none of it.

"I don't want any Jell-O, I just want to go home," Olivia says. "That's all I want, okay?"

Okay, sweetie, Roger tells her.

## 35

What Roger chose not to share with Dr. Avalon was that he'd gone back a second time to the Rebbe Schneerson's grave with another one of those carefully considered notes, this time a very brief one:

Dear Rebbe,

Please save me and my beloved family from the hopelessness in which I find myself engulfed.

You will have my gratitude—
Roger

He realized too late that he'd forgotten to include "son of Beverly" after his signature, as required, and still had his fingers crossed that the Rebbe wouldn't take off too many points for it.

"Let's hear about your week," Dr. Avalon was saying during Roger's last appointment. Avalon was seventy now, and no doubt contemplating retirement, Roger thought. He was chewing gum, very discreetly, but Roger took note of it nevertheless, and thought how unprofessional it was.

"In high school, my French teacher once caught me chewing gum," Roger heard himself say. "And she made me stick it on the tip of my nose and keep it there until the end of class."

Much to Roger's surprise, Dr. Avalon went on chewing.

"I was seventeen years old, and I felt like a fucking idiot with that gum stuck on my nose," Roger continued. "It was Bazooka. Bright pink."

Dr. Avalon nodded. "Something so intensely humiliating is hard to forget."

"I couldn't get up there and deliver a eulogy for my sister," Roger said. He folded his hands into fists. "How's *that* for humiliating?"

Dr. Avalon bent over in his armchair facing Roger, and using his fingers like tweezers, picked up a piece of lint from the oriental carpet at their feet.

*He was talking about his sister's funeral but Dr. Avalon just had to get that lint off the rug.*

Roger contemplated firing him at that moment, that gum-chewing, lint-picking shrink who said little, mostly nodding his head for a living for three hundred bucks an hour which, frankly, *he* could ill-afford these days.

Now he was telling Roger that he and his wife were going on a ten-day trip to Portugal, Spain, France, and the Netherlands. "So I won't be available for a while, even by phone."

"Me either," Roger said. "But can you renew my prescription for Xanax before you go?"

Playing with the lint he'd captured, rubbing it thoughtfully between two fingers, Dr. Avalon said, "You did once tell me that your goal was to eventually feel a lessening of anxiety without the meds. Does that feel like a realistic goal right now, Roger?"

He considered telling Avalon that he'd been doing some thinking and that, barring a miraculous intervention by the late Rebbe Schneerson, he and the doc would not be seeing each other again, that it was time for them to go their separate ways. He was getting sentimental in his old age, and thought, just for a moment, as his anger evaporated, of cradling Avalon's hand and thanking him for the many, many expensive hours he had listened, in the soothing, mostly nonjudgmental way of his, to Roger brooding about that ache of uneasiness that could not be quieted. No matter what.

He was that kid with the bubble gum stuck to his nose, all these years later.

$S$he was emptying the dishwasher and he was poised at the entrance to the kitchen and brooding about public school—*all those crappy third-rate teachers with degrees from crappy third-rate colleges*, and parents forced to pay extra for the art teacher and art supplies, and, unbelievably, there was no music teacher at all . . . And of course the classrooms weren't air-conditioned and were probably steamy in the early fall and late spring . . . *Compare that*, Roger instructed her, to Olivia and Will's old school, where the tenth-grade chamber music group would be performing in China in the spring, and seniors who were enrolled in Hungarian and Czech classes would be traveling on a two-week cultural tour of Budapest and Prague. *Hungarian and Czech!* Roger said admiringly; then his face darkened.

*It kills me*, he said, *to think of all those lost opportunities for Olivia and Will.*

To study Hungarian and Czech?

What was he talking about?

Olivia was in kindergarten and Will was only in preschool, Stacy pointed out. *What* lost opportunities?

He declined to answer her with anything more than a wistful shake of his head, and she went on stacking the glass salad bowls and dinner plates—one of which had a chipped rim and needed to be trashed—in orderly piles, clearing out the dishwasher until it was completely empty and Roger had turned and started to walk away.

"Come back!" she called after him, but he waved a hand over his head and continued on his way to somewhere else.

Lately it seemed that Roger just couldn't keep his eyes off those family pictures of his. He examined them obsessively, but only after Stacy had crashed for the night and he'd struggled in vain, and for too long, to get to sleep.

Here in a leather album stuffed with photographs—arranged so painstakingly by Stacy over a succession of ice-cold winter evenings—was a grinning Will standing in his crib dressed only in a diaper, a colorful beaded necklace drooping nearly to his knees, a visible stream of saliva trailing from his chin all the way down his bare chest to the waistband of his Huggies. Overhead a mobile of dolphins balancing balls on the tips of their snouts—a gift from Clare and Marshall—hung gaily. And here was one of Olivia and Will sharing a kitchen chair, both of them in pajamas, Will's face turned toward Olivia's and held against her cheek, Olivia resting her chin on her brother's shoulder, a large red box of Sun-Maid raisins in the middle of the table like a centerpiece. Here on one of the last pages was a photograph of Roger seated on the piano bench in their Park Avenue living room with his kids crowded into his lap, their faces reflecting identical, supremely goofy smiles while Roger himself stared, deadpan, at the camera. He could not remember the day the photo had been taken last year, only that Stacy had told him the picture would be funnier if he didn't smile. So as his children mugged joyfully for the camera, he'd worked hard to keep that impassive expression on his face.

Mesmerized by these images at three and four in the morning while his family slept so soundly, it was as if what he'd been looking at were scenes from someone else's lucky, lucky life, a life that hadn't, even for a moment, ever been his.

∽

*The timing is right: both kids are asleep in their beds, and Stacy is in the shower, which she has decided to take now instead of tomorrow morning, when things will just be too hectic, she predicted, what with last-minute packing and a quick visit to the pool so Will, and Olivia—if she's feeling up to it—can get in one last swim before leaving for the airport.*

*Roger takes the elevator down to the deserted lobby and walks to the rented Toyota that sits in his parents' covered space in this parking lot, a mere sixty-second walk from the front door. The lot, at ten P.M., is empty of people, all of whom, he would bet, had dinner at one early bird special or another at five o'clock, then came home and got directly under the covers of their neatly made beds.*

*He opens the driver's side of the Toyota, gets behind the wheel, and pops the glove compartment; sliding over, he hunkers down in the passenger seat and takes out the Glock. He loads the magazine and shoves it into the handle of the gun. Then eases himself carefully out of the car, the gun concealed in a small, environmentally friendly paper shopping bag that he'd left under the seat.*

*The night is muggy; the air smells of rotten eggs. Above him, the moon is partially hidden by a thin veil of clouds.*

*There is no one in the elevator as he rides upstairs, no one to ask him whatcha got in that small shopping bag you're carrying so close to your heart? He's back at the apartment moments later, closing the door quietly behind him and making his way down the hallway to the master bedroom.*

*Standing just outside the bathroom now, he can hear Stacy singing a Beach Boys song in the shower.*

*"I wish that every kiss was NEV-er end-ing," she croons in a sweet soprano that's only slightly off-key.*

The day before the flight out of Kennedy, Stacy met with Magnolia, the seventy-something neighbor whom she'd hired to feed and water her Persians. Though she thought of Keats and Shelley as overgrown kittens, they were, at fourteen and fifteen, elderly now. Most of their time was spent as it had been in their youth, chilling on Roger and Stacy's bed, front paws clasped together devoutly, the delicate, reassuring rise and fall of their fluffy backs as they slept letting Stacy know that they were, despite their chronic indolence, doing just fine.

In addition to their chicken-and-rice-flavored cat food, Stacy told Magnolia, pointing to the list of instructions she'd printed out for her from the computer, Keats and Shelley were each to get a teaspoon of melted ice cream every day.

"They're not too keen on strangers," she warned Magnolia. "So when you come in and they're hiding under a bed or behind the blinds in the living room, please don't take it personally."

"Oh, I never allow myself to be insulted by animals," Magnolia said. "Only people." She began to tell Stacy about her grandson, whom she'd raised from infancy entirely on her own, only to have him join a cult somewhere in Oregon, the kind that allowed her no contact with him whatsoever. "Not even a measly phone call once a year," she lamented. "I'd be better off if he were in prison . . ."

"Oh God, how cruel!" said Stacy. She still hadn't finished packing the kids' suitcases, and had barely started on her own, for that matter, but how could she let Magnolia leave without offering her *something*? "Would you like a cup of coffee?" Stacy asked her. "I'm not a coffee drinker myself, but that doesn't mean I don't know how to make it."

"Sorry, can't. Gotta go upstairs to the thirteenth floor and get that Norfolk terrier who's waiting for me to take him out for a walk. His owners were in Hawaii, and he just got back from a week in the VIP suite at the Luxury Pet Resort down in the Village."

Rolling her eyes, Stacy said, "What do they get in the VIP suite? Manis and pedis for dogs?"

"Not sure, but I know they have story hour every night."

"Crazy!" Stacy said, and laughed. Then she said, "Okay, look, after I go to the ATM later, I'll have your money and will leave it for you in an envelope on the kitchen counter."

"No need," Magnolia said. "Pay me when you get home, no worries. And I can e-mail you every other day just to let you know how the cats are doing," she offered.

Stacy thought of Magnolia's grandson, imagining him in a cabin deep in the woods of Oregon, without electricity or running water, never, not for a moment, thinking of the grandmother who longed to see him. Impulsively, she hugged Magnolia, whose black sweatshirt was coated with dog hair and who seemed to stiffen slightly in her brief embrace.

"All right, all right, see you when you get back," Magnolia said, and tapped Stacy on the shoulder awkwardly.

Stacy returned to the big suitcase that lay open on the bedroom floor; it was hers and Roger's and since he was at his office, trying desperately, she knew, to get investors together for another development project, she decided she would do most of his packing for him. She started with his pajamas and boxers and T-shirts, and packed in neat, careful layers, with tissue paper placed meticulously in between, as if she were a sales clerk in a luxury department store, doing her job and doing it well.

She worked for nearly half an hour, then stopped to check in with the two mothers who were supervising her kids' respective playdates today, promising them both that of course she would reciprocate when spring break was over. After the phone calls, she allowed herself to take a quick look at the e-mail on her laptop; mostly pleas from the ACLU, Doctors Without Borders, and websites asking for money for breast cancer research and for the prevention of cruelty to animals—organizations that, in better days, had been the recipients of her generosity . . . And now she was startled to see Rocco Bassani's e-mail address; she hesitated for a moment before clicking open his mail, as if it might have been spam, or the work of a hacker who had every intention of stealing from her—her money, her social security number, her identity, her life. She opened it anyway, and was relieved to see the playful letter from Rocco, which included, inserted directly into the e-mail, a photo of his two-year-old, Dylan, who had red hair and looked nothing like him. They hadn't seen each other in nearly a decade, she calculated, not since the night they'd had farewell sex and smoked weed together. She wanted to write back immediately to tell him that just seeing his e-mail address there on the screen had reminded her of how much she missed being young. The e-mail itself opened with the salutation "Wass up?" and mentioned Rocco's divorce and his hope that they could catch up in person sometime in the not-too-distant future. He signed it "xox" and she had to smile when she saw it, recalling very clearly now the two of them in Rocco's bed sharing that joint, and the path of dark-blond hair that led from his stomach down to his groin.

It was the joint that brought to mind Olivia's friend Jazzmin and her pothead father and how Stacy had meant to follow up after the call she'd made to the Administration for Children's Services. She'd made the call but had never heard back from the social worker who'd answered the phone and promised that someone from ACS would look into it.

One more thing to take care of when she returned from Florida.

She didn't want to think of herself as someone who was merely well-intentioned. Because she had always hoped she was better than that.

## 39

Stacy's just out of the shower, standing in the bathroom doorway barefoot, wrapped in a peach-colored velour bathrobe that she swiped from his mother's closet. Her toenails are painted a color Roger would call mauve.

At first she thinks it's a joke when he points the Glock in her direction, but then he explains to her that though up until just a few days ago he'd planned to kill only himself tonight, he's come to realize, after a great deal of agonizing deliberation, that it's best to take her and the kids along with him. To rescue all of them from the mortification of his failures.

"We're bankrupt," he says. "And I mean totally, irretrievably, down the crapper. I didn't want to tell you, but now I have to. We have nothing. *Nada.* There's no hope for us, babe."

"Put. The. Gun. Down," Stacy says. She's panting, trying to catch her breath.

His love for her is infinite and he only wishes there were another way out. He tells her this, and just for an instant, hearing the word *love,* she looks relieved.

"Oh God, I love you, too," she says. Her breathing is still labored, as if she's just finished a four-minute mile. "And that's why you have to put. The. Gun. Down."

He doesn't appreciate it when she talks to him like this. He's not a child, and there's nothing wrong with his hearing.

"You love me," he says, "but do you love me with a full heart? Do you love me 100 percent?"

Stacy slaps her right hand over her heart. "One hundred percent," she tells him. Her voice sounds warbly and thin. "With a full heart, absolutely," she says, voice stronger now.

Walking closer toward her, he continues to point the gun in her direction; he backs her toward the side of the bed, where she trips over her own feet and falls, pathetically, to her knees.

"Stay right there," Roger tells her. "*Don't* move."

## 40

He's looking at her with those turquoise eyes of his, suddenly startlingly beautiful to Stacy again. But she can see that he's in an altered state, that his mind is ablaze, and that these are the baby blues of someone who, except for those eyes, is unrecognizable to her. A man she no longer knows. And perhaps—it occurs sickeningly to her now—never knew well enough, deeply enough, not really. This man she's loved for years: how many? Her heart is beating so fiercely she can't think, can't even remember how long they've been married.

Then it comes to her. *Nine, nine next month*, she says to this man who is going to kill her, and her children, too, unless she can persuade him otherwise.

He stares at her. "Nine years," he says, nodding his head.

The gun is still pointed at her.

"Waitwaitwait," she says, "just try and explain again why you think you have to do this."

"I've already told you," the man holding the gun says, and looks at her with a combination of exasperation and pity.

He says that he will never be able to give her and the children the sort of comfortable life they had before.

That he cannot live with these failures of his to provide them with what they deserve.

There is simply no way out. "No way out," he repeats, staring at her apologetically now. "I don't want us to starve," he says, "don't you see?"

*Starve?* What is he *talking* about?

It can't be true, can it, that this distorted thinking might actually prove to be the ruin of them all, Stacy asks herself. Or maybe she's said it aloud; she doesn't know. Doesn't know anything except that she must pit herself against this stranger, this *psychopath*, whom she cannot allow to harm her children. *Their* children.

She has never seen a gun before except in the movies or on television, and is sick with ice-cold terror at the sight of it. Sick with disbelief.

She is shivering, but has sweat through her mother-in-law's bathrobe and can feel the perspiration collecting in the hollows under her arms, in the creases behind her bent knees, and beneath her toes. She wants to ask the man who is pointing a gun at her where he got it and when, but doesn't it seem best not to focus attention on it?

"Will you just listen to me, please," she says. She can feel her mouth twitching. "I don't care at all about those things—that life—that you think the children and I deserve. I don't care at all about what we had before, all those trappings of living well—it's nothing, it means *nothing* to me! *Less* than nothing! I just want the four of us to be together," she says, and hates both the quivery sound of her voice and the modest nature of her desperate request. "And don't worry, I'm going to find a job as soon as we're back in the city. I promise," she squeaks. Wishing she sounded a lot more confident.

The man is shaking his head sorrowfully. The gun is still pointed at her as he says, "Get real, Stacy, you're a social worker! Your salary was peanuts. You think you can rescue us with whatever pitiful money this imaginary job of yours is going to bring in? Listen to me—there's no way out."

Though he may think there's no way out, Stacy can't possibly let herself believe that he's right. Under other circumstances, she already would have said, *How dare you insult me and my career like that!* But these particular circumstances don't allow for hurt feelings, she understands. And so she tells this man whom she no longer recognizes just how much she and Olivia and Will love him, never mind his business failures. Which are nothing to their children, nothing to *her*, she repeats. "They do nothing to diminish you in our eyes, baby, you understand that, right? We adore you!"

"Thanks for the vote of confidence, Stace," he says, but he sounds unconvinced.

She asks him, quietly and politely, in a whispery voice, for a drink of water.

Backing into the adjoining bathroom, with his 9 mm semiautomatic pistol still aimed at her, he fills up a Lucite cup with southern Florida's idea of cold water and offers it with a hand that trembles slightly.

This much he can do for her.

Stacy takes a few sips, and, using both hands, sets the cup on the floor next to the bed, on the moss-green textured carpet where she is sitting on her knees, her back rigid against the side of the king-size mattress. Drops of water fly over the top of the hard plastic cup as she sets it down with those shaky hands and hears herself pleading for her life now.

And the lives of her children.

*Their* children. Olivia and Will.

*Pleasepleasepleasepleasepleasedontdothis. Imbeggingyou. Beggingyoupleasedont.*

"Olivia and Will," she says. "Will and Olivia."

She's struggling painfully to talk and breathe at the same time, but, even so, she reminds the skinny man with the gun how much he loves these children of theirs.

But that, he explains to her—with genuine, profoundly felt sadness evident in his voice—is precisely why he must do what he must do.

Because he loves all three of them more than life itself.

## ~ 41 ~

Listening to Stacy beg for her life is one of the hardest things Roger's ever had to endure. Right up there with the death of his sister.

The look of absolute astonishment on her face—nicely tanned from the Florida sun, her nose a little burned—when he actually puts the pistol to her head, well, that, too, is terribly hard to take.

Absolute astonishment turning to pure terror, and who can blame her?

No matter what he says to Stacy, no matter how much effort he invests in trying to explain himself, it's clear she just doesn't get it.

She keeps telling him that his thinking is distorted, completely wrongheaded, *just plain crazy.* And keeps pleading pleading pleading until both of them are worn down by her appeals, and he has to ask her, as graciously as he can, to please, *please* shut the fuck up.

# ~ 42 ~

As he presses the muzzle of the Glock against the left side of her head, where she can feel a vein pulsing feverishly, she allows herself to believe that her beloved children will be spared. Because she just doesn't have it in her to believe otherwise—that this man she no longer recognizes will do exactly what he says he's going to do.

Not to her children.

And not to her.

This man she's loved every day of her life for the almost-nine years of their marriage.

*Pleasepleasepleasepleasepleasepleaseplease.*

She has the feeling she's talking out loud but she's not sure; her head is filled with ugly static and it's so hard to think.

In the smallest of voices, Stacy asks him now if she can please go to the bathroom; like a child, she simply can't hold it in any longer. He is patient with her and says, "Of course," then walks with her—the Glock still held to the side of her head—the few yards to the bathroom. She raises the bathrobe slightly, and he stands there with the pistol pointed straight at her, gazing at her lovingly for a moment, then turning away. Because even though the two of them have had, in his estimation—and hers, too, he thinks—a pretty wonderful marriage, it was never the sort where either of them would feel comfortable watching the other one pee.

And he knows, even as he turns away from her, affording her a momentary opportunity to grab the gun, that she will never do it, never reach for it. Because her thinking is warped by terror and confusion, and she's just not capable of altering his plans.

## ~ 44 ~

"Remember our wedding?" she asks him. Anything to remind him of the best parts of their life together, their history. Anything to persuade him to let go of the gun he's raised to her temple, to let go of the very *idea* of the gun.

"Nine years ago," he says.

"Nine years ago next month," she corrects him, and thinks vaguely about the trip to Paris and Vienna and Berlin they'd once—before things went south—planned to take in celebration of their anniversary.

"Lots of great food," he says. And, to her surprise, enumerates, like a well-schooled waiter, the filet mignon, the truffled halibut, the Seafood Newburg filled with lobster, shrimp, and scallops . . . For their vegan pals, let's see, there was chickpea polenta cake with roasted vegetables.

But the desserts were the best, she reminds him, and together they're able to conjure up the peanut butter ice cream with Concord grape sorbet and caramel popcorn crunch, then the lemon ice cream with raspberries and almond nougatine.

"This is almost making me hungry," he says, smiling slightly.

"Me too," she lies—lying through her teeth, really—and suggests he go out and get some dessert for them right now; you know, a quick trip to Baskin-Robbins, or maybe Carvel?

"I'm sorry," he tells her, and he really does sound regretful. "I wish I could, but I'm sorry, Stace, no can do."

"Are you sure?"

"I *said*, no can do. Case closed, babe."

## 45

She finds herself wishing she believed in God, or Jesus Christ, or Buddha or Allah or Krishna or Vishnu or Shiva— any one of them will do, any deity at all who will rescue her and her children.

When the doorbell rings, it isn't God, of course, but only Mrs. Feinsilver. The old lady rings the bell two, three, and four times, yelling out their names until finally Stacy says to the man holding the gun, "She's going to wake up the kids. We've got to answer the door."

He rests the barrel of the gun against the base of her spine and instructs her to get up and walk toward the front door. He's right behind her, and gives her a hand as she rises from the bedroom floor. She walks obediently, on wobbly legs, to the door, and, with his permission, opens it.

*Help me!* she mouths, but Mrs. Feinsilver isn't paying attention.

"Oh, thank God, I was worried you weren't home," the old lady says. She's here to return the two bucks she owes them. Stacy reaches for the dollar bills, and thanks her, her hand trembling so violently that Mrs. Feinsilver asks if she's all right.

Stacy opens her mouth to answer, struggling to seize upon just the right words, just the right gesture, anything at all that will arouse Mrs. Feinsilver's suspicions but not the gunman's fury.

*HELP me!* she tries again, but clearly Mrs. Feinsilver is no lip-reader. The old lady may even be a little out of it, Stacy thinks, but she tries once more, opening her mouth wide, shaping the two simple words more deliberately this time.

*HELP ME!* And hears herself say, "Would you like to come in for a cup of coffee?"

"What the fuck?" the gunman murmurs. The barrel of the gun is being pressed painfully into Stacy's lower back now as he says, "Actually, Mrs. Feinsilver . . . we were just getting ready for bed. Maybe another time, okay?"

"One of the washing machines swallowed my money but wouldn't start," Mrs. Feinsilver complains. "Don't you hate it when that happens?"

No one responds.

The sound of Stacy's pulse ticking is deafening, but why is it that no one else can hear it? She considers grabbing Mrs. Feinsilver by the arm and yanking her farther into the apartment, but then what? What is she thinking? That this shrimpy little octogenarian with her too-short housecoat and those pale, vein-laced legs, is going to knock the gun from the madman's hand and save the day?

She shoots Mrs. Feinsilver what she hopes is a look fraught with sheer desperation, a look that shrieks *911!* Mrs. F., however, gives no sign of having received her message, and is already halfway out the door.

"Okay, back to the bedroom, you," the man with the gun orders Stacy; he's still behind her and puts one hand at her waist to turn her around, then steers her, with a surprising gentleness, in the right direction. "A cup of coffee? *Really?*" he says, and it almost sounds as if he's laughing.

Olivia and Will are asleep in their beds no more than twelve feet from the living room. Stacy wants, more than she's ever wanted *anything*, to gather each of them to her and then take flight. Right out the eighth-floor window, the three of them flying, on their own steam, through the night sky and all the way home.

But there's a loaded pistol nudging the small of her back, and the only place she's going is where that pistol leads her.

"Please, no!" Stacy is telling him.

As she speaks, her breath so close to his face, he can actually smell what can only be described as the scent of fear; he would never have known that there *is* such a thing, but, he's discovered, there really is.

"Dont*do*this to us! Pleasedontdothisto*yourself*."

What Stacy fails to comprehend is that he doesn't have a choice. He has been over this numerous times with her tonight, but, smart as she is—and don't forget she spent four years at Harvard—*she just doesn't get it.*

He's been patient with her, this woman he loves more than anything on earth.

But his patience is running out; there's just been too much talking back and forth. He needs to get down to the terrible business at hand, though, God knows, he wishes he didn't have to.

First the doorbell, now Stacy's phone, which is playing her new ringtone, acquired just a few days ago—Beethoven's "Ode to Joy." From her seat on the bed, she can see the phone there on the night table, and that she has a call from her sister, probably just something about double-checking their flight number or arrival time tomorrow.

Stacy asks if she can take this call, please, but the answer, unsurprisingly, is *Sorry, babe, I can't let you do that.*

She asks the gods to bestow upon Lauren the miracle of clairvoyance, for the power to see, from a distance of thirteen hundred miles, what must be fixed here.

"Look, why don't you sit down?" she suggests to the armed and dangerous guy standing over her, hoping he'll relax, let go of his gun, and, perhaps, his devastating lunacy.

The Glock still in hand, he pushes a brocade armchair toward her, and settles himself in it, close to the side of the bed where he'd instructed her to sit.

Not for a second in the fifteen minutes or so since the gun has been in his hand has it been pointed in any direction but hers.

Not for a second has he given her an opportunity to make a run for it, to make a run for their sleeping children, who are still at the other end of the apartment, in the den. She's convinced herself that if it comes to pass (and she's praying now to anyone who's listening that it won't) that she doesn't survive this, Will and Olivia will thrive in Brooklyn Heights with Jefrie—their legal guardian as designated in her will—and Jefrie's partner, Honey. A decision that was made shortly after Clare's death, and made despite what Stacy knows will be Lauren's hurt feelings over not having been chosen to take Clare's place as guardian. The simple truth is that Jefrie, her best friend, is someone with whom she's always felt more of a kinship than with her own sister; and, too, no way would Stacy consent to have her children raised in the suburbs! No way! And Roger finally, after all their years together, had come to accept this . . . Years from now, Stacy imagines—because she cannot and will not permit herself to believe that the lunatic in the room with her will actually take her children's lives—Will and Olivia will attend a good public high school somewhere in the city with a couple of thousand other students and will do just fine, both of them, she believes, unusually bright kids who will make their way in the world with enthusiasm and confidence and discernment . . . But what about her cats, she spends just an instant or two thinking. What will happen to Keats and Shelley back in New York? They're senior citizens, and they will be undone, in their way, if she disappears from their lives. They may very well stop eating, and even drinking, and spend all their time circling the apartment in bewilderment, looking everywhere for her.

If Will and Olivia end up with Jefrie and Honey, and if they beg hard enough, maybe—even though Honey is slightly allergic—maybe they'll be allowed to take Keats and Shelley with them to the townhouse in Brooklyn Heights.

To their new lives.

But it's impossible not to harbor hopes for an outcome even more miraculous than that. And so she wonders now who will rescue not just her children, but all three of them.

Who will throw them a lifeline? Jefrie? Marshall? Her sister? Her ninety-two-year-old grandmother? Rocco? Professor Dave? Every one of them safely up north in the New York metro area, thirteen hundred miles from her mother-in-law's condo just north of Miami Beach.

Her pulse has gone haywire, but she will keep her wits about her and will not—WILL NOT—allow herself to surrender to this stranger who is going on and on and on about his in-fucking-surmountable problems, not a one of them that can be remedied, he keeps telling her, his voice grim grim grim.

Not one?

"That's right, not one," he says. He sounds very certain of this, very sure of himself.

When she tells him how much she loves their children, he reminds her that *he* loves them, too.

They're the most precious things in the universe to him, he says mournfully. And he just can't allow them to starve.

He is weeping now, standing over her, barefoot, in his sweatpants and Harvard B School T-shirt, with the Glock pointed straight at her—though the barrel is not, for the moment, touching her, and that, at least, is a relief.

For the moment, anyway.

The next moment may hold something entirely different.

Sure enough, after he switches the Glock from one vis-ibly sweaty hand to the other, he leans over across the bed and places the barrel slightly above the slender tip of her left eyebrow, a brow so dark it is very nearly black.

She is paralyzed; she can't even move her lips to speak, to say the simple word *Don't*. She's *scared stiff*, she thinks, able to grasp that these are words she has never really under-stood before.

*Pleasepleasepleasepleasepleasedontdothis. Imbeggingyou.*

*Beggingyoupleasedont,* she wants to say but can't. It's as if she's suffering from locked-in syndrome, she understands—she can think but she can't move a muscle. Not even if it means saving herself so that she can save her children.

"You love me with a full heart, don't you?" he says.

*A full 100 percent,* she thinks she hears herself whisper, and it hits her again that this man who loves her, who loves their children, won't actually take their lives. It simply isn't possible.

But now she hears him say, "Listen, you get that it's just that everything's spun out of control, right? You get that I love you, Stace, and wish to God there were another way out, but I swear to you there isn't. There just . . . isn't."

Her heart has shattered, like fragile bone, into a thousand weightless slivers; this is the husband she'd loved so ardently, and now she sees that he means every word.

In the few moments that are left to her on this earth, just before he slips a small throw pillow between her head and his gun, she is flooded with a terrible, sorrowful disappointment— there are no opportunities left for salvation. Not even one.

She longs for her parents, and wishes, without hope, that they were here to save her.

There is still time to absorb one last thing, and that is the crushing, unendurable thought that she will never again see her children, never again run her fingertips along the satiny skin of their darling, child-sized hands, their bumpy little wrists and knees . . .

Most excruciatingly, she will not be there to comfort them at the moment of their own deaths tonight.

She cannot bear it.

# ~ 48 ~

There are things he will remember from this night, things he would prefer to forget.

Watching the hope drain from Stacy's eyes in the moment just before he set the pillow against her head to soften the sound of the gunshots.

The blood spatter that sprayed the bedroom ceiling.

The blood-soaked linens he left Stacy lying in.

After she died, he put his lips to the outline of the purple heart tattooed beneath her wrist.

Now that Stacy is gone, he discovers—greatly relieved—that it simply isn't possible for him to kill his children, as he planned to. Seeing Will's head resting on that red-and-yellow Winnie the Pooh pillowcase, Olivia's against a lavender, star-sprinkled Tinkerbell, he just can't. Cannot take the lives of his beloved children. When push comes to shove, he's not up to the task. Not able to rise to the occasion.

*So be it*, as his mother likes to say.

Tiptoeing in his bare feet away from his sleeping children, he realizes, as well, mostly with embarrassment but also with a bit of relief, that he is not yet ready to die. At least not by a gunshot to the head. He thought he was ready, but then that moment passed, and it turned out he was mistaken.

*You're a fucking coward*, he tells himself disgustedly. And he really needs to clean up all those gleaming shell casings that litter the carpet beside the bed where Stacy lies so still.

⁐

He's taken a bunch of Xanax already today, but now he goes into the kitchen cabinet to get more, a generous helping of those cantaloupe-colored pills—ten, to be exact—that he swallows down with a few swigs of Diet Coke, Stacy's favorite drink. *The American Champagne*, he recalls a waiter in Italy teasing her on their honeymoon.

He's hoping to die now, hoping that all that Xanax will quickly and painlessly do him in. Because now that Stacy is gone and his children most certainly will be taken from him, why on earth would he want to live?

He dials 911 and tells the bland voice at the other end what he's done. He's suddenly eager to turn himself in, though the truth is, he's hoping to die before the cops arrive.

He's ready to die this instant, in fact, but no such luck: the cops are already at his doorstep, along with a couple of neighbors, who are told by the cops—a rookie and a middle-aged guy, both strawberry blonds—to go home and mind their own business. The rookie's badge says "McDonough," the older guy's "Rosenfeld." Roger explains to them, apologetically, that he'd meant to clean up, because he knows that his wife, though not what he would call a particularly zealous housekeeper, would, nonetheless, be more than a little humiliated at the thought of strangers coming through here and seeing the god-awful mess. The blood-soaked linens, the bloody fingerprints on everything he's so carelessly touched: the refrigerator, and the countertops, faucets, and cabinets in the kitchen and bathroom. And please don't forget, he tells the officers, his voice softening, falling to a whisper, there's all that blood that has already congealed in the dark hair of his beloved wife. Though not in the pale hair of his children, whom he'd meant to kill, but, in the end, simply could not. *Could not.*

*Jesus fucking Christ*, one of them says when Roger shows the cops what he means, shows them the bed where Stacy, no longer alive, still lies.

He apologizes tearfully to the cops for the mess he hasn't yet managed to clean up.

The rookie slugs him, hard, and Roger falls to the floor, surprised at how much it hurts.

It hurts, too, God knows, to see the way Olivia and Will are whisked out the front door half-asleep and still in their pj's, out of the apartment and out of his life, denied the chance to offer even a simple good-bye from their plump, rosy lips.

In a day or two, after the news of what he's done—and what he'd planned to do—hits the local TV stations, readers will begin leaving messages on a popular crime story website.

ROTT IN HELL, YOU SICK BASTARD!!!!
FORGET DEATH ROW AND FRY THIS
FUCKER TONIGHT!

The cops, though, can barely bring themselves to even speak to him.

# ~ 49 ~

Later, after his stomach has been pumped at the hospital, and the arresting officers who take his statement that night go home to their wives and families, both cops will note how polite Roger Goldenhar had been, gentlemanly, almost. And how at first he'd been mistaken for a victim, with all that blood spattered and smeared across his cheekbones and into and above his brow and under his nose like a small blot of vividly red marinara sauce from a veal parmigiana and angel hair dinner that might have been prepared for him by what their former neighbors on Park Avenue in Manhattan will describe to the media as his smart and funny and loving wife. But this Roger Goldenhar—vacationing for the week with his wife and young children at the condo on South Ocean Drive still owned by his elderly mother—kept insisting, again and again, in a voice dulled by pain and bewilderment, that he was no victim, that the blood was not his own, and that some might say what he had done was, hands down, the worst possible thing a husband could do.

## ~ 50 ~

Lauren is calling from her cell phone to let her grandmother know that she is in Brooklyn, downstairs in the lobby, as a matter of fact.

"All the way from Connecticut? Well, that's a nice surprise!"

But then Juliette says she doesn't like the sound of Lauren's voice, and asks if she has a cold.

No, she doesn't have a cold, and will be upstairs in a minute.

There's an elevator in the building, but it's not working today, and Lauren is surprisingly breathless after climbing only a single flight of stairs. And she is somewhat disheveled; her hair is in a careless ponytail, her lipstick has worn off, and her eyes, which have been burning all day, are dimmed and watery-looking.

She opens the door with the key Juliette made copies of several years ago for both her granddaughters.

Lauren stands in the minuscule foyer and stares and stares at her grandmother, who is seated in a straight-backed wooden chair in the modest kitchen that hasn't been updated since the fifties.

"What is it, babydoll?" her grandmother says.

*Go ahead, you're perfectly capable of doing this*, Lauren imagines Stacy urging her, as if her sister were a ghostly presence by her side, nudging her on.

Lauren opens her mouth, but all she can manage is the single word, "Gram?"

D r. Avalon, having just returned with his wife from a trip both entertaining and educational to Portugal, Spain, France, and the Netherlands, stammers into the phone when Buster Ostrofsky, Roger's attorney, reports that Roger would like to schedule a call from his jail cell, where he is awaiting arraignment.

"What? What the hell is he doing in jail?"

Fingering a small Royal Delft vase imprinted with windmills that he picked up in Amsterdam, Dr. Avalon allows the vase to fall from his grasp onto the kitchen floor and break into three pieces when he hears what Roger is being charged with.

"Fuck!" he says.

In the nearly four decades he has been in practice as a psychiatrist, not a single patient of his has ever done what Roger apparently did, though a number of them have fantasized aloud about doing so.

As he bends down to pick up the blue-and-white pieces of the vase, distracted by the horrific news about Roger, Dr. Avalon lacerates his index finger so badly, he and his wife have to take a cab to the ER at Roosevelt hospital, where he is forced to wait around for nearly an hour before his finger is finally stitched up.

*Should have seen it coming*, he muses aloud. And later that night suffers what he understands to be a full-blown migraine, his first ever.

## ~ 52 ~

When Rebecca, his office manager, comes into his opera-tory to inform him that there's an urgent call from his son, Marshall is with a patient, a pretty twenty-five-year-old whose teeth have shifted back despite the three years she wore metal braces as a teenager. Marshall is enthusiastically recom-mending clear plastic aligners that are a popular alternative to braces, but Rebecca won't allow him to finish his pitch, and, instead, interrupts him, saying, "I really don't think this can wait even a minute, Dr. Tuckman."

"Back in a jiffy," Marshall promises his patient, but, in fact, he will have to close down the office for the rest of the day and go home to comfort Nathaniel. Who got the news from Stacy's best friend, Jefrie Miller, after she left a weepy, hysteria-tinged message on the digital answering machine in Marshall's den just before Nathaniel arrived home from school this afternoon.

Nathaniel tells him, over the phone, in his adolescent, grief-cracked voice, that he had to play the message over and over again until, at last, he finally understood what he was hearing.

Stuck in midday traffic on his way home in a cab now, Marshall thinks of Clare, and how devastated she would be knowing the unforgivable thing her brother had done. But would she have forgiven him?

Will he himself think of her every day for the rest of his life? He believes at this moment that he will. *And now Stacy.* Marshall remembers her leaning forward to offer his wife a kiss as Clare lay, just a few months ago, on a gurney in Sloan Kettering, waiting to be wheeled into her final surgery. Stacy had bent toward Clare, and the curtain of her hair swung forward, grazing Clare's pale cheek before Stacy could flip it out of the way. *Good luck, sweetie,* he can hear Stacy saying. *Good luck!* With all the cheery hopefulness of someone seeing a beloved friend off on a cruise ship and calling out *bon voyage!*

# ~ 53 ~

Dave is shopping for a Big Wheels tricycle in Toys R Us for his nephew's birthday when the call comes from someone named Jefrie Miller on his cell phone.

"Professor Sarno?" she begins. "Dave?" she says, and gets right down to it.

For the very first time in his life, Dave feels as if he is going to faint; right there in the tricycle aisle, he sits down on the floor, and puts his head between his knees for a while. When, a few minutes later, he pushes his head upward so that blood can flow to his brain, he overhears a guy his own age saying to his companion, "Hey, I feel bad for the jerk because he's got two stupid parents. Not one, but two. She's an idiot, and so's he."

He thinks of Stacy, and her blond kids, whose pictures he's sneaked looks at on Facebook. And that husband of hers who will probably be in the slammer for the rest of his miserable life. *Fucking psycho dude.*

He lets himself smile now, thinking of the first time he and Stacy helped themselves to one another in the walk-in closet at the back of his classroom, and how he'd kept the light on.

*To see how beautiful you are,* he'd told her.

In a way, Dave thinks, after two and a half years, they'd just recently been getting to know one another.

Reaching for the phone in the rear pocket of his jeans, he calls Elisabeth, his ex-wife, because he needs to talk to someone right now, even if it's someone who no longer likes him very much.

"Hey," he says into the phone, but Elisabeth tells him she's been trying for more than an hour to get her step-daughter to bed and can't talk about anything right now.

"Please just listen," Dave says, but what's the use, she's already hung up on him.

*Call her back*, Stacy would probably like him to say. *Call her back and make her listen.*

# ~ 54 ~

Smiling, Roger's mother, Beverly, listens as a young kid and a gray-haired man talk about someone named Stacy. She thinks she may know a person by that name, someone who used to come and visit her and bring her music in a very thin box the size of a candy bar. It had wires attached to it and little plastic things that this someone-named-Stacy put into Beverly's ears so that she could hear the music. Music from *My Fair Lady*, which Beverly saw in 1956 on Broadway at the Mark Hellinger Theatre; don't ask her why she remembers this—she just does.

*A very lovely person, this Stacy*, Beverly remarks.

Then she will say to someone they tell her is named Nathaniel, a handsome, dark-haired kid she thinks she may have seen before, "Do I know this Stacy? Is she coming to visit today? Or maybe tomorrow?"

No one bothers to answer her.

*So be it*, she hears herself say. Don't ask her why—she just likes the sound of the words, that's all.

# ~ 55 ~

Jefrie Miller is wearing a borrowed pair of sunglasses today when she takes her seat, along with her partner, Honey, in the front row of the funeral chapel on the Upper West Side, just across the aisle from Stacy's sister and brother-in-law. (Who, she bets, are probably both insulted and relieved that Stacy's will has named her the legal guardian of their niece and nephew.) Jefrie's eyes are so swollen, they're no more than the narrowest of slits, really. Because that's what happens when you begin to weep and find that you just can't stop, no matter how many times your partner takes your hand and says, "Look, you've got to get hold of yourself, okay, kiddo?"

Jefrie ignores Honey each time she says this to her, and ignores, as well, the hundred or so mourners who have filled the chapel to pay tribute to Stacy, slaughtered by the man who is still insisting, according to a couple of nightly news broadcasts, that he loved her more than anything on earth.

She closes her swollen eyes at the sight of the glossy coffin resting on its gurney, barely ten feet in front of her—thanks to Stacy's deranged, deluded, narcissistic, pathetic psycho of a husband, who, in truth, Jefrie had never really warmed to. Not completely, anyway. She'd always found Roger a little too self-absorbed, a little too intense, and, in retrospect, way too concerned with keeping a firm hold on what he considered the good life.

Though a fervent opponent of the death penalty, Jefrie finds herself secretly hoping that the state of Florida will treat Roger to one of their lethal cocktails, the sooner the better.

This is what she's thinking as the rabbi, dressed in a dark suit and surprisingly bright blue tie, ascends to the podium and murmurs something in Hebrew that Jefrie can make neither head nor tail of; it might as well be Farsi or Tagalog or Romanian or Mandarin, for all she knows or cares.

Because her dearest friend is gone, and she's gone for good. Let Jefrie cry all she wants, there's no getting her back. And how the hell is she ever going to figure out the right way to explain that to those two little pip-squeaks she and Honey will be raising as their own?

## ~ 56 ~

Here he is in his cell in a Broward County jail, awaiting arraignment.

He's heard through his lawyer that a couple of experts have diagnosed him—after a quick look at his suicide note—as severely and lethally depressed, not to mention pathologically narcissistic. They think he fits the mold of a certain kind of killer they've seen time and again, the sort who is so intensely narcissistic, he couldn't even turn the gun on himself even though he wrote the damn suicide note.

Fine, let Dr. So-and-So and his colleagues say whatever insulting things they want to about him.

What these shrinks don't understand is that at least he's saved his beloved wife—if not his treasured children—from the sad and difficult life they were all facing in that modest apartment on Third Avenue. A far cry from their luxury three-bedroom on Park, where he and Stacy spent the best years of their life together, wanting for nothing.

He's been here in his cell for several days now, missing his family every moment of every day.

How could it be otherwise?

If only, he thinks, the powers that be would take pity on him and let him kill his worthless self. Right here in his cell, with twice as much Xanax as he took the last time around, but this time washed down with a nice fruity Cabernet. The perfect combination for a guy like him, someone who's more than ready to say *adiós, au revoir, auf Wiedersehen. Till we meet again.*

Eventually he will be arraigned on a charge of first-degree murder; even though his attorney, Buster Ostrofsky, originally thought he might be able to get him off with an insanity defense, Roger will wind up pleading guilty and later be handed a life sentence by an angry judge who will use the words "diabolical" and "hellhound" when referring to him. Yet after the sentencing, when the local media shows up, Mrs. Feinsilver will make sure to note that the night of the shooting, Roger very kindly lent her a couple of dollars so she could do her laundry.

"A generous young man," she will add, and Roger will predict, mournfully, that this just might be the last compliment ever to come his way.

In his cell, he's finishing up the insipid bologna sandwich that is today's lunch, and finds himself thinking of Olivia, his firstborn. A five-year-old who adores bologna on Pepperidge Farm oatmeal bread and would have had it for lunch every day of the week if only Stacy had allowed it. He thinks of Olivia not as she was one of the last times he saw her, sleeping so serenely against her Tinkerbell sheets, but years earlier, when she was just eighteen months old. The family had gathered in their old apartment on West End to celebrate his mother's birthday, and Olivia—who was standing on a chair for a better look at the festivities—was clearly enthralled, her face lit with pleasure at the sight of the cake and all those blazing candles, which she must have mistakenly assumed were for her. Because an instant later, hearing the lyrics *Happy birthday, dear Grandma Be-ee*, his daughter's face fell in confusion and then defeat in that moment of recognition as it hit her that the song and the cake and the candles weren't for her after all. Roger saw, perhaps for the very first time, as he swooped Olivia up from the chair and into his arms, just how much he wanted to spare this child of his even the slightest pinprick of pain or disappointment.

*Don't let them say you weren't a good father*, he tells himself. *Or husband.*

He is entirely bereft, and overcome now with the taste of fresh grief at the corners of his mouth, the underside of his lips, and all the way down the back of his throat; it's a bitter taste that's never going away. And that will, he predicts, stay with him until the very last moment of his life here on earth.

# EPILOGUE

On a particularly humid late-August afternoon, years from now, Jefrie and Honey will move Olivia into her dorm room in Matthews Hall in Harvard Yard, into a suite with two other freshman girls. Will, sixteen years old, quieter and less rambunctious than he'd been as a child, will decline to join them, more than happy to spend the weekend back home in Brooklyn with a couple of his high school buds.

As it happens, Matthews is the dorm where, in the last century, Jefrie and Stacy first met, and entering Olivia's suite, Jefrie will instantly remember Stacy seated at her sturdy oak desk in their fourth-floor freshman digs, already homesick on their very first day in Cambridge. She will remember Stacy with her head bowed forlornly over a loaf of homemade chocolate pound cake in its flimsy, throwaway aluminum pan. Believe it or not, she was already pining for her parents, Stacy had confided—with, Jefrie saw, just a whiff of embarrassment. As she talked, she was eating the cake with her fingertips, though at first in a delicate, ladylike way. Stacy's fingers were long and thin, her unpolished nails dipped in dark chocolate. She offered the pan to Jefrie, who thanked her and pinched off some cake, awkwardly feeding herself with one hand and then the other until, eventually, she and Stacy had polished off the entire pound cake together. Jefrie had to smile, had to lead her brand-new roommate to the full-length mirror at the back of the closet door. Where the two of them, their mouths rimmed in chocolate, their teeth coated with it, their nails painted with it, took a gander at their ridiculous-looking, freshman selves and cracked up. What a mess they'd made of themselves, eating with their hands like babies! Like chimpanzees! Like squirrels!

Stroking Olivia's thick, sweat-dampened hair on this sweltering afternoon, absently lifting it off her smooth pale neck and letting it fall back again, Jefrie will swear she can still see Stacy doubled over in joyous laughter, slender arms wrapped around her middle; can still hear the sound of the two of them laughing their heads off in a room just like this one. *As if it were yesterday*, Jefrie will say.

And Olivia, the daughter she and Honey have nurtured so tenderly—as Stacy knew they were meant to—will nod and say, *I believe you.*